SORROW'S KNOT

ERIN BOW

Arthur A. Levine Books
An Imprint of Scholastic Inc.

Library of Congress Cataloging-in-Publication Data

Bow, Erin.
Sorrow's knot / Erin Bow. — 1st ed.
p. cm.
Summary: Otter is a girl of the Shadowed People, a tribe of women, and she is born to be a binder, a woman whose power it is to tie the knots that bind the dead — but she is also destined to remake her world.
ISBN 978-0-545-16666-9 (hardcover : alk. paper) 1. Magic — Juvenile fiction. 2. Identity (Philosophical concept) — Juvenile fiction. 3. Identity (Psychology) — Juvenile fiction. 4. Knots and splices — Juvenile fiction. 5. Fate and fatalism — Juvenile fiction. [1. Magic — Fiction. 2. Identity — Fiction. 3. Fate and fatalism — Fiction.] I. Title.
PZ7.B67167Sor 2013
813.6 — dc23
2013007855

10 9 8 7 6 5 4 3 2 1   13 14 15 16 17

First edition, November 2013

Printed in the U.S.A. 23

Book design by Jeannine Riske

Like a baby named for her midwife, this book is dedicated to Seánan Forbes, who walked me through all the stuck spots.

CONTENTS

PART THREE

PART FOUR

PART ONE

Chapter One

THE GIRL WHO REMADE THE WORLD

The girl who remade the world was born in winter.

It was the last day of the Nameless Moon, and bitterly cold. For as long as she could, the girl's mother, whose name was Willow, walked round and round the outside of the midwife's lodge, leaning on the earthen walls when pains came fiercely. Willow's hair was full of sweat, and her body was steaming like a hot spring. She was trailed by a mist of ice that glittered in the bitter sunlight. She looked like a comet.

She looked like what she was: a woman of power.

Willow was a binder: a woman whose power and duty it was to tie the knots that bound the dead. But her knots could do more than that. When the time was right, she went into the midwife's lodge, and there, as the last binder had taught her, Willow let her power turn backward and undid the knot between herself and her baby, and made an easy birth.

"Ah," said Willow as the babe was placed on her belly. "Ah, look! Look at you!" The baby gave a great squall and started to cry. "Look at you," said Willow, touching the little face. The baby turned toward the touch, rooting for milk. "Just look."

"A girl," said the midwife. "A beautiful girl. And in the lucky moon too. What will you call her?"

Willow touched the black hair, which was spiked into small peaks with dampness and looked like the thick, wet pelt of an animal. "Otter," said Willow. She kissed the closed eyes, and they opened, fathomless. Willow cupped her daughter's little face and gave a mother's blessing: "I name you Otter. May you be clever and happy. May you have a fierce bite. May you always be warm."

She touched the dark hair again, and at the touch of her power — still backward, still — the straight spikes sprang into curls. The baby gurgled. The midwife frowned. But Willow did not see, and only smiled, falling into those dark eyes. "May you live with joy."

⋀⋁⋀⋁⋀

So Otter was born, and so she came to girlhood, among Shadowed People, the free women of the forest, in the embrace of mountains so old they were soft-backed, so dark with pine that they were black in summer. A river came out of those mountains, young and quick, shallow and bone-cold. Where it washed into a low meadow, the people had cleared the birch saplings and scrub pines and built a stronghold of sunlight.

The name of their pinch — a forest town was called a pinch — was Westmost, because it was the westernmost human place in the world. If one traveled farther west, upstream, the mountains rose, and the rivers were too small to run in the cold winters, and only the dead lived long.

The dead. Otter grew up almost without fear of them. After all, her home was the safest place in Westmost: the binder's lodge. Otter and Willow lived there with the first binder, Tamarack, who was old by the time Otter was born: a woman with hair as soft as milkweed seed and fingers as strong as rawhide knots.

Tamarack, as first binder, was a woman of status; when people came up to her, they covered their eyes. But for Willow — though she was only second binder — for Willow people did not simply cover their eyes. They told tales. It was said that Willow was the greatest binder since the days of the Mad Spider, whose time was sinking from memory to legend. It was said that she had given birth without a single sound. It was said that her ward knots were so strong they could stop the very dust, and leave it hanging, glittering, in the air.

They lived a quiet life, Otter and Willow and Tamarack. Inside their lodge, no one visited, and they were easy with one another: daughter and mother and something near to a grandmother. Outside it, they were honored.

And so Otter grew up as a princeling might grow, or the acolyte of a great priest. Her shirt was made of the skin of a white deer, embroidered with quills and silver disks. But though she could have held herself apart, held herself proud, Otter did not. She was a tumbling child, strong and happy, like the best puppy in the litter. She was the one who led the children in sledding down the snowbanked sides of the earthlodges in winter, splashing in the cold river in summer, spearing fish with sharpened sticks. Her fine clothes were always mud-smeared and tattered. Her mother mended them, and sometimes the embroidery curled loose in Willow's hands, sinewy threads springing free from the shirt, twining around the binder's fingers like questing tendrils of morning glory.

Otter was a child; she did not notice the clothes unstitching themselves. Tamarack was old, and her eyes were failing. She did not see it. Willow saw it, watched it, and dreamed of it. But she said nothing.

At the edges of Otter's childhood, the black trees cast shadows, and in those shadows, the dead were always hungry. But Otter did not look too closely at the shadows. As her mother had wished for her, she was clever and warm-hearted and fiercely happy. For a while.

Chapter Two

THE THING IN THE CORN

Otter and her friends were in trouble again.

There were three of them: Otter, Kestrel, and Cricket, who was the only boy. They were not related by blood, but they were close in age, and they'd grown up together like wolf pups. Now they were the oldest children of Westmost, and a solid little pack.

On that day, they'd been given the work of pulling up last year's cornstalks — muddy, messy, hard work — and they'd done quite a bit of it. But the gardens of Westmost were large, and the day was lovely: earliest spring, the Sap-Running Moon. There was a warm breeze and the sun was soft as a blessing, though snow still clung in the shadows under the pine trees. After the long winter in the lodges, such a day tempted them.

Kestrel had started it. There had been one thrown mud-ball, and then another — and then a storm of them, and a broken hoe. And now they were facing down the cold and careful judgments of —

"Who started it?" asked Thistle.

Otter would never betray one of her pack to one of the stiff, serious adults of Westmost — particularly not this adult. Thistle was the chief of Westmost's rangers, one of the most powerful women in the pinch, and the person who had given them the work in the first place. And, though Otter rarely thought of her so, she was Willow's mother, Otter's grandmother. There was something old and broken between Thistle and Willow. Otter did not know what had happened, but without even wondering, she took her mother's side.

She would not turn in Kestrel. And even if she had, Thistle would not have believed her. Kestrel started it? Kestrel was dutiful and upright. Only Otter and Cricket knew how mischief would slip out of that sober exterior like a turtle poking out of its shell. Only Otter and Cricket knew: Yes, Kestrel started it.

"Well?" said the ranger captain. "Speak. Cover your eyes and speak."

The three of them each covered their eyes. Otter saw Cricket sneak a sidelong look behind his lifted hand — over Kestrel's head, his gaze met Otter's. His eyes were dark and bright as a chickadee's and he had mud streaked across his nose. Otter had to swallow her grin. "Lady Ranger," she said, "I don't know what you mean." A clump of mud chose that moment to slide down the front of her shirt and plop at Thistle's feet.

"Binder's daughter," said Thistle, "I mean there is a hoe broken. There is a field half-done."

"I tripped," said Otter.

Cricket was trembling with silent laughter. Kestrel dipped her dutiful head and appeared to study the knots in the yarn that wrapped the foot of Thistle's staff.

"You tripped," said Thistle. "And your friends?"

"Helped me up," said Otter sturdily. It was quite true. She left out that her friends had also knocked her down.

Thistle put up both eyebrows. Otter, Kestrel, and Cricket stood united in their silence. Mud dripped from them, incriminatingly.

"Do it without the tools, then," said Thistle. She took the broken hoe from Kestrel; Otter and Cricket surrendered their digging sticks. "These come from the forest. Such things are not without cost."

And off she strode.

The three of them watched her go.

"There are tales," said Cricket, tugging on one ear, "of a woman who was never young. I think I now believe them."

"Are there stories you do not believe?" asked Kestrel as they walked back into the squelching corn. "I didn't know."

Cricket was in love with storytelling. He'd been known to spin the wildest ones with a perfectly straight face.

"There's one about a binder's daughter," said Cricket. "She *tripped*."

Kestrel laughed her sweet and secret laugh, the one she used for them alone.

"It's only a stick," said Otter. She spun her yarn bracelets, making sure the mud hadn't snagged them — a somewhat sulky gesture, in a place where yarn meant safety. Cornstalks, even the half-rotted ones of the end of winter, had a sullen grip on the earth. Clearing them without their digging sticks and rakes would not be easy. "A hoe is bit of wood and a bit of bone. How costly can it be?"

Experimentally, Otter tugged at a cornstalk. It didn't budge. It was lifted on its little roots, standing above a small cage of shadow, and it looked fragile, but it was going nowhere without a fight. Otter braced her foot against the corn hill and pulled hard. The stalk, of course, gave way suddenly, and Otter stumbled backward.

Cricket caught her. "Clearly, Otter, you are growing into a woman of grace and power."

"There is still mud to throw, Cricket."

Kestrel was tugging at her own cornstalk, and she too was struggling. "I side with Otter," she said. "Sticks" — tug — "are not" — tug — "so scarce."

"Thistle is thinking only of your safety," said Cricket. "I was planning a devastating surprise attack."

Otter's second stalk gave way then, and she fell again. The clots of earth tumbled down the little hill around her.

"Grace," sighed Cricket, shaking his head, "and power."

There was a clot the size of a snowball right by Otter's hand. She threw it. It splatted against Cricket's heart and slid goopily down the already-mud-slicked deerskin of his shirt. "Tsha!" he said. "My hand was out to help you!"

"Grace and power, you say," she said, rising to her knees among the clots.

Cricket's eyes widened and he dodged backward, tripping and landing on his tailbone in the sticky mud. Otter was laughing even as she stood up, armed.

"Otter!" Kestrel's voice was stretched between delight and caution. "Oh, Otter, don't. . . ."

Cricket was a pole's length away, and the low spot gave him shelter. He stretched a hand behind him, seeking a clump of dirt.

Otter was laughing so hard it was bending her up like grief. She was hiccupping. Cricket fumbled, reaching — and in the place he was reaching toward, Otter saw something.

Something was resting in the nest of shadows under a cornstalk, something stirring as Cricket's hand came near. Something gawk-stretched and ugly as a new-hatched bird with no feathers and skin over its eyes. Something that moved subtly, like the earth moving above something buried. Something struggling and starving.

Cricket reached backward, fumbling toward the shadow-cage, and the dark thing opened its dark mouth like a baby bird, like a snake. It opened so wide that if it had had a jaw, its jaw would have broken. Suddenly it was all mouth, and it was reaching —

There was one heartbeat in which Otter couldn't move. She was still hiccupping, though her heart had nearly stopped with horror. Kestrel shouted: "Cricket!"

Cricket grinned up at Kestrel, groping unknowing toward the shadow — and Otter dove to save him.

Anyone in the pinch would have counted her as a child. But it never occurred to her that most people would have dived the other way.

"Ware!" shouted Kestrel.

Cricket's smile froze, his head whipped toward the

warning. He was halfway to his feet by the time Otter hit him. She'd meant to knock him sideways, but because he was twisting she hit him wrong. He fell full backward, into the corn.

Onto the dead thing.

It vanished under him for a moment, and in the next heartbeat it was coming out of the muddy trail over his breastbone, where Otter's latest mudball had hit him. It had pushed up through him like a shoot breaking free of a seed.

"Ware!" shouted Kestrel, her voice cracking then ringing out: "Ware the dead!"

Otter, meanwhile, had thrown herself backward, out of range of the uncoiling darkness. She fell into the cold, sticky mud — and Cricket gave a single raw scream.

A shadow fell across Otter and her heart lurched — but it was Kestrel, yanking her to her feet.

Cricket was thrashing. He managed to roll over onto his stomach, but the dead thing only moved with him, rolling him as a wolf rolls a deer, breaking now out of his back. Kestrel's fingers dug savagely into Otter's arm.

Otter yanked free, pulling at the yarn that wound her wrists. In three drumbeats, she had the long loop hooked around her spread fingers and was making a pattern of crossed strings in the air.

Cricket pushed himself up on his hands for just a moment — and then fell, his face in the mud. By then, Kestrel had her bracelets free too. "Not the cradle," said Otter, looking at the pattern Kestrel was casting. It was a cradle-star, the simplest of casts; done well, with intention and power, it could both detect and repel the dead. "Not the cradle — we have to pull it out." If they repelled the thing, it might only seep back down into Cricket's body.

The fallen boy was gulping in panic, swallowing earth.

"I can't cast anything else," said Kestrel.

Very few could.

There was an instant when they simply stared at each other. Kestrel shot a look at the ring of earthlodges. From the ring, and from the river and from the ward gates, there came shouting and movement. *Ware the dead*, Kestrel had called. It would bring help running. But the garden was big and they were on the far side of it, just a pine's length from the ward itself. Even Thistle had long since left them. It would be a hundred heartbeats before they had help.

And Cricket did not have that many heartbeats left.

"Is there only one?" said Kestrel.

"I only saw one."

That meant nothing. The dead were drawn together like raindrops into greater drops. There was never only one.

Kestrel looked down at Cricket, at the shadows he was lying in, the little pockets and knots of shadow cast by the jumbled earth. Any one of them might have contained something hungry and nearly invisible, something deadly. And yet Kestrel dropped her bracelets, which were her only defense, went to her knees in those shadows. She lifted Cricket by the shoulders, jerking his head into her lap so he wouldn't drown in mud. She took both his hands. She looked up at Otter. And she said: "Pull it out."

So Otter stood over her two friends, with help coming, but not quickly enough, and the dead thing close enough to taste in the air. The world seemed to narrow. Wind beat wings in her ears: the only sound. The strings dug into the roots of her fingers. They crossed and opened: the only movement.

Kestrel's fingers were laced around Cricket's fingers, two tangles of knuckles, white with panic. Her hands were still. His hands jerked open and closed even as she held them. Otter could hear him gulping, see his back arch like a torn deer trying to rise.

But he could not rise. The dead thing rose out of him. It was an arrow tall now. It had thickened until it almost had form — twisty like smoke, gelatinous like frogs' eggs, rising up from Cricket's spine. It was so close to Kestrel that her breath seemed to stir it. It wove in front of her frozen eyes like a snake rearing. But still she did not let Cricket go.

Otter's pattern had come together. The tree: roots in one hand, branches in the other. She braced herself and lowered the hand that held the roots into the sticky-looking shadow.

The dead thing flowed up into the strings.

It was the first time Otter had held the dead. She'd made the loops dance around her fingers before; she could cast patterns fast and fearlessly, but she'd never before used them. Until that instant, she hadn't known what it meant to use them. Whether she *could* use them.

But she could. The cords between her fingers felt to her, suddenly, as real as her fingers themselves. As real as if her blood vessels had been pulled outside of her skin and held stretched open. The touch of the dead thing on those cords was like plunging the hand into winter water. A shock, and then a slow-building pain. That was power: the ability to feel that cold. And beyond that: the ability to feel that cold, and stand still.

Otter lifted her hands. She held them high, and as far from her own body as she could. She pulled the dead thing up, stretching it thin — and then it came free of Cricket's back. The boy made a wet and broken sound.

It was all in Otter's hands now. She started to shiver, and then shake as if taken by a seizure. How long could one stand in such cold? The tree she'd cast made the dead thing climb — it could no longer reach down for Kestrel and Cricket. *Good,* she thought, but her hands shook as she moved the pattern, trying to change the tree to the scaffold. Her fingers were nearly numb. They would drop the cast — they would drop it and then . . .

The narrowed world was tiny now: Otter could see only the blue cords and the black eel of the dead thing pulsing and struggling inside them.

And then she saw other hands reaching into her pattern.

"Otter. Otter, give it to me."

It was her mother's voice: her mother, the binder, Willow. Willow's fingers seemed to shine as they reached in and mirrored her fingers, slipping into all the right places. Otter's vision was fading: She could see willful darkness pulse around the cords, and the cords themselves flaring like lightning and beating like red hearts. She knew she was close to passing out. Breathless, she managed the last twist — the one that would move her pattern from her hands onto her mother's.

And then she found herself sitting on the cold wet earth.

Cricket was curled up on his side, with Kestrel still clutching both his hands. His mouth was black and dribbled with swallowed earth. That black mouth moved. For a moment Otter was frightened, but then realized it was good news, that moving mouth. Cricket was still breathing.

She was still breathing. She looked up and saw the blue cords of her casting on her mother's hands. They were silhouetted against the pale spring sky — the whole sky looked fractured by them. Willow spread her fingers, pulling the scaffold pattern long. The thing inside them went long too. Willow made one more twist, turning the scaffold into a pattern called sky. The narrow black thing burst open, like birds from a tree, and was gone.

Otter blinked, and blinked again, and looked around her.

Help had come: the strong and quiet and practical women of Westmost. They stood tall among the cornstalks, that upright and almost that still. There were rangers in both inward- and outward-facing rings, their staffs held ready. There was Newt, the bonesetter, kneeling now by Cricket. There was Otter's mother, Willow, who was casting a figure with Otter's yarns. And there at her mother's side was Thistle, looking weathered and strong as a digger pine.

"Get up," said Thistle. "Let us see the earth."

Otter had almost forgotten the danger they were in, sitting in shadows. All her life she'd known — everyone in that place knew — that any patch of shadow might be home to the dead. And yet, exhausted and terrified, she'd forgotten.

She flinched at Thistle's words and tried to get up. Her knees buckled.

Willow had the cradle cast across her hands now. She thrust it up in Thistle's face: three clean diamonds. The strings did not shiver or twist, as they would have in the presence of the dead. "There's nothing here," Willow said. She pulled the yarn free of her fingers and coiled the loop in her palm. Then she reached down and took Otter's hand. Otter felt the warmth and scratch of the yarns between them. Willow pulled; Otter came wobbling to her feet.

"Daughter," said Willow, "those were strong knots."

Otter was still breathing in weird gulps; they made her feel as if she were still laughing or beginning to cry. "Cricket?" she asked.

"He's alive," sniffed Newt. She seemed almost offended by the fact. Healer she might be, but Newt the bonesetter had not a soft spot in her whole body.

On the other hand, silent Kestrel was all soft, suddenly. Tears were running down her face.

"Alive," said Otter, half in wonder.

"And you, daughter?" said Willow. "It is no small thing, the scaffold."

"I'm alive," said Otter. She spread her hands then, looking over her own skin for the mark of the dead. But there was nothing. "I'm alive," she said.

The rangers scooped Cricket out of Kestrel's arms and carried him toward the bonesetter's lodge.

Otter turned in her mother's arms and pulled Kestrel to her feet.

Thistle looked them up and down. "Come," she said shortly. She had the manner of someone accustomed to being obeyed. Kestrel wrapped her fingers in Otter's. They were both shaking. Surely they had no more need for courage. For surely they had no courage left.

"Come," said Thistle, more sharply still. Willow laid a palm against each of their backs. "Ch'hhh," she soothed them, soft as a breeze. "Best to." So they went. They trailed behind the women carrying Cricket's body like the drummers at the end of a funeral.

Inside the lodge, the rangers set Cricket wobbling on his feet. Newt pulled Cricket's shirt off over his head. The boy tottered and tipped to his knees, groaning. There were marks on him: white. One just below his breastbone, one over his spine, as if something had burst from within him, back and front. He pushed both his hands over the mark on his chest — a scrabbling, desperate gesture, as if the white mark were a gaping wound. He folded forward over his knees. Otter held on to Kestrel and stared at Cricket's bent back. The hunch. The spine like a cord with knots tied in it. The way the waist dipped inward that was different than the way a girl's waist dipped. The panicked heave of the ribs.

"What shape had the gast?" Newt the bonesetter asked Kestrel. "Did it have hands?"

Otter's heart skipped. The mark on Cricket's back was formless, a blotch, but it was the right size to be a handprint. "No," Kestrel said. "No hands." It was not clear if she was saying what she remembered, or begging for what she hoped was true.

"Hmpf," said Newt, and looked up at Otter. "Well? Did the dead thing have a shape?"

Otter said: "No shape. It had no shape."

Thistle turned toward her. "Are you sure?"

Otter was not sure. She looked at Thistle, whose eyes were flint gray and hard. She looked at her mother, whose face was set and sad. "It was strong," said Otter. "But we caught it — we held it. Surely it cannot have been . . ."

Kestrel tore herself from Otter's side, then, and knelt with Cricket, wrapping her arms around him. "He is not turning," said Kestrel, and this time it sounded like pure will. Newt seemed far too willing to see a handprint in that blotch — far too ready to cut Cricket's throat with her healing knife. "It is not inside him. He will be healed."

Otter looked around. The little space was full of women, looking carefully down at one gasping, trembling half-grown boy.

Otter knelt beside Kestrel. She put her hand over the white mark on Cricket's back. "Cricket," she said, and her voice broke, "it's gone now. It's not in you. It's gone."

/\/\/\/\

For days they waited to see if it would be true.

They were not sure, not quite sure, what had touched Cricket.

The dead were of three kinds. The commonest were the slip. They had no more form than a clump of roots and earth.

They had no more will than hunger. Their danger was that they gathered together: Where there was one, there were usually many.

The gast were different: They had form. A limb, sometimes. A way of turning that, though blunt and blind, suggested eyes. They had cunning too. Eyeless, but they could watch. Brainless, but they could wait. They were stronger, rarer. The thing in the corn, with its open mouth — gast, probably.

But they were not quite sure. Because they had not seen its hands.

Who knew what the slip had been in life, or even the gast, with their blunt cunning. But the Ones with White Hands had once been human. And alone among all creatures, humans could be cruel.

Even slip could kill, of course. The touch of one made a numbness and a weakness, and many a ranger had a little limp, a lost finger, a gray place hidden beneath their green leggings. The touch of many slip was a mud to drown in. The touch of a gast could blast open all the knots in a limb. They could weaken a lung, chill a heart. It was rare to take such a touch and live.

But better to be touched by the gast than the Ones with White Hands. The slip and the gast — their touch went to the body. The touch of a White Hand went to the mind.

There are wasps in this world whose sting paralyzes but leaves alive. Inside the bodies of their caterpillar prey they lay their eggs, and later, while the inchworm lies — paralyzed, alive — the young wasps eat their way out. And so the White Hands were also called Wasp Kind.

Their touch did not kill. It weakened, it dazzled, but it did not kill. It was said indeed that Mad Spider herself had been touched and touched and touched again as she fought the White Hands away from her last ward. Touched and touched and touched and still she drove them back, and with a knot made from her own belt she caught and unmade them. Then she went back to her pinch — not Westmost but a different and greater place: Eyrie, the city of dreams. She went back to her home, back to her lodge, undid its lashings, with her power pulled the poles down, and buried herself alive.

The touch of the White Hands does not kill. It transforms. Those touched by a White Hand become Hands themselves.

In the beginning it looks like madness. Probably one of the Sunlit People — a buffalo hunter from the prairies, say, or a Water Walker with his travois and feathered spear, would take it as madness. But the Shadowed People, the free women of the forest, know that it is not madness. It is the White Hand, eating its way out from the inside.

Chapter Three

THE FIRST UNBINDING

Newt the bonesetter kept Cricket confined and waited for him to go mad.

"She's looking for a chance to kill me," said Cricket, when Otter and Kestrel came to visit him inside the bonesetter's lodge. "One of these mornings I'll choke on my porridge and she'll see the foam on my lips and pull out a knife."

"Try a rising block," said Kestrel with an arrow-straight face. "I am sure you can best her."

"Oh!" Cricket gasped. "Don't make me laugh!" He twisted sideways where he lay on a sleeping platform, propped up on a pile of buffalo robes. He pushed a hand over the white mark on his breastbone, as if pushing the air back into himself.

"All right," said Otter. "Possibly you can't best her. But we would avenge your death."

"We would," said Kestrel. "It would be epic. A tale for our granddaughters. There would be stars for you, Cricket."

"On the dark side of that," said Otter, "you *would* still be dead."

"That does seem dark." Cricket, grinning, sprawled backward onto the robes. The gast in the cornfield had unwoven things inside him, and Newt had wrapped him in red-dyed cords, carefully knotted. He still had his hand pressed among them, and for a moment he panted helplessly.

"How are you, Cricket?" said Kestrel softly, when the boy had his breath back.

Cricket's smile faded and he shook his head.

Otter touched the cords around him and felt their power stir softly, as if she'd touched something sleeping.

Where Otter saw power, Kestrel saw pain. She turned to the heavy clay pot that was nestled in the embers of the fire pit. "Is this willow bark?" When Cricket nodded, she dipped a gourdful and handed it to him. "You're hurting," she said.

Cricket took the gourd, slipping his fingers among hers, smiling. "Ch'hhh, I'll be all right," he said. "So long as I don't talk in my sleep, like Red Fox in the story, and wake up with my throat opened."

Otter stuck her finger in the brew pot, and then into her mouth. The bitterness made her suck in her cheeks. "Is there no honey for this?"

"Oh, the home of Newt needs no honey," said Cricket. "She's that sweet."

"Well" — Kestrel smiled, taking the gourd back from him — "don't go mad."

"Keep visiting me," said Cricket.

Kestrel hooked the curve of the gourd stem over its stick by the fire, and when she turned around her expression was fierce. "Cricket: It had no hands." She glanced at Otter.

"We held it," said Otter. "Two children held it. It was no stronger than that. It had no hands."

Cricket's face softened, and he reached and took one of each of their hands. "If such a large seed were planted in me," he said, "I would know it."

Would he?

"Always in the stories," said Cricket, "they know it."

/\/\/\/\

And indeed, as spring spilled into summer, Cricket did not go mad.

He continued not to go mad until even Newt seemed to give up hope that he would. She tightened her bindings around him — which made him wheeze — but she also began to let him out into the air.

The first day, he went leaning between Kestrel and Otter. Because winters in Westmost could be bitter, earthlodges were built with small tunnels for entrances, with a curtain at one end, and a curtain at the other. They were not built for three to go abreast. Otter's shoulder hit one of the supporting poles in the half-darkness. A moment later, there was an *oophf* from Kestrel, and she stopped too.

"We're stuck," said Cricket. "Like a baby too big to be born. We're doomed."

"The rangers got you in here somehow," said Kestrel reasonably.

But none of them wanted to think about that moment. Just the mention of it made Cricket shiver. "I've gotten fat since then," he said, though the lightness in his voice cracked a little. "Newt slips me sweets."

They shifted and went sideways, and they got out. That first day they only leaned on the southward flank of the earthlodge, and Cricket breathed in the sun, closed his eyes, and smiled.

Soon enough he was walking under his own power. Nearly every day that summer, Otter or Kestrel or both would help him go walking, or sit with him on the grassy roof of the earthlodge while he tried out one of his new stories — he'd been much visited by the ancient woman Flea, the pinch's storyteller, for whom Cricket had long been a favorite.

The beginning of the Moon of Ease saw him drowsing in a patch of crown vetch — his black braids tangled in the dense lavender flowers, while Otter sat guarding him and Kestrel picked the feathery leaves of mayweed and the first fist-and-feather flowers of bee balm, to tuck into his straw pillow. The mere scent on her hands in his hair was enough to wake him. He caught her by the wrist, turned his head, and breathed deep.

The Moon of Ease closed and the Sunflower Moon opened. Strength came back to Cricket's body; he and Kestrel would walk the whole rim of the pinch, inside the ward. At first they went hand in hand because he was breathless from the knots around his ribs. But later they went hand in hand without that cause.

Otter watched them and wondered. It would probably be the last summer of the sunflower years, as the Shadowed People called the space between childhood and adulthood, after girls shot into their height, but before they were given their women's belts. When the sunflower time passed, the girls would join a cord — becoming a ranger or a binder or a dyer or some other thing. The secret learnings and solemn duties of each work would claim them — separate them from one another. And Cricket . . . Well. That was harder still.

/\/\/\/\

By the time the Corn-Cut Moon began to wax, marking the beginning of harvest, Cricket moved almost as well as if he'd never been injured — but still Newt kept him confined.

Every day Otter and Kestrel worked hard in the garden for the morning — in the harvest, everyone worked hard. They took rest, and then one or both of them would rescue Cricket.

One day, all three of them went. It was a fine day, warm. They wandered along the little river, kicking round stones into the bright, shallow water, climbing boulders for no better reason than that they were young and they could. They drew out the wander, Otter and Kestrel batting a ball back and forth, Cricket practicing sleight of hand with a chipped arrowhead he'd found.

They went down the river as far as they could — which was not far. Between the pinch and the shadows of the forest was the ward.

The ward was like a fence whose fence posts were full-grown trees: a ring of slender birches that circled the pinch. From tree to tree went blue cords of braided rawhide, knotted and knitted together, tied here and there with that most precious of things: yarn. The cords dove into the earth to knot unseen roots. They reached three times a woman's height. The ward thrummed in the wind and cast strange shadows in the sun.

The ward was the crown of a binder's work. It was a glory. It was the only thing that kept the whole pinch from filling with hungry shadows. But just then, it was also a fence that was keeping them in.

Kestrel, Cricket, and Otter did not really consider themselves trapped: That they had never left their village, that the dead could be anywhere — it was simply the way things were. Still they pushed a little: They followed the river to the gap it made in the ward. No dead would come through there — the dead could not cross running water. There was not even, that day, a ranger at guard.

"We could go right out the gate," said Cricket, looking at the open space in wonder.

"Yes," said Kestrel. "If we were seeking horrible death, we could find it, right over there!"

"Handy," said Cricket, and sighed. There was, just there at the very edge of their world, a big slab of granite, smooth as a shell, that slanted lazily down to the water. Cricket sprawled on his back on the sun-warmed stone, and Otter and Kestrel sat on either side of him. Strings of shadow danced over them, and they talked the sun down the sky.

It was the last of their sunflower summers: They stood on the edge. As soon as that fall's great fire — or the next year, or the next — they would be taken into the cords. They would be given a belt — a woman's belt, an adult's. They would learn secrets. And then the silences between them, the warm and easy silences, would fill and change. Otter's heart wrung, just for a moment, thinking of that, even while chickadees still flitted overhead.

Cricket, meanwhile, was holding his arrowhead up against the bright sky. He kept pinching it between two fingers and closing the fingers to tuck the little object into his palm. The third time the arrowhead dropped and went skittering down the slope of granite, Otter sighed at him. "Cricket, you know that I love you, so trust me in this: That's hopeless."

"It's part of my work," said Cricket, which was true: Many storytellers used sleights of hand and other small magics to knot a gasp or a laugh into a well-known tale.

Kestrel picked up the arrowhead and handed it back to the sprawling boy. "That doesn't mean you're not bad at it."

"Do you think so?" Cricket grinned up at her. He turned his hand over and opened it. There was an arrowhead there already. He closed his hand again, flipped it, righted it, opened it, and there were two arrowheads. He closed his hand a third time, and when he opened it there were three. "Keep near me, Kestrel," he said, still looking into her eyes. "I'll show you wonders."

And Kestrel — unexpectedly — blushed from her hem to her hair.

Cricket dropped his eyes from hers, as if out of kindness. One by one he made the arrowheads vanish. "I will be a story-teller," he said. By the measure of their people, he should not have said it. The status of a cord should be given, not claimed. But Cricket walked always at the edge of the forbidden. Being a boy, but not a weak one, he could hardly help it.

"I will be a storyteller," he said again. He looked up at Otter and took one step further: "And you?"

Otter had the blood of a binder; she had never wanted anything else. The work of binding the dead was terrifying and dangerous and difficult — but it was her work, and her heart claimed it fiercely.

And yet . . .

That day in the corn had changed things. Otter had power now — she had power the way a puppy has feet. It came too early. It was too big for her. It made her conspicuous, and clumsy. It marked her out. After she saved Cricket, the people of Westmost watched her carefully. A child who could cast a scaffold? A sunflower girl who could lift and hold the dead? It was extraordinary. Behind her back they whispered: "Here is a girl who will save us." And: "Here is a binder born."

But Willow watched Otter practice her loops and casts with a new and cold gleam in her eye.

For years, Otter had helped her mother and Tamarack with the simplest parts of their work. She'd been very small when Tamarack had first pulled her into her lap and showed her how to use a drop spindle to whirl the buffalo hair into yarn. She remembered laughing as she learned it — the little spinning top was harder than it looked. Once, it flew off and hit Willow on her dignified nose. Tamarack had laughed and Otter had laughed, and Willow had made a show of outrage, like a bluejay, before dissolving into laughter too. As Otter's hands had grown bigger and stronger, she'd spent long winter days braiding rawhide into cord. The binder's lodge was always warmed by a good fire, well-lit with pine-resin glims, cozy with the coiled cords and knives of the binder's trade. The three of them often sang, and when they were silent, the silence was well-lit and rich as amber. It had been Otter's whole life. She'd been warm and safe inside it.

But since that day in the corn, Willow's gaze had turned sharp and the silence was first ice: thin and brittle. Otter felt uneasy under that gaze, that silence. Uneasy, and even ashamed. What had she done?

"I will be a binder," she said, to the silence, to Cricket's question, to the world. It felt like defiance. But she said it again: "I will be a binder."

The words hung there. The air was warm and the sun came in long slants. Cricket reached out for her. His hand was empty now, and it seemed to hold light and time. "Otter, you will be a legend," he said. "There will be stars for you."

When Cricket said it, it sounded true. Otter looked down at him, for a moment caught in wonder. Then he grinned and pulled the arrowhead from her ear.

"Will you go this year?" she asked him. Another breach. She was sure they had each thought about the day Cricket would leave Westmost, but they had never spoken of it.

But Cricket surprised her. "I'm not going," he said.

Otter saw Kestrel grow very still. She turned. The two girls looked at Cricket.

"Why should I go?" said Cricket. "Westmost is my home as much as yours. My mother was born here, my mother's mother."

"But you're a boy," said Otter.

Cricket faked a startle and reached up, fumbling for the telltale knob in his throat. "I am?" He widened his eyes and dropped his hands to his private parts, checking there too. "You're right!"

Otter spluttered and threw the arrowhead at him.

He caught it, one handed, easy, and tossed it back to her.

"Some stay," said Kestrel, quietly.

And that was true. Most boys left the Shadowed People when they came of age, going with Water Walkers, the traders who plied the narrow safety of the river, or joining the Sunlit People, following the buffalo herds on the prairies. Binding power ran in the female line, and few people untouched by that power cared to live in a place so deadshadowed.

But some stayed. Even among the boys, a few stayed.

Otter looked at Kestrel looking at Cricket, and saw a reason he might want to be one of the boys who risked Westmost.

Cricket looked back toward the corn and sighed. "Oh, look: Here comes the joy of my life." It was Newt, with red cords wrapped around her shoulders and a look as sour as willow bark on her face. "Tsha! If ever again I am blasted open, don't save me." Then he put on a smile like Red Fox's smile and said: "Hail, Lady Boneset."

"There you are," said Newt. "You know I need to tighten your bindings."

"Ah," said Cricket. "I *thought* I could breathe." But he stood up, shrugged off stiffness, and then shrugged off his shirt.

"Have you no modesty, boy? You're not a child anymore."

And he wasn't. Otter found herself staring at the narrow chest crisscrossed with red cords. They were startling as wounds against his bare skin. He didn't look like someone who had been hurt. His skin was the dark sweet color of old honey; his hair was glossy. And while the pain had cost him some weight, it seemed as if it had merely polished away his boyish softness. He looked lean and strong and not at all like a child. The white mark of the gast looked like a star above his heart.

"These are my friends," said Cricket. "And I don't want to go back into your lodge, today or tomorrow or in the next moon, Lady Boneset. I think I am well healed, and I'm tired of darkness."

Newt harrumphed but didn't press the point. And, after all, she'd brought new cords with her. She hadn't, though, brought her second. She looked Kestrel and Otter up and down as if selecting a cut of meat. "Binder's daughter," she said, "I imagine you can hold the end of a bit of rope?"

Otter nodded. She was not keen to help Newt, but she was ready to help Cricket.

"Then take —"

And something burst from the ripe corn behind them.

Everyone whirled around. The corn in that season was thick, almost pine-black where the shadows hit it. It rustled and thrashed, and then opened, and something came out of it. A living person: a woman. Otter's mother, the binder, Willow. She was running.

She was wild-eyed, almost stumbling as she ran. For a moment the three friends could only stare. Then Kestrel swung around, pressing her back to Otter's and pulling her bracelets off. She cast a cradle — a bit lopsided — and held it up, into the dark face of the woods beyond the ward. Otter lifted her own cradle between herself and the running form of her mother. Cricket — though he was so powerless that he did not even bother with his bracelets — took the third point, making the three of them into an arrowhead. Now nothing would come on them unaware.

"Newt!" Willow shouted. "Newt!" Her breath was ragged, her voice wild: It raised the hairs on Otter's scalp. But she hadn't said what they'd dreaded she would. She hadn't said *ware the dead.*

"It's Tamarack," said Willow, stumbling up to them. Behind them, the ward itself seemed to shiver to her voice, and a sudden wind moaned through it. "Newt: Her breath is failing."

Newt paused, and then slowly lifted a hand to cover her eyes. She bowed to Willow before she spoke. "Tamarack our binder has long been halfway out of the world. A blessing if she should go the rest of the way, and peacefully."

"I am not ready," said Willow. "Newt, I am not ready."

Otter felt Cricket shift beside her. She glanced and met the boy's dark eyes: *Not ready? The greatest binder since Mad Spider, not ready? Not ready for what?*

Newt had a similar bewildered look. Her mouth narrowed, then she gathered herself: "I must finish with Cricket. Then I'll bring my medicines."

"Quickly," demanded Willow.

"Most likely she cannot be saved." Newt nudged Cricket forward, beginning the long and fiddly work of undoing the healing knots. "If it's her time, she'll go, whether you're ready or not."

"I'm not," said Willow. And she reached forward and put her hand, flat, in the middle of Cricket's chest.

Cricket gasped and stumbled back. The red cords that bound him — the healing cords that had been intricately knotted, alive with power — had come loose in a heartbeat. They sagged around his waist, looped down his legs.

Newt lifted her braceleted wrists against Willow, as if Willow herself were one of the dead. "What did you do?"

This was not a binder's power: It was the dead who undid knots. A binder's power was to wrap and tie. To hold tight and to fix. One of the most difficult things a binder could do was undo her own work without being caught in it. It was of course possible — a spider does not get caught in her own web. But even a spider must know where to step. An unbinding was a slow and careful thing, like pulling out the lowest stick in a pile without letting the pile fall.

But what Willow had done had not been slow and careful. It had been instant, instinctive.

Terrifying.

On Otter's fingers, the yarns were stirring, restless, as if in the presence of the dead.

"What did you do?" said Newt again, swallowing her way toward calm, lowering her hands.

"Come, Boneset," said the binder. "Now."

Chapter Four

SCAFFOLDS

Tamarack died that night.

There is little a knot can do for someone coming loose from the world, and Newt could not hold her. In truth, she did not try. There was no reason to try. The old binder seemed at peace as she worked her way loose, one breath, one pause between breaths, one breath at a time.

So Tamarack was at peace and Newt was at (as usual) gruff indifference, and only Willow was frightened. She knelt beside the sleeping platform, her hand on Tamarack's hand, and when the pause between breaths stretched, so did Willow's fear. "Please," she said, clutching at Tamarack's hand, shaking it. "Please."

The old binder's eyes turned to hers. They'd gone filmed as a dead fish's eyes. "Let me go, Willow," she rasped.

Willow stopped begging but didn't release the hand.

A death, like a birth, can take a while. In the binder's lodge, through the warm night, Otter watched as Tamarack labored with her death. When Otter slipped into sleep, it was the silence that woke her, woke her with a jerk of fear: Willow holding her breath as Tamarack didn't breathe.

And then Tamarack started breathing again.

Let me go, she'd said.

But Willow didn't. The night grew tighter and tighter, like leather shrinking as it dries.

Tamarack. She had braided Otter's hair, embroidered her shirts with the quills of porcupines. When she claimed the lodge's share of wood to burn she'd kept an eye open for cottonwood, and slipped Otter bits of the inner bark to chew, just for the sweetness. She was upright and mostly silent, but to Otter she was near to a grandmother. It was hard to watch her die.

Like most of the children of Westmost, Otter had seen a death or two. But her mother's fear made her fearful, and the little space of the binder's lodge became unbearable. She remembered the feeling she'd had when she'd held the dead thing in the corn: that her nerves had left her body and were held stretched as yarn between her hands. She felt that now, though she cast no patterns.

And finally Otter could not watch it anymore. She went through the two curtains of the earthlodge and out into the warm night. At the center of the pinch, inside the double ring of earthlodges, was the palm: a flat open space where the dancing and the games of hoop-and-lance kept the earth bare and packed. It was a friendly place, even in the darkness: well-known and safe as a mother's hand. Otter walked along its edge, where the bird's-foot flower made forays into the clay. It was a quiet night, smelling of smoke and cooking and human life. She could hear the murmur of the river, the sleepy rattle of the summer-stiff corn, the crickets singing about the coming fall.

A hoop — a bent wood hoop from the hoop-and-lance game — rolled across the open ground toward her. Otter caught it and flicked it rolling back into the darkness, and by the time it was halfway across the palm, its roller had strolled up to catch it, just at the edge of sight: Cricket. He spun the hoop up into the air, caught it, spun it a few times around his wrist, and walked over to Otter.

"Spider knows you need practice," she said, "but I hope you left the lance at home. If you hurt yourself in the dark, there will be no one to save you."

"I'm a storyteller," he said. "I would holler at the top of my highly trained voice." She could see the flash of his smile, white in the darkness. "But, yes, I just have the hoop."

Otter leaned back on the flank of the nearest earthlodge and Cricket leaned with her. They were silent for a while, then Cricket said: "Is she dead?"

Otter shook her head, unable to put words to what she feared.

Cricket slipped his hand into hers. "It has been too long since I saw the moon." He sighed and tilted back his head. His hand was dusty and warm.

The moon was a little past half, and waxing. It was riding like a boat up the river of the Milky Way. Otter considered that Cricket probably hadn't seen it all summer. In her mind, she counted the moons off: Sap, Blossoms, New Grass, Ease, the Sunflower Moon, the Moon of Thunderstorms . . .

"She won't let Tamarack go," said Otter. The words seemed to burst from her, to come from nowhere.

"She should," said Cricket.

I'm not ready, Willow had said, and touched Cricket above his heart. The boy had looked gutted as he staggered back.

"Are you all right?" Otter asked. "My mother — did she hurt you?"

Cricket was silent a moment, as.if turning the question over like a flintknapper. "It didn't hurt." He considered again. The moonlight seemed to bring his answers more slowly. "It didn't . . . exactly hurt. I was frightened. I thought: *Perhaps it was a White Hand in the corn after all; perhaps this is the moment it eats its way out of me.* I felt as if a gast were touching me. But still it didn't hurt."

Otter tightened her hand around his. Wings flashed over them suddenly, silent and very close, golden in the moonlight. "Look!" called Cricket after the vanishing owl, and a heartbeat later came the death-cry of a rabbit. All their lives, rabbits made no sound, but in death . . .

"She won't let Tamarack go." Otter shuddered. "Why should that . . . Why is that so frightening? There's no story like that."

"I know one," he said. "I know one a little like that. But it is not a happy story."

The cheatgrass growing on the earthlodge was prickly against her back. She shifted, uncomfortable. "Something is wrong. Cricket, something is . . ."

The boy didn't answer, but wrapped his arm around her shoulder. She folded against him. Even through their clothes, his body was warm. For just a moment, she wished they were small again, that they could tumble in the dust of the plaza and have it mean nothing. So small that she wouldn't have glimpsed whatever dark thing was beginning to happen.

When Otter went back to the lodge, Newt was gone and Tamarack was dead. Willow was still holding her dead hand. The new binder of Westmost leaned her face into the body of the old binder and whispered: "Don't go, Tamarack. Don't go."

The whisper, more than any howl, made Otter's hair stir like a cast pattern. She was sure, for a moment, that something was listening.

Inside the binder's lodge, which had been Tamarack's and Willow's and was now only Willow's, Otter put on her finest shirt, and found that she had grown since the last time she'd had any need to be fine. The soft leather pulled taught across her shoulders; it made her arms feel half-pinned. When Otter turned, she found her mother watching her with eyes so fierce that she almost flinched. She swallowed down something like shame — what had she done? — and crossed her arms over her chest to hide the way the smock both crushed and showed her new breasts.

"The plain would be better, I think," said Willow. "Tamarack will — Tamarack would understand." She ran a finger down Otter's sleeve, over the white suede. "Look at you, my fierce lovely one: You're all grown."

Otter was not quite sure when she had stopped being a child. That day in the corn? Or only yesterday, when Willow had touched Cricket, when Tamarack had died? She was certain that she was no sunflower now.

She turned away before she pulled off her smock and put on her plain one.

Willow, meanwhile, dressed herself in red: skins made pale with brain-tanning and dyed with bloodroot. Over her ribs were embroidered ribs, porcupine quills stark white against the vivid leather. A binder's funeral gear. Willow fussed over her belt, newly threaded with three silver disks: a binder's belt, echoing the three stars in the belt of the constellation Mad Spider. She hung the binder's knife from the loop at her hip. Otter caught herself staring at the knife. It had a blade of white chert and its handle was a human jaw.

"Daughter," said Willow. She raised her hand to touch Otter's hair. "It would be all right to weep."

Was that it? Otter wondered. Was the fear and strangeness she felt only sorrow?

Or was her hair stirring, all by itself, where her mother's hand had touched it?

So it was that the first thing Otter did as a woman was go out to bind the dead.

Tamarack had been the Binder of Westmost. There was not a woman in the pinch who did not honor her by walking with her this last time. When they gathered at the gap where the river went through the ward, Otter found she was not the only one who was newly being treated as an adult: Kestrel was there too, standing quietly. Otter went and stood next to her and was glad she was there.

And then the drums began to sound.

To walk the dead out, the Shadowed People played a deep drum that they played at no other time. It sounded like the heartbeat of the world.

Tum, thum — Kestrel reached out and took Otter's hand. And the procession gathered itself, and stepped into the river. To Otter, the water where she'd so often splashed seemed bitter cold that day. The ward, now that she was about to pass through it, seemed taller. It did not feel like something that was keeping them safe. It seemed like a thing with its own power, its own intentions. Going through its gap was like going through its mouth.

Otter was not sure if they were being spit out or swallowed.

She tightened her hand around Kestrel's; Kestrel's hand tightened around hers. They went out.

The Shadowed People had always bound their dead to rest high in trees. In the time of Mad Spider, they had learned not to do it too close to home. It was some way, therefore, to the scaffolding grounds — the distance gave the pinch safety, warning, if the dead did not stay bound. Outside the ward the scrub meadow went on a little farther, and they passed between birch saplings and digger pine. Then, sudden as passing through a curtain, the procession was in the forest itself.

The forest. Bare and straight, darker than skin, the trunks of the pine trees stood in ranks. They went back and back, until they made a blur, like dark mist. The ground under them was mostly bare, cloaked in needles. Gray stone broke from it here and there. It was more than quiet: It ate sound. It was more than shadowy: The shadows watched.

At the back of the procession, the drum beat. The splash of many feet made a constant living sound against it. Someone began to play a bone flute. *We are here*, the drum said, the flute said, *We are alive.*

Soon the bitter water had soaked through even the best-greased of boots. The round stones of the river were difficult underfoot. The women carrying the bier staggered. One of the oldest women — Flea, the storyteller — fell, and from there had to be helped along. But no one left the river. The water could only kill you. The forest could do worse.

The procession left the river and went up, climbing beside a splashing rivulet, through wet ferns. On either hand was a rough fence of knotted cords, just a strand or two, strung from trunk to trunk. The path grew steep, and the fern and pine needles gave way underfoot to scoured slopes of rock. Finally the procession came into a stand of lodgepole pine that clung to a cliff edge, high above a black lake. Across the lake rose great gray spires of granite, round-topped and steep-sided as fingers. It was as if something huge had been buried there, and was digging its way out.

Willow stopped. The people bunched and gathered behind her. They were surrounded now with a warding: not a few token strands but a constricting snare of knots. Unlike the ward of Westmost, this ward pushed inward. The scaffolding ground was tight with that power, airless and almost hot. Otter shivered. The drums beat.

And Otter saw that she was standing in bones.

There were pebbly finger bones. There were femurs like fallen branches. There were skulls. Otter looked up. High in the trees were loose-woven platforms, some piled with squirrel nests and lost in leaves, others showing still the shapes: the red lumps of the bodies.

The drums stopped.

And Willow turned around.

To Otter, it seemed her mother was wearing a mask: Her face was stark. Her hair stood out around her like the hackles of a wolf. The women of the pinch edged backward, away from Willow, away from the body of Tamarack. Only the body bearers stood still, silent.

Willow stalked up to the red bundle that was Tamarack and peeled back a wrapping. A bare hand flopped free. It had gone gray and loose.

Otter swallowed. The hand was so . . . She had known Tamarack. She did not know this hand. But Willow did not hesitate. She opened the palm and slipped her fingers among the dead fingers.

"Tamarack," she said.

It was the first word in the grove; it startled like a slap. Otter shook back at the ringing voice. She could see the bearers trembling with their effort to stand still, and the body trembling too. "Tamarack, your name is done with the world." She dropped the dead hand and it swung from the frame.

From around Willow's arm, a single cord unwound itself, slinking through the air under its own power. There was a muttering of fear.

Willow did not seem to notice. "Hold fast to your name," she said. "Follow it from this world and do not return." She touched the wrist once as if in blessing, then bound it to its platform with a harsh jerk of rope. Otter could feel the power of the knot as if it were around her own neck. The bearers shook, and sweat sprang through the black paint of their faces.

Willow fell silent. She lashed Tamarack wrist and wrist, ankle and ankle. She stepped back. "Raise her." And the rangers began the hard work of casting ropes into the trees, raising the new dead one to rest among the old. The red looked harsh against the black trees, the soft summer sky.

"May the wind take her into the wind," said Willow when they were done. "May the rain take her into the water. May the wood hold her away from this world. May the ravens fly her far."

The drums began.

"And when she comes back," said Willow, under the drumbeat but not quietly enough. "When she comes back, may she tell me why."

Chapter Five

WHEN THE ROPE ROTS

The binder is mad.

The whisper had started even before they got back to the pinch.

The old binder is dead; the new binder is mad. She called back the dead. The one whom the dead obey, she called one of them back.

For Otter, it was as if her mother's whisper had stolen her voice. Under the scaffolds, her throat closed. Her body shook. With Kestrel holding her elbow as if to hold her up, she walked back to the pinch like a woman struck blind. She was that lost. That frightened.

And even inside the safety of the ward — but was it safe? — the cords pulled at her. She felt them twang against some sense she didn't know she had, something deep in her body, signaling her as a web signals a spider. Even inside the safety of the ward she felt as if dead eyes were on her, as if something hungry were watching.

In truth, there were indeed eyes on her. Willow had stalked off to her lodge, silent, majestic, unconcerned. The women of Westmost had watched her go. They stood around in threes and fours and whispered. Often they looked at the binder's lodge. Often they looked at Otter.

Otter just kept walking. She wanted to get away from the ward, its strange and stirring power. But where to go? Not into the darkness of the binder's lodge. Not into the whispering knots of women standing on the packed clay of the palm, the open space at the center of the earthlodges where dances were held and gossips traded. The corn was thick enough to hide in, but she had a cold thrill at the thought of what could be hidden in corn. Kestrel walked beside her and was silent even as she slowed and stumbled — and finally stopped, leaning on a pile of rocks by the edge of the sunflower patch.

Otter tried to breathe deep, but each breath made her shudder and shudder. Kestrel put her hand between Otter's shoulders: steady. The summer stones were rough and warm to the touch. They were not alive, but if they were dead, it was a simple kind of dead: They were only themselves. They needed nothing.

Otter was thinking this and not watching the world, and so when someone moved just behind her, her heart leapt like a startled grasshopper. She spun and had her bracelets thrust up before she saw who it was.

"What happened?" said Cricket.

"Once our dogs were wolves," said Cricket, when no one answered him, "and though we loved them, we watched them carefully."

Kestrel half laughed. "They're watching Willow."

"No, they're sure she's rabid." He turned to Otter. "They're watching you."

Otter trailed along the edge of the sunflower row, away from the lodges and the open space of the palm. She could feel the eyes of the pinch on her back. "I didn't do anything," she said. "It's only that I'm — I'm —" *This girl is a binder born.* "— her daughter."

Slowly they walked away from the lodges of Westmost, as if they were deer browsing. As if they were not afraid. Kestrel put out her hand and skimmed it along the top of the grass as the meadow became wilder.

"What happened?" said Cricket again. "Have mercy on a storyteller: Tell me a story."

"It's not just a story," said Otter. Something broke out of her that sounded like anger.

"They never are," said Cricket softly.

"My mother . . ." said Otter — and she could say nothing more. It was Kestrel, then, who spun the tale: Kestrel, four-square as flint, plain as that, unornamented. She told the story of how the binder had turned around wearing the face of a wolf. Of how her cords had moved by themselves to make the knots. Of how she had bound the old binder to rest. Of how she had closed her eyes and called the old binder back.

Silence fell in the meadow.

"Oh," said Cricket.

"What does it mean?" said Otter. "Cricket — you said you knew a story like this." The night Tamarack had died, he'd said that. "A . . . an unhappy story."

"No, I don't know this story," said Cricket. "But —" He touched the tip of his tongue to his upper lip, as if he suddenly was unsure. They watched him, silently, and when he spoke again he sounded tense. "Otter, think a moment before you ask me. It is a serious thing. Do you want to hear a story?"

"Tell me a story," said Otter.

In answer, Cricket turned around three times, like a wolf seeking rest, then sank into the grass. His turning had made the grass into a little nest around him. He sat cupped in it, cradled like a fawn.

Otter sat with him, not so neatly. Kestrel sat too.

The grass here on the ward-side edge of the meadow was tall, full in that season of drifts of purple aster and goldenrod just opening, sweet smelling in the sun, loud with bees. Sitting in it they were tucked away, hidden. Hiding was not a thing people did much in Westmost: It was better to stay in sight. Better to be able, at any instant, to see the shadows on all sides, to be able to summon help.

Kestrel had pulled off her bracelets and was casting patterns between her fingers. Even children in Westmost might cast patterns to amuse themselves, to practice — but Otter knew that Kestrel was not practicing. She was keeping watch for the dead. Otter herself kept her face toward the palm, to watch for the living. And Cricket's eyes turned inward.

"Now," he said, softly — and there was a strange tremble in his voice, as if he was afraid. "A long time ago, before the moons were named, there was a binder named Birch. And she had a daughter, a binder named Silver. And she had a daughter, a binder named Hare. And she had a daughter, a binder named Spider, who later was Mad Spider, and a hero, and that is as far as the memory goes.

"Now, Mad Spider was not a hero born. As an infant, she did not sing instead of crying. As a child, she did not run and make the wind jealous. As a sunflower, she did not cook for the queen of the bees. She was a living woman, and she had power and she worked it well, but she was human and sometimes she was a fool."

There was a prickly cluster of narrow-leaf yucca growing beside him: this year's spires green- and yellow-blossomed, last year's black as wet flint. Cricket snapped off one of the dark ones.

"So." Cricket rolled the black stem between his hands and the seedpods rattled. Hissed and rattled. "So. Little Spider, who was not yet Mad, was not much more than a sunflower when her mother died, and her mother's second too, in the winter fevers, a fever of blisters. And so she became first binder of a great pinch while her hair was still wholly black. Oh, young. So young. She was frightened. She did not want to let her mother go."

Otter swallowed.

"She was frightened, but she went out anyway," said Cricket. "She went out to bind the dead." The yucca pod, spinning like a drop spindle, made a hiss. "Now, it was said of Little Spider that she could tie a knot in living bone. She had that much power. What she bound stayed bound.

"But what does a spider do when it catches a rabbit?

"Little Spider bound Hare, who was her mother, high in the scaffolds, under the pale sky. But the wind did not take Hare. The rain did not take Hare. The ravens did not fly her far. She was bound there, with her bones knotted, and she stayed bound.

"Little Spider's knots were troubled. She felt the pull on them. She began to be afraid. And then, in the moon where the sap rises, she realized why. One night she went out to the scaffold grounds, alone. And when the moon rose, she saw it: bound high above, neither living nor dead, a thing with white hands."

Cricket fell silent. The three of them sat there a moment, knee to knee. Kestrel lowered her bracelets slowly and said: "I have never heard this story."

Cricket looked away. "It is a secret of the storytellers," he murmured. "A great secret."

"Cricket," whispered Kestrel, shocked.

"Flea has been teaching me," he said, with his face still turned aside. "She has — she will not live much longer, and she has no successor."

But to teach in secret, to teach a *boy* —

"You think the pinch can survive without its stories? That because there are no knots in them, they are not important? If you think that, you are wrong." He looked over at the earthlodges, at the handful from which no cook smoke rose. "There are not enough of us. We must hold on."

"But a secret of your cord —"

"Yes," said Cricket. "I know. They could take my status —
such as it is — and keep me forever a child. They could tear
out my tongue. They could send me to walk into the West
alone, under the eyes of all the dead. I know."

"Cricket," breathed Otter. This was nearly as shocking as
what Willow had done, though Cricket's soft voice, and the
flush that was creeping up his neck, made it less so. Willow
hadn't been fearful, embarrassed, shy. She had snapped nor-
mality in half like a twig, and dropped it like a ripped shirt.
She'd been past any shame. Otter was afraid for Cricket.
But she was not afraid of him.

"They won't, though," said Cricket. "Flea would have
to . . . Flea wouldn't. And this is the story, Otter. This is the
story you need, I think. You are my friend and I am a storyteller. I will tell you the story you need."

Kestrel leaned forward and put her hand on Cricket's
knee. Cricket flinched, flushed, turned. "We will keep your
trust," Kestrel said.

"For you . . ." He looked up into her eyes. There was a
cupped, still moment — and then Cricket gathered Otter in
too, with a touch of hand on hand. "For you — for the two of
you — I would break any rule in the world."

"Tell us — tell me," said Otter. "Tell me the rest."

Cricket turned his head in the direction of the ward. The
grass blew in billows around them while the storyteller gathered his strength. "In the moonlight Little Spider saw it: the
One with White Hands." He swallowed, and the story broke.
"In truth I need a drum for this, a rattle — some stories are

too big for one voice. And mine isn't much." He turned the yucca pod. "I can only try."

He began again, and this time his voice was faint, like someone barely brushing a drum. It was soft, but there was no doubting its power. Otter leaned forward to hear him above the whispering grass, the buzz of the cicadas. "In the moonlight Little Spider saw the white hands, and she thought: 'It is only bone; my mother's hands have gone to bone, and that is as it should be. That is the way of things.' And then in the moonlight she saw the white hands move. Bound high above, they opened and closed. They begged and they beckoned."

The summer world around Otter seemed to fall away. She could feel only the points of warmth on her knees, one against Kestrel's knee, one against Cricket's, and the shivery brush of the story over her whole body. Her hair was rising on end.

"Now, this was long ago, in the great pinch of Eyrie, before the moons were named. Always there have been the dead, always the shadows have been hungry." Cricket touched his own heart, where the gast had scarred him. "The little dead are the crack in the pot, the tear in the curtain. They are here because the world is not perfect, and they mean nothing more than that. Little Spider had seen many little dead. She had knotted them away from her home; she had knotted them out of the world. But never before had one beckoned to her. One that once had a name, though the name was done with the world. One that had once been her mother.

"Never before had she seen One with White Hands. No one had seen a Hand — because that was the moment in which they entered the world."

"What?" said Otter, even as Kestrel said: "Cricket!"

It was impossible. It was like hearing that yesterday there had been no such thing as the sun. They both stared at Cricket — who closed his eyes, a fine shiver running over his whole body. But he said nothing to their shock, and kept speaking.

"Little Spider called to it," he said. "She sent her voice up into the trees. She said: 'Mother.' The thing had no voice — or at least, it did not answer. She saw the hand still and cup itself into an ear to listen to her. 'Mother,' said Little Spider, 'come down from there. Why are you up a tree in the moonlight? Why are you in the living world?'

"Still the thing did not answer. Little Spider stood in the moonlight. She moved her toes through the snow and the bones. A long time she waited, and still nothing answered.

"She could have climbed into the tree, but she did not. She could have summoned her rangers, but she did not. She called up to the scaffold: 'I will see you when the rope rots.' And she went back to the pinch, and she began to cast a ward.

"It was the first ward, and it was a great ward. All that spring she worked, while the sap rose and the grass unfurled. And the people of Eyrie said: 'Little Spider, what are you weaving?'

"And she said: 'I am weaving a web to keep back the dead.'

"And they said: 'But the dead are everywhere: They are both in and out.'

"And she said: 'There is one who is out.'

"All that summer she worked, while the corn grew tall and the pumpkins fattened. All that fall she worked, while the deer grew plump and the geese grew restless. And by the time the snow came they called her Mad Spider, and they always would, but the ward was ready.

"And then the White Hand came."

Cricket fell silent. Otter had to blink three times before she could see him — she had been caught in his story, and seeing only that. In front of her now, Cricket was trembling and sweating as if he was holding up a great weight, putting forth the whole effort of his body. "And that," he said, in a voice that was more like his, and less like a whispering drum, "that is another story."

Otter swallowed what felt like a mouthful of spider silk, dry and sticky. She saw Cricket's throat work too. How Mad Spider, greatest of the binders, had learned to make a ward, had held back the White Hand when no one else knew what to do — that story, that story she had heard before. But this story was new. This story was strange and secret. It seemed to turn her upside down.

The three of them sat there for a long time, silent, wide-eyed, shaking.

"This world is a door tunnel," said Cricket. "There is a world behind and a world ahead. What the storytellers say is that White Hands are those that should pass through the curtain — but are bound halfway. Those caught in the door."

Otter looked at Kestrel. She knew they were both thinking the same thing: of Willow saying, *When she comes back, may she tell me why.*

"So the storytellers say," said Kestrel. "What do the binders say? Do they know this tale?"

"My mother . . ." said Otter. "My mother hasn't taught me anything."

Otter could do the simplest pieces of a binder's work: the weaving of rawhide cords, the casting of patterns between the fingers. No more than any dyer or rope worker could do. No more than any child. Of the great work of binder's knots — the lore of them, the power of them — her mother had never said the least word.

Kestrel blinked at that, surprised. Otter could see from Kestrel's face that she knew a thing or two about the work of a ranger that she should not know. And Cricket knew a storyteller's secrets. All her life she had wanted to be a binder. She had a binder's power, she claimed a binder's work in her heart. But here she was with her friends, and she alone was still wholly a child, wholly untrained.

"Will you be her second?" said Kestrel.

"I —" said Otter. "We have not spoken of it."

She had always just known.

And now — her mother's look made her fear something that she could not put a name to. Made her flush at something she had done, and did not understand.

The binder is mad.

The old binder is dead. The new binder is mad.

"What shall I do?" Otter asked — but it felt useless to ask. She had nothing to do but go back to her lodge. Back to her home. Back into the darkness, where her mother was waiting.

She looked in that direction. A summer wind was picking up puffs of dust. It made the curtain of the binder's earthlodge — adorned in disks of silver — shimmer like water.

Kestrel was watching Otter. She must have seen how the shivering curtain held Otter transfixed, like a rabbit entranced by the weaving of a snake. "I will go with you," she said.

And Cricket said: "We will both go."

Otter looked back at her friends. No: It was no fairness to them. Cricket had already risked his status, his body, his very life that day, giving away secrets and lending his voice to a dangerous story. Kestrel had walked her down a cold river as if she were a woman in labor. "Stay where I can find you," Otter said, and got up. She brushed her palms — they were clammy — down the suede of her leggings. And she went home.

Otter went through the first curtain and into the darkness of the door tunnel. She could feel the open air behind her, and smell the smoldering fire ahead. She paused long enough to breathe hard for courage. Then she went through the second curtain.

She stopped.

Tamarack's grass pillow was burning in the fire pit. The lodge was full of a thick and clotting smoke. Through the smokehole the sunbeam came down like a solid thing. In the brightness and dimness, Otter could just barely see that her mother had strung cords — from sleeping platform to sleeping platform, from fire bench to pot hook, from the rough bits of wattle that made the walls themselves — there was a web of cords, everywhere. Her mother stood at the center of it, her hair moving with no air to move it.

"I want you to know," said Willow, "that I will never hurt you."

Chapter Six

HOMELESS, HOME

"I will protect you, Otter," said Willow. The binder's hair moved around her — as if little fingers of breeze touched her here, there. But the air in the lodge was thick and still.

"Protect me from what?" said Otter.

"From this," said Willow, and spread her hands. The web of cords around her jerked. Otter flinched back toward the door tunnel. Even there she could feel the curtain stirring at her back. "From binding."

"From binding?" Binding was itself a protection.

"From —" said Willow. Then suddenly her voice changed, became something small and lost: "Something is wrong, Otter. The knots are wrong."

Otter did not know what to say. The smoke was scorching her lungs, making her lightheaded, as if with fear. "Come —" she stuttered, reaching out. "Come out into the air, Mother. The smoke is . . ."

Willow cut her off. "Therefore I will not take you."

Otter froze. "What?"

"I will not have you as my second. You will not join the binding cord. You will not be a binder."

Otter felt as if something heavy had struck her without warning. All her life — she'd wanted nothing else, and she'd always assumed . . . *Here is a binder born*, they said of her. At her mother's words, the very fact of her birth seemed to spin away. She was not who she had thought she was: She had not been born. She was no one.

"You will not be a binder," said Willow. "You are my daughter and I will save you: *You will not be a binder.* Now. Get out."

Otter turned and ran.

She went blindly through the ring of earthlodges, dashed across the palm without meeting any of the eyes that turned to her. She went past the gardens, back into the meadow. She almost wanted to scream, but a scream would bring people running — she would have to explain — have to tell, to say the words and make them real and give up everything she'd ever wanted: *You will not be a binder. Not a binder.*

The grass grew thick before her, and grasshoppers whirled up on all sides, on hissing wings of yellow and brown. The thickness of the grass slowed her headlong bolt. She stumbled, she stopped. Without thinking, she'd come back toward the last place she'd been: the hidden nest Cricket had made in the grass. She did not see Kestrel and Cricket now — did not want to see them. Did not want to have to speak. She didn't think she could stop herself from sobbing if she had to speak.

She went to the nest in the grass, and she sat down.

She huddled there, hidden. She was so still that a yellow-throat flew in, perched sideways on a grass stem, and twittered around her. She watched the gnats, fine as dust, rise in spirals over the river as the sun went slant.

The shadows had thickened and swung to the east by the time Willow came rustling through the meadow. The aster and goldenrod parted and closed behind her. She was dressed plainly again, her hair braided down her back, her face soft, as if she'd been weeping. "Otter," she said.

Otter said nothing.

The birds were beginning to stake their evening territories — *My tree, my tree, I'm a blue jay!* The *thk thk thk* of a woodpecker rang out of the forest.

"Otter," said Willow, and sat down. There was a bundle in her arms, tied with an extravagance of yarn: blue-dyed, binder-blessed yarn, the most valuable thing in the world. Willow set the bundle down and put her finger on the knot. It snaked itself open.

The outer wrapping was a buffalo robe, new, the leather side soft. Willow lifted it aside. Inside the bundle was everything Otter owned.

"You cannot come back," said Willow. "I am so sorry."

Otter gaped at her.

"I love you," said Willow softly. She had been weeping. She was beginning to weep again, slowly, as slowly as evening was falling. "Oh, my daughter."

"Where will I go?" whispered Otter.

"You should go down the river," said Willow. She tried to catch Otter's hands. Otter yanked them away. "You should go with the Water Walkers: Go into sunlight; go as far as you can. . . ."

To leave the free women of the forest and become one of the Sunlit People. To leave her mother and her friends and everyone she knew. To leave the work her heart still claimed. To leave Westmost, as if she were no one, as if she were a boy . . .

No.

Unbidden, Cricket's words came back to her: *There are not enough of us. We must hold on.* He'd looked toward the earthlodges from which no smoke rose.

Well, then. Let one of them have smoke again.

Otter picked up the awkward, opened bundle with both hands and walked away, leaving her mother bent double in the grass. Overhead, the swallows swerved from shadow to shadow as the evening rose. Their pipping cries went over them all.

The earthlodge Otter claimed was a small one, left abandoned in an outbreak of blistering fever, four years before. It was near empty: Every basket and blanket, everything that could burn, had been burned. The sleeping platforms looked as bare as scaffolds. The stones around the fire pit were smoke-black and cold. Dust and silence had been sitting together on the fire bench. Together they rose and watched her come in.

Home.

The earthlodge was so empty. The wattle of the walls was almost bare of blessing knots. The ones that were left had become like the egg cases of spiders: shapeless, dry, brown.

Otter had nothing beautiful to hang on those sad walls. She had three shirts, one of which — the fine one, made from the skin of a white deer — no longer fit. She had a small box of feathers and beaded thongs for her hair. A corncob that had once been a doll that she was far too old for. A rattle made of a turtle shell that had been hers since she was a baby. Why had her mother not kept that? Surely she must want something of her daughter's? Had she thrown everything away?

Willow had sent three baskets. They were the best of the baskets Tamarack had made. Tamarack had been good at baskets, had had a deep patience for plaiting them, a sharp mind for seeing what patterns could be made from the tuck and weave of the light and dark rushes. The baskets — one little, one big as a pumpkin, and one bigger even than that — were each different, each beautiful, each tight enough to carry water.

Tamarack, thought Otter. *Don't go.*

Then: *Don't come back.*

She lay down on the dusty platform alone, too bewildered to cry. Evening came, then twilight, then night, and then emptiness. It became bad, that emptiness. She wanted to get up and pace around the fire pit, but it was too dark, and she was too proud. She wanted to bang her head against the bare wood of the sleeping platform and let daze and pain pass for sleep.

It was nearly dawn, the smokehole becoming a ring of gray, before fatigue was strong enough to take her.

Sleep. No dreams.

Otter woke exhausted, with a leap of fear: She was not alone.

She sat up gasping. Kestrel was sitting across from her, building a fire. "I am coming to live here," Kestrel said.

Otter gaped at her.

"Don't argue with me," said Kestrel.

"And anyway," said Cricket, lifting the curtain and easing in, "you appear to have plenty of room." He was cradling a big clay cookpot in his arms. He set it down beside Otter. "Why did you not find us?"

She had been too afraid. Afraid to say out loud what her mother had said to her. *You will not be a binder. Get out.*

She didn't say it, even now.

Cricket gave her a smile that made his mouth narrow. It looked like sorrow. He dropped a hand on Otter's head. She felt the warmth of his long fingers brush through her hair. A motherly gesture.

"There's more to fetch," said Cricket. No one said anything to that. He shrugged. "And so I'll fetch it."

Kestrel watched him go. Otter watched Kestrel.

"We have talked," said Kestrel, coaxing up the fire. "Cricket and I have talked of *okishae* — at the great fire, next moon."

Okishae — an odd word, an old word. It meant mate, it meant pair, it meant knot — but it was a pairing and a knotting that was meant to last a lifetime. It was a startling idea, to Otter: that humans should pair like wolves or swans. Most human couplings in Westmost were not like that at all. Otter's own father was presumably one of the Water Walkers:

the men who brought trade up from the Sunlit Places. She didn't know, and no one cared. *Okishae* were rare, and thought rather strange.

But on the other hand, perhaps it was not so strange. It was Cricket, after all.

"*Okishae*," said Otter, trying out the word.

Kestrel gave the fire a last poke and rocked back on her heels. "We'd need a home," she said. "We thought: here."

"Here," said Otter. Her voice sounded rough. All the tears she hadn't let out were making her throat ache.

"With you," said Kestrel. She flashed Otter the wicked smile that few in the pinch had ever seen. "Not that I propose a three-rope tying. That boy — he's all mine."

That jolted a laugh out of Otter — and the laugh turned suddenly into a spring of tears. They startled her, and she was helpless against them: They just broke out of her, bubbling. Kestrel came and wrapped her arms around her as she shook. For a moment, Otter didn't even know why she was crying. That Kestrel was making a pairing — why would that make her sad? Then she heard herself say: "She will not have me as her second. She threw me from our lodge." Kestrel was still and strong and warm: Against that stillness, Otter could feel herself shaking. "She will not . . . I cannot be a binder."

Otter pulled back and swallowed down the tears, trying to breathe, trying to speak, to make sense. "Something is —"

"You do not need to say it," said Kestrel softly. She leaned her forehead against Otter's forehead a moment, and put her fingers in her friend's hair. "The whole pinch is saying it."

"That she rejects me?"

"No," said Kestrel. "That something is wrong." She paused. "When they hear she will not have a second . . ."

Otter had not looked at it that way. It would come to the pinch as disastrous news. Only one binder — not even a girl in learning. Only one binder, and something wrong with her.

"I think I will not be the one to spread this story," said Kestrel.

Otter nodded.

Cricket came back, staggering under the weight of three buffalo robes, and they set about making a home.

/\/\/\/\

Through the wax and wane of the Corn-Cut Moon, the three of them reclaimed the earthlodge from its dusts and silences.

Kestrel, as it turned out, could have joined the cord of people who cleaned. She knew how to make a broom of birch twigs to sweep down the cobwebs, a smudge of kinnikinnick to case out the staleness, a garland of sagewort to bless the door. She had them split new pine for the sleeping platforms. Lay new stones in the fire pit. Cut new rushes to line the cache pits. Pick scouring rush to rub on — absolutely everything. After two days of this, Cricket flopped down on the sleeping platform. "Mercy," he gasped. "You two are going to kill me."

"It's mostly her," said Otter, putting down her hyssop broom, and glad to have the excuse. "But, you know, together we outnumber her."

"There's a thought," said Cricket. "Tsha, Kestrel! Together we outnumber you."

"I think —" began Otter,

"— that it's clean enough," finished Cricket.

The three of them looked at one another. And slowly, between them, bloomed a ward of smiles.

So opened the last moons of their sunflower years. Already things were shifting. Nearly every day Cricket would walk with Flea up and down the river. He had a new rattle, made of a turtle shell painted red and black and collared with black curling feathers. He practiced with it until Kestrel swiped it and hit him over the head.

Kestrel, meanwhile, slipped away often with the rangers. The cord of the rangers were the warriors and hunters and foragers of Westmost, women of sharp eyes and steady nerves. Rangers, alone among the free women of the forest, went into the forest itself. They brought back the dyes and herbs, the game, the wood for the fires. They worked with arrows, with staffs wrapped in knotted yarn, and with their own bracelets, under the constant, shifting threat of the dead.

Kestrel's mother had been a ranger — lost, and no one knew how or where — lost as many rangers were, some years before. Kestrel, then, had the bloodline, had the power. Her calm made her seem fearless — though Otter knew she was not. Often when Otter looked for her she was nowhere to be found. One day, she came home with two fingers blistered from learning to use a bow. On another, with sweet smell all around her.

Cricket slipped his hand into hers and found it sticky — her skin caught and stretched his as he tried to pull away in surprise.

"Oh dear," he said. "I think we are stuck together."

"Yes," said Kestrel. "You are mine forever." But she lifted their joined hands and blew between them, as if trying to nurse a little fire. When their hands were both warm she jerked free. The separation of their two palms made a *squelch-pop*.

"What is that?" said Otter. And then backed off — for surely whatever it was must be a secret of the ranger cord. "I mean . . ."

Kestrel hesitated a moment, then took something from the pouch at her hip. "It's this," she said. "Look at this."

It was a lump of something golden-brown, like honey crossed with clay. Kestrel set it in the bowl of an empty stone lamp and handed it to Otter. Cricket pulled a splint from the fire. In Otter's hand, the little glim sputtered and smoked and then began to burn with a clear orange flame.

"See," said Kestrel. "Today I learned where the light comes from."

"Where the light comes from," said Cricket, bending close in wonder.

"It's sap," said Kestrel. "It seeps out in knots, from white pine trees. It's pine sap. It's not a secret: You cut it free with a knife."

The stone bowl in Otter's hand was starting to become warm. She set it on the bench. "Your mother would have been proud," she said, and had to swallow hard.

Only Otter, then, had no cord at all. As if she were the one who was motherless.

Though she wasn't.

The pinch was not big: Otter saw Willow often. Sometimes she had her face scrubbed and her hair braided tight, so tight it pulled at her temples, making her look like a child. Sometimes she had her hair unbound and a knife in her hand.

She and Otter did not speak.

Otter worked — far more than her share, merely to be busy — in the great gardens of Westmost, plucking the rattlesnake beans that grew twining up the cornstalks, gathering the first of the thickening ears of corn. She received glances but not questions.

Often, Cricket worked beside her and told her stories — not great dark tales, but silly things, stories anyone might tell, though no one could tell them so well as Cricket: "The Goose Who Got Lost Going South," "How Moon Forgot Her Name," "How Red Fox Was Double-Crossed." They worked with one basket between them.

/\/\/\/\/\

Kestrel and Cricket were each making, secretly, new shirts to give to each other at the fall fires, when they would stand together with all eyes on them, and do this strange thing: *okishae*.

Only Otter knew they were both making shirts. Only Otter — and the dyers — knew they had both chosen yellow leather dyed with prickly poppies.

Only Otter knew that neither of them could sew.

It ended with both Cricket and Kestrel secretly requesting help. It ended with Otter sewing both shirts. She tucked one or the other away whenever one of them came into the lodge. It was good to have her own secret work to smile over. It was good to have knots in her hands. They came to her easily, and they made her feel as if she had been singing.

There was, in short, a little while in which she was warmly happy. She was happy one day lounging on top of their earthlodge with Kestrel, watching Cricket and nearly all the children of Westmost play hoop-and-lance. He stuck up from them like a sapling from a meadow, and yet they ran circles around him. He was good enough at rolling the hoop, but when he threw the lance the first time it went wide, and somehow swerved, hit a windpole, and went tumbling end over end.

"Behold, your future mate," said Otter to Kestrel as the players pounded past. "Behold his aim. Were you hoping for children?"

"Oh," said Kestrel, spinning a bit of grass between her fingers. "In that game the hoop can help the lance along."

Otter laughed and was happy.

And she was happy at the great fire that opened the Pumpkin Moon. Happy to give the yellow shirts and see both her friends laugh helplessly. Happy to help Cricket fuss over his crown of sweetgrass. Happy to put ocher into the part of Kestrel's hair. Happy to see them — they had each been in seclusion — see each other at last, and grow suddenly shy, as if they were pledging to strangers. Their eyes were very wide as the cords wrapped around their hands.

As a wolf loves another wolf. As an eagle loves an eagle. You only, mine only. Through our whole walk through this world. Okishae.

Chapter Seven

FAWN

Soon the corn was cut and the beans were harvested. The days grew shorter. It was the season in which the Water Walkers came.

The Walkers came up from the prairies, and across the snake lands where no one lived, and into the spreading skirts of the black-shouldered hills. There, where the thin shadows of birch and aspen began to thicken with the dead, they sought and struck the River Spearfish, thirsty for the protection of running water. They went to Bluehold, the great pinch famous for its lupine dyes. They went to Little Rushes, where the silver was panned. And in the end they went to Westmost, the last human place in the world.

On their backs, and on the travois of their great, wolfish dogs, they brought the bounty of the prairies: Bales of buffalo hides, and skin bags of buffalo hair gathered after the spring molts. Cured meats and certain prairie herbs — coneflower against toothache, snakeweed against coughs. These they traded for the things only the forest could give: Silver hammered to look like running water, and said to repel the slip. Arrows by the bundle, for the prairie had neither wood nor flint. Herbs of taste and medicine. Ornaments of mica and quartz and porcupine. And above all, above everything, the dyed yarns, binder-blessed, to hold back the dead.

The coming of the Walkers transformed Westmost. For half a moon, the pinch was filled with new folk and new food and new stories. There was shouting and splashing as the travois were unloaded, there were new songs, there were dogs everywhere. From the poles of their travois, the Walkers pitched conical tents, and the ring of the earthlodges was circled by another ring: lighter and taller, and more full of music. The rolling hoops of hoop-and-lance and the shouts of players filled the palm. Fires burned in the open, extravagant of wood, and in the careful, modest pinch, no one was careful or modest.

Through it all strode Willow. Her unbound hair was full of silver disks, she had silver on her belt. She flashed like fast water. Her stride ate the ground, her laugh was hawk-wild. The people of Westmost watched her with an unease that looked like awe. To the Walkers, she was the forest made flesh: She was beauty and darkness and power.

Otter watched her from the roof of her earthlodge. She did not go to the palm to hear the stories, to try the new dances. She watched Willow and she waited. The fall fires were only days away. Kestrel would take her woman's belt. And Cricket too: He would become the pinch's second storyteller. Otter's unbelted shirt felt loose around her waist. What would she do?

And what would the pinch do? How could the binder be without a second?

There was no one else.

And then, suddenly, there was.

Through the first half of the Pumpkin Moon, the people of Westmost and the Water Walkers gathered together. They traded news, goods, glances. But as the moon came full, they built the fall's great fire, and there they traded their children.

The folk of Westmost were mostly women, of course. The Walkers were mostly men: young men, breaking free from the hunting or the wool gathering, looking for adventure. There were always a few Westmost boys, proud as young stags, who would walk away down the river. There were always a few half-grown girls from the Sunlit Places, seeking a place among the free women of the forest.

That year, the people of the prairies had sent only one new child, a small and quiet girl, narrow-wristed and large-eyed. She was dressed in the fashion of the Sunlit People, in a shirt that fell impractically to her calves, and her legs bare. There was a stripe of red painted down the center of her nose, dots of yellow around her eyes. To Otter, she looked as strange as a new kind of bird.

It should have been the binder who welcomed such a child. Tamarack had always done it with great seriousness — to come into such a shadowed place as Westmost was no small thing — but also with great grace, and a secret smile slipped to the girls like a sweet. Willow, though, stood by the edge of the fire, staring at the new girl like a wolf at a rabbit.

She stayed silent so long that people began to shift from foot to foot, as if the binder's silence were a weight they were trying to hold.

It was, in the end, Thistle, captain of the rangers, who spoke, looking the small stranger up and down: "How old are you, child?"

"My name is Fawn," the child said. "This will be my sixteenth winter."

"Hmmpf," said Newt. "You don't look it."

Fawn said: "I don't lie."

Otter felt Cricket, beside her, turn a laugh into a cough, and that made her smile too. She was prepared to like this strange girl.

Newt, though, looked as sour as one of her medicines. "And what can you do?"

Fawn paused, then lifted her chin and said: "I am a binder."

Otter's heart lurched.

A huge silence opened like a pit in front of Fawn. No one could have stood on that edge without teetering a little. Fawn looked down, flushing in the firelight.

"Well," said Newt. "In sureness, we need —"

"Show me," said Willow.

Fawn looked up, startled.

Willow took a step forward. The light caught on the silver disks of her belt, and the disks in her hair shone as if she had a dozen eyes. "Show me," she said.

Fawn was done teetering. Looking at Willow, she unwrapped her bracelets. She cast a cradle, then flipped her fingers and made the pattern change: the fourth star, the woman running. Then the pattern that drew up the dead: the tree. When Fawn made the tree into the scaffold, Willow stepped closer still. She slipped her fingers into the yarns beside Fawn's fingers. She spread the scaffold open so that it became the sky. The two of them stood there, both trembling a little, with the wildest and widest of patterns cast between them.

"You know that this will kill you," said Willow.

Otter could just see Fawn's eyes, so wide they showed white all around.

Willow seemed to let the pattern loosen a little, and her voice came more gently: "It is very dangerous, to be a binder. There are other things a girl of knots might do."

Thistle spoke: "The binder must have a second." Otter saw the ranger's gaze flick toward her. *My grandmother*, she thought, as she rarely did. *My mother's mother.* There was something . . . soft . . . in the look Thistle gave her. Grim but sweet, like a mother brushing back the hair of a dying child. "Willow: You must have a second."

Standing there, shining with silver, her hands in the knots, Willow seemed to consider. "Your name is Fawn?"

"It is."

"Fawn. Do you want this?" It was almost a whisper. The strings shivered between them.

"I want this." Fawn's voice had come out as a whisper in turn. She shook herself, pulled the sky taut again, and proclaimed: "I want this."

Willow yanked her hands out of the pattern, leaving Fawn gasping as the power surged and changed. The girl fumbled to pull the sky back to the scaffold before the slack made the yarns drop free.

"Well, then," said Willow, and watched her for a moment: a small girl struggling with a great power.

Otter thought her mother's face looked both sane and sad.

"Welcome, Fawn: daughter of my power, bound to my cord. Fawn, binder of Westmost."

PART TWO

Chapter Eight

THE WARD IS RENEWED

So. The time of ceremonies passed: the fall fires where cords were joined and pledges made. Otter's shirt stayed unbelted. It had always been unbelted, but now it felt strange, as if she had lost something. A dream of something.

What was she going to do?

Her mother made no announcement, no proclamation that she had rejected her own daughter, but when the time came to tie the new cords, the fact that Otter joined none of them could not be missed. There was whispering. There was outright talk, and some of it to Otter herself. Pokeberry, the midwife, said ridiculously: "She's just forgotten." Hart, the silver-worker, said, with black comfort: "That other one won't last long." And Newt, the bonesetter, Newt of all people, said gruffly: "In my cord, Otter, you would be welcome." A kindness.

The kindness was the hardest thing to take.

The kindness and the fear.

Because now that the fall fires had passed, it was time to renew the ward.

That year, for the first time, it struck Otter how thin the ward was. She had grown up knowing only its power, its knots and its silver disks, a binder's strength and pride made visible. Now she saw the rest of the truth: The ward was made of rawhide cords, each no thicker than a finger. They had held the snow all winter; they had borne the summer wind. Now they drooped, and here and there ripped or slipped or simply gave way. The ward was only skin, and it sagged.

Therefore, beginning on the day when the Store-Up Moon was full, it was renewed.

The morning of the renewal, Willow was among the last to emerge. When she did come out, the women sitting together on the sunny bare clay of the palm, braiding corn, fell silent to watch her. Willow stretched, blinking, in the egg-yolk yellow light, then set off toward the ward without a word, little Fawn trailing her, looking pale and small. When she came across the palm, the women watched her as if she might suddenly spin away from her shadow and become a thing of twigs and teeth.

But she did not.

Willow did what she was supposed to do: She walked up to the place where the river came through the ward, and she stood there, waiting. And softly the word went around, and the women of Westmost got up from their baskets and put down their tools and came together at the river's edge. They looked at Willow. They looked at the ward.

The tired and rotting ward.

What should have happened was this: Willow would take out her binder's knife, the one whose blade was white chert and whose handle was a human jawbone, inlaid with silver. The people would gather, she would give a blessing, ladders would be raised, and the long work of renewal would begin. Taking the one piece of the ward between the first two trees and recasting the barest threads of a new one would take all day. To do the whole ring would take the moon and more. It was a vulnerable time, full of openings and known for its bad dreams.

Anyone who could walk was meant to witness the first blessing, and so Otter went, and Cricket went with her. Kestrel was among the rangers that day: They would join nearly shoulder to shoulder in the weak section of the ward, lest the shadows pour into Westmost like water through a crack in a pot. It was not unknown for a ranger to be lost in the Store-Up Moon, when the ward was weak.

That morning, Otter and Cricket had both watched Kestrel get ready. She sat with her ranger's staff in her lap, her hands going slowly over the knots that wrapped it. There were cords of rawhide and tendon and yarn itself, richly dyed in reds and yellows and greens and blues. There were binding knots. There were silver charms that made the staff shiver like spring rain. Knots and silver: A strike from such a weapon should drive back any but the most powerful of the dead — at least for a moment.

Cricket watched Kestrel, sometimes silent and sometimes more quick-tongued than he should have been — as if the words were birds that rose from him, frightened into flight. Otter wanted to tell him to be calm, but how could she? She had only held the dead in her knots. Cricket had held them in the heart of his body, and barely lived. What did she have to tell him, really?

Nothing. And so they went out in silence.

They hung to the back of the gathered people and watched as Willow climbed onto a round-backed boulder by the tree's roots. The stone was big as a buffalo, and so the binder stood high above the crowd, her blue shirt like a thickening of sky, her fringe of white weasel tails shivering in the wind. The Shadowed People looked at her, and slowly their silence went from solemn to uneasy.

She reached down and pulled Fawn up beside her. The young binder had her hair done in a strange style: braids coiled around her head, with the two little tips sticking out above her eyes like quail feathers. They were trembling. Everything else was still.

Willow did not say the words she was meant to say. She looked from face to face, black eyes wide. She did not look like a binder about to give a blessing. She looked like a woman waiting to be run through with a spear.

Finally, she lifted her hands. Sunlight glared off the clear stone blade, and for a moment she seemed to be holding a star. "So," she said softly. It carried only because of the drum-tight silence. "So. Let the ward be renewed."

She reached out and touched the birch tree.

The tree shivered as if its skin prickled. A faint gust of whispers swept the watching women: Did they imagine that little movement? Then all at once, the birch shuddered and shook, groaned like a laboring animal. And the cords of the ward . . .

The cords of the ward unbound themselves and dropped free.

∧∧∧∧∧

Otter felt raw power lash through her — she took a step back and Cricket caught her, hugging her from behind. Stunned but steadied, Otter looked up.

For just a moment, the section of the ward hung unsupported in the air, the cords drifting through one another as if they were watersnakes, dancing. It was startling, lovely —

And then it fell. Not the whole ward, but the piece between the birch Willow had touched and the next. She had been about to take it down anyway, but this . . .

The cords were rotted like frost-blasted pumpkin vines. They lay in a tangle on the cleared earth. The heap seemed to shift and sigh like a wounded thing. And then it was still.

Everything was still.

Someone — just one person, for the free women of the forest were brave — screamed. Once. And then again it was still.

Otter felt Cricket's breath catch. "What are you weaving, Little Spider?" the storyteller murmured.

Willow stood on the rock staring at the ruin she'd made. Fawn lifted her head. Her voice was small and tight and strange, but she said: "The ward . . . The ward will be renewed." And she put the first of the blue cords into Willow's hand, the way a mother might work a rattle into a baby's fist.

Willow lifted it, stared at it. And then wrapped it around the birch tree.

And very slowly, as the rangers of Westmost gathered to stand against the seeping, reaching shadow that spilled from the forest, the two binders, the young and the mad, restrung the ward.

The breaking and remaking of the ward went on all through the wane of Store-Up Moon, the moon of fine weather and bad dreams. The weather was fine that year, and the dreams were bad.

Over and over, Otter dreamed of Tamarack bound in the scaffolds. Sometimes she saw the body high above, and saw its hands. In her dreams, she stood waiting to see the hand move. Always it was about to move.

It never did.

Kestrel came in from her days at the ward, some days blank-eyed and some days shaking. The rangers had it hard that moon. The ward came down when Willow touched it, undoing itself as should only happen in nightmares. And when each ward piece came down, the dead came sniffing around.

Shadows oozed out the edge of the forest like lymph from under a scab. As evening lengthened, the gast pressed close, then closer. They shied back from the rangers' staffs like kicked dogs, and then again came forward.

Kestrel returned to the lodge with her staff frazzled and frayed, its cords hanging loose in great loops. She worked at those knots into the night until her fingers grew so dry they bled.

Cricket sat beside her and rubbed yarrow paste into her roughened skin. He told her stories. And Otter, who had no belt and no cord, had nothing to do but watch.

Until one day, Kestrel said softly: "Your knots are better than mine." And she handed Otter her staff.

At first Otter could only stare at it. A ranger's staff should not be held by anyone except a ranger. It was as strange as holding a rainbow. And she could feel the stirring of the knots on it, almost as if it were alive. Rangers' knots. Secrets of the rangers' cord. "I should not take this," she said.

"I should not ask you to," said Kestrel.

A weight hung from those two *should nots*.

What would happen if someone came through the curtain in that moment? Kestrel could lose her status. Otter could lose a finger, if not a hand. But no one came. No one ever did. Kestrel leaned her head against Cricket's chest. He wrapped an arm around her, then met Otter's eyes.

The day they'd bound Tamarack, Cricket had tucked his chin and risked his life for Otter, to tell her the story of Hare the White Hand, and Mad Spider before she went mad. He'd blushed as if shamed; he'd panted as if terrified, but he'd done it.

And now: "Show me these knots," Otter said.

And Kestrel did.

From that night on, Otter did the forbidden work, and if Kestrel's staff was stronger than it should have been — if it had so much power that it was more like a sky full of stars than a spring rain — no one noticed. The rangers were hard-pressed, and for all their stoic silences, they were frightened.

Still, they kept Otter's work secret. It was a serious business, a deep wrong, that she should know the secrets of another cord — of any cord. It was so wrong and so strange that they did not know exactly what would happen to them. There were tales — the storyteller with her tongue ripped out, the fletcher who lost three fingers. Punishments for giving away the secrets of the cord. If they were found out . . . But how might they be found out? Their lodge was quiet, and the curtain never lifted unexpectedly.

Until, one night, it did.

Cricket was making a porridge and Kestrel was drowsing. Otter had Kestrel's staff planted between her feet, and yarns wrapped around both hands. The curtain moved.

Otter jerked, power running down her fingers and up her arms — and there was no way to lay such power down quickly.

The curtain stirred aside, and in came Fawn.

She stopped with her back to the curtain and looked at them. Kestrel sat up. Otter had managed to wrap the yarns around her wrists like bracelets, though one cord still tangled the staff, even as she tried to set it aside.

Fawn shook her head. "Don't. I have seen already."

Around Otter's wrists the yarns itched as if they were crawling with insects.

They all stared at one another. It was Cricket who spoke: "What now, then?"

"It does not matter to me," Fawn said. "Let those who can knot tie knots. That is the way of the prairie."

It should have been a fear lifting — and yet Otter flashed with anger. "We're not on the prairie," she said. "You came here. We are the Shadowed People, and you came here."

Fawn paused. She was dressed in the manner of the Shadowed People now — a shirt and leggings, not a dress; her face unpainted. But her hair was still coiled around her head, almost as if it were short as a child's. The ends of the braids quivered like wolf ears above her eyes. She still looked strange. Her voice was soft and child-high: "Need we be enemies, Otter?"

They had never given each other their names — but, of course, in a place so small, they knew them. As Otter knew Fawn, the binder's apprentice, so Fawn would know Otter, the binder's rejected daughter.

There were three drumbeats of silence.

"We need not," said Cricket firmly. "Come to the fire, Fawn, binder of Westmost. We welcome you."

So Fawn came in. She perched daintily on the bench by the fire. Otter, defiant, pulled Kestrel's staff into her lap. The little binder watched the cornmeal bubble for a few moments, and then said: "I come to seek your help."

"With what?" said Otter.

"The binder," said Fawn, as if the word were difficult. "Your mother, my master. Our binder. Something is wrong."

"So they say . . ." said Cricket.

"But they haven't seen," said Fawn. "Her power is . . ."

She fell silent, and they were silent with her. Cricket leaned forward to stir the cornmeal. He sat back and said: "Here is what you've seen: Her power turns backward. It pulls too hard, and breaks its travois. It turns too fast, and it entangles her."

Fawn blinked at him.

Cricket tilted his head. "It does not take a binder to see it."

"No one else sees it," said Fawn.

"The day the last binder died, I was still wrapped in healing cords," he said.

Fawn looked blank, and so he pulled his shirt up a moment. The firelight showed the slickness of the scar between his ribs. "A gast," he said.

"In the corn," said Fawn. "I heard."

"The day Tamarack died, Willow came to us," said Cricket. "She was frightened. She touched the healing cords — she touched me." He tugged his shirt straight. "It is not a binder's power, is it, to make knots undo themselves like snake-balls in the spring? That is something gone too far. Something backward."

A pause.

"She cannot dress herself," said Fawn, very softly. "The brown shirt — the one that laces . . . ?"

"With the shells on the collar," said Otter.

"It laces across the top of the arms," said Fawn. "And she cannot lace it. When it touches her, it — the cords — come loose. They move by themselves. Her — her shirt fell off."

Otter stared at her.

"Is she marked?" said Kestrel.

"Marked?" said Fawn.

"A handprint — a white handprint. Anywhere on her?"

Otter felt the knots of Kestrel's staff pulse in her hand.

"No," said Fawn. "I . . . do not think so." It was clear she had not looked.

"She wasn't," said Otter. "When she touched Cricket, when she bound Tamarack. She wasn't then."

"It is not a White Hand," said Fawn.

"You are from the sunlight," said Otter. "You have never seen one."

"Neither have you," said Cricket gently. The White Hands, the horror at the heart of all horrors. They were that rare.

"It is not that," said Fawn. "It is . . . an unbinding. It takes all my power to lace that shirt," said Fawn, spreading her little hands. "And I do have power. I know I do not look it. But I do. To lace her shirt is the barest edge of what I can do, Otter. I cannot go further — and yet Willow goes further, every day. I need your help."

Otter looked down at the staff in her hands. "What can I do?"

"You are a binder," said Fawn. "I know you are."

Otter laughed bitterly. "I'm nothing. Haven't you heard?"

The cornmeal had thickened now. They could smell it coming to sweetness, hear it glub. Cricket leaned forward, branch in his hand, and nudged the pot to a cooler part of the fire. Fawn looked at the yellow, stirring stuff.

"Do you know a story," said Fawn, "about a rope that rots?"

All three of them looked up, sharp and silent, like deer when they hear a twig snap. They looked at one another, and then Cricket said: "Will you tell it?"

"I don't know it," said Fawn. "Maybe it is secret? We do not speak much, my master and I. But she begins sometimes to tell this story — or perhaps it is the end of the story. She says that Mad Spider bound her mother too tightly. She says everything is too tight but the rope is rotting."

The cornmeal gave a last great *glub*, like someone drowning.

A silence tightened, and Fawn said: "She says it will be soon."

Chapter Nine

THE WHITE HAND

So, winter.

The summer — the last summer of Otter's childhood — had been dry. As the winter grew colder the river ran shallower and slower than it should have. Somewhere in the Moon of Wolves, it froze solid.

The frozen river was a thing to fear. The dead were shy of running water, but they had no fear of ice.

The Wolf Moon passed and the Hunger Moon grew fat while the slip clotted together in the shadows, and the gast lingered like wolves just under the forest eave, waiting.

"What do they wait for?" said Cricket, when Kestrel reported it. A storyteller's question, and a good one.

"There is something coming," said Fawn.

She was often with them. It was like living with a little owl: her watchful eyes, her strange, silent presence. She said she could no longer breathe deep in the binder's lodge, that the backward powers that surged there made her braids undo themselves. So, often in the evenings, she would bring some of her work, and Otter, no longer shy of her, helped as she could: braiding rawhide, boiling saxifrage to set dyes. Fawn did not offer the secrets of the ward knots, and Otter did not ask for them. But sometimes she watched Fawn's hands closely as the young binder practiced casting figures, keeping her hands busy as the corn roasted.

"Willow says something is coming," said Fawn.

Cricket looked at Kestrel and Otter. "So the rope is rotted."

It was what Mad Spider had called to the bound form of her mother. *I'll see you when the rope rots.* Tamarack's rope was rotted.

Kestrel's face grew tight and thoughtful. "The rangers have seen something. Out near the scaffolding grounds, sniffing its way toward us. They track its coming. It will be here when the moon is full."

"But that is only three days," said Otter.

Three days.

/\/\/\/\

By the next morning, and who knew how, the tale was all over the pinch.

They did not panic, the free women of the forest. They prepared.

The binders were sent out to cast a ward — in so short a time, it could only be a weak one — across the river gap. Fawn did it willingly, spending her power until it pulled the color from her skin: She looked pale and small. Willow did it fitfully, and often fell simply to staring into the forest.

All the women of the pinch rewound their bracelets. Those who could shoot tied dead-knots around their arrows.

Rangers renewed their staffs. Plans were made to send the men and the children into the binder's lodge. It was one of the largest lodges, and the best warded. Lodges were built of woven wattle overlaid with clay, then sod. On their inner surfaces the women of Westmost tied knots for luck and protection. In the most ancient of the lodges, generations of knots lined the wattle as feathers line the nests of birds. In a binder's lodge, of course, those knots would have power. Even the most powerful of the dead, surely, could not burrow into a binder's lodge. They would have to strike at the door. And a door could, in a last effort, be defended.

Three days was too short, but they did what they could. On the last day, toward sunset, Cricket and Otter and Kestrel shared a roasted pumpkin, stuffed with corn and bits of venison and sage — a feast. "Well," said Cricket, who was the cook among them, "you'll need your strength."

He looked at Kestrel with fear plain on his storytelling face. Not fear of the White Hand. Fear for her. He stumbled through stories that day as he never did, as Otter wove a few last knots around Kestrel's staff and Kestrel wound and unwound her bracelets, casting the figures she'd learned: the tree, the scaffold, the sky.

Outside, a drum sounded three times. Cricket broke his story mid-sentence. He reached out and wrapped his fingers around Kestrel's wrist, weaving them in and out of her bracelets. She looked up from her careful fingering of the knots.

"Ward me well," he said.

Kestrel caught his wrist in turn, so that they were joined as if to pledge *okishae* again. "I'll be careful."

She let him go, and he raised a hand to his chest, and then held it out to her. "Do you need two hearts to be so brave? Because you can have mine."

Kestrel covered her eyes to them, and she went.

Cricket was not a child. But he was male, and had no power — could not possibly defend himself. And Otter had no belt, no status. So they went with the children.

Otter and Cricket went to the binder's lodge as the light poured out of the sky. They could see the women of Westmost as black figures against the white gleam of the frozen river. They were gathered at the river gate — all of them. The rangers in front, but all of them. The Shadowed People did not hide from danger.

"I could help them," said Otter. "If they'd have me."

"Oh," said Cricket, his voice too light. "Come help me, instead." He lifted the outer curtain of the binder's lodge. The silver disks on it fluttered red in the setting light.

Otter had not been in the binder's lodge since the day her mother had cast her out. It seemed different. The deer-hoof rattles on the door curtains — so often they had clattered a welcome — now seemed to jangle in her ears. The door tunnel seemed small and tight. Inside it was . . .

She remembered how it had been to go into the empty lodge, the first night of her life alone. Silence had been like a thing that watched her enter.

Fear was the thing here. Thick, choking fear. Something winding through the air.

Her mother wasn't there. And Otter was glad.

The children of Westmost — a moon-count or so, from babies to girls in their sunflower years — were already gathered. Otter knew them all, at least to call by name, though she did not really have friends among them. They looked up at her and Cricket in the dimness of the lodge, their eyes shining dark and big like rabbits' eyes.

Cricket paused at Otter's side, then moved with quick kindness over to the children. She watched as he threw a few planks of sweet-smelling larch onto the sleepy evening fire. The new wood smoked and then flared, and with words and nudges he herded the children close to the leap of light and the fragrant smoke. Soon he had them all seated near the fire and was telling them something small and silly.

Otter should have gone too: should have helped the children, cast figures with them, led them in string games and singing. She didn't. She stood with the curtain against her back.

The lodge was warm with the fire, and with the breath-heat and heart-heat of the many who sheltered there. But Otter stood at the curtain, and the air that came under it was bone-cold.

Westmost's handful of grown men sat together on one of the sleeping benches, talking quietly. One of them had an infant in a sling, another bounced a babe on his knee, little fingers wrapped around one of his big fingers.

Helpless: They were all helpless. The firelight picked out the inner wattling of the lodge, and all the blessing knots tied there: a small ward, almost, it must have looked. It must have made the others feel safe. But Otter could feel something restless and rotten coiling around Westmost. She had seen sparrows huddle under the eyes of kestrels. Kestrels can take a bird from the air, but not from a tree. And yet, always, always the sparrows broke first — flying into cold fear, into their own deaths.

Something was coming. Something was about to strike. The men sat talking, and Cricket told "Mad Spider and the Stuck Sheep," while all around them the blessing knots undid themselves, one by one.

All at once the deerskin curtain behind her jerked and its rattles glattered. Probably it was only the wind, but for a moment Otter felt a fear as if something dead had a hand on her throat. She gasped —

The feeling was gone.

This time, she hadn't been the only one to feel it. Cricket was looking at her, his eyes wide, his story stumbling. In fact, everyone was looking at her, and past her at the door.

The door that could, in a last chance, be defended.

And it was a binder's lodge, after all. There were cords.

Otter took loops of blue yarn and rawhide from a hook on the wall. She went out.

Otter went into the door tunnel and let the inner curtain drop. For a moment she was in darkness, and she was alone. She paused there a moment, and then slipped a hand between the great smooth log of the doorframe and the edge of the deerskin curtain, making a cold little eye that looked out into the night.

This is what she saw: The white birches of the ward. The river gap, like a hole where teeth had been knocked out. Her mother, standing there, her shoulders tight as if she had been carrying something heavy for a long time. It seemed to Otter that her mother was looking back — not to the forest, not to the danger, but back. To Westmost. To the binder's lodge. To her.

Then Willow turned, her form dark against the silver ice of the river that gleamed in the rising moonlight.

Willow turned and faced — nothing.

Something.

Otter only glimpsed it: a lightning flash, a nightmare flicker. Against the moonlit ice it twisted: a human shape, but pulled into lumps and long places, like a shadow cast on rough ground. It looked as if it were made of shadow: a hole in the air, a hole in the light, a place of refusal and rot.

Willow lifted her hands, with the cradle-star strung across them. The thing lifted its hands, which were not like the rest of it, but white.

Cold hands touched Otter's neck. She spun, thrusting up her bracelets as she turned: But it was only Cricket. He flinched back from the lifted yarn. "Sorry," he said, soft. And then, softer still: "What did you see?"

Otter swallowed and stared at him: He held a lit pine glim in a stone cup in one hand, as if he were turning into a constellation, as her people said happened to the most honored of the dead. His face was golden by its light, but hard, pinched with fear. She didn't know how to tell him. It was real. It was here.

"A White Hand," he said.

And she said: "I saw it."

For a moment, he looked foolish with fear.

Something outside made a sound, a howl or a moan that might have been human.

Cricket's breath caught high; he took Otter's arm. "Come away from there," he said. "Come away from the door." He lifted the inner curtain. But Otter didn't move.

"We should ward it," she said. "I should — a White Hand. If it breaks through —"

"Ch'hhh . . ." Cricket whispered. Otter turned and saw, beyond the open curtain, many wide eyes catching the light, many small faces.

"The binder will stop it," said Cricket, his voice pitched strong. "This is so: Willow is the greatest binder in many generations, the greatest among the Shadowed People, the greatest since Mad Spider, who once stood on a rock in the river and made a ward of no more than raspberry canes, and in that place held back the dead for three days. The binder will stop it. Willow will stop it."

Willow had called it. Willow had made it.

But the sureness and steadiness of Cricket's words made it hard to doubt him. It was as if he knew the story already. He was holding thirty people together with the barest skein of words.

Otter was amazed that she had ever thought him powerless.

Outside, there came a moaning like the sound of wind across a smokehole, and a distant shuddering sound that might have been a wolf. They both looked at the black stirring curtain. They might lift it, to see if Willow had fallen, to see if Kestrel had fallen. To see if, right outside, the One with White Hands stood reaching.

They did not.

"Master Story," said Otter, trying to match his certainty, "go back to the fire. Take care of us. I will ward this door."

He covered his eyes, formal and strong. Then he bent and kissed her, just at the hairline. "Lady Binder," he whispered, his breath warm and stirring. "Be careful."

He handed her the light. He went.

The inner curtain shivered closed.

So. Between curtain and curtain, between firelight and fear, between childhood and womanhood, Otter cast her first ward.

She did not know how, not properly. She had no belt, no status. She had learned things from Kestrel, and from Fawn, both in haste, both in secret. She knew nothing well.

But though she didn't have knowledge, she had power.

Power had grown inside her that year, the year in which she should have become a woman. She had not taken a belt, but it had grown all the same. It had grown restless. Like a stomach with no food, it might have made her sour, made her frightened. It hadn't — she'd fought that. But it had grown, and it was ready now. It leapt into her hands, into her heart.

The tunnel was low, and the peeling logs had plenty of rough bits where a twine could be attached. She drew the cords through her hands and felt as if she were drawing them from inside her own body, as spiders do. She made the line cross itself one, two, three times: the cradle. She added new strands to bend and transform it, to hold the power of the knots suspended like a wall in the air.

A ward. By fear and by pride, by instinct, in near darkness, between the children of Westmost and the outer door, Otter cast a first ward.

And her power carved its channel into her, straight and deep, from the heart to the hand, like a streambed. Like a scar.

/\/\/\/\

When Otter lifted the inner curtain again she saw the faces of the men watching. She knew they saw her silhouetted against her own ward like a spider on a web, but they said nothing.

What the women would do, when they found someone with no status had cast a ward, Otter did not know. It would not be nothing. She staggered at the thought. She staggered, the power draining out of her. Cricket stood up, wrapping her against his body. One of the children started to cry. "Easy," said the storyteller. "Rest and easy."

He settled Otter on the bench by the fire.

She was startled that the others had kept the bench open for her. As if she had status. As if she had power.

She did have power.

Cricket sat beside her.

Some of the smaller children were asleep, all piled on one platform, tangled up like puppies. The older ones were playing string games, in tight and wary silence. "Once," said Cricket, as if to begin a story — and then broke off as Otter leaned on him. Power was still draining out of her. She wasn't sure how much she could lose, and live. "Oh," he whispered to her, his hand slipping around her back as she put her head in the soft hollow under his shoulder. "Oh, Otter."

What would the pinch do when they saw her ward?

They might kill her, send her walking down the frozen river into the West, under the eyes of all the dead. But she hoped they would see her ward. She wanted them to see it. She wanted them to know her. And she wanted them to live.

/\/\/\/\

Otter would not have thought she could sleep. Not in the thick air of the binder's lodge, not in the waiting, not in the listening to the sounds from the curtain and the smoke-hole: distant babble, a single scream.

But she did sleep, leaning onto Cricket's side. She was, after all, only a child. She had cast, by herself, a powerful ward. She slept.

And meanwhile, the women of Westmost stood through the night, against the thing that was the root of all their fear.

Only one of them fell.

Chapter Ten

THE WARD ON THE DOOR

Otter woke. The smokehole showed sky the color of still and shadowed water: earliest dawn. Someone had lifted her onto a sleeping platform and tucked robes around her. It was warm under the soft sheered fur of the buffalo robes, and everything seemed like a dream.

But by the doorway, the other children had gathered, and some of them were weeping. And outside, many voices sounded like bees. Otter got up and stumbled over. The others fell back from her as if in fear.

Both curtains stood open. Down the door tunnel, the dawn air stood like a square of tarnished silver. The cords of her first ward were like strands of darkness against it. And into it, suddenly, a dark shape shifted. Otter went still with fear, her eyes searching out the shadow's hands. But they were dark like the rest of it, and they held a spear of darkness: a ranger's staff. A ranger. Otter went into the tunnel, until she could see the face.

It was Kestrel.

"Kestrel," said Otter. She had an instant's pure relief, pure joy: Kestrel was still standing. But the young ranger was bleak-faced, drawn in the dim light. Before she knew what she was asking, Otter said: ". . . My mother?"

Kestrel swallowed, tried to speak.

Cricket came up behind Otter. "*Okishae* —" There was a softness in that voice, a warmth that could melt ice. The storyteller reached past her, as if to put a hand through the cords and touch her face.

"Don't!" Kestrel brought her staff up fast. "Don't touch the ward." Carefully, she touched her staff tip to a central knot, which shifted as fast as a spider springing and wrapped the wood in a snarl.

Otter tilted away. She felt Cricket's warmth against her back.

Kestrel withdrew her staff, shaken.

"A binder should undo her own work." The voice was hard and seemed to come from nowhere. Otter turned her head, but pointlessly: She could see only the close walls of the door tunnel. Then Thistle slid sideways into the door frame. So narrow was the view from the tunnel that it was as if the ranger captain had appeared from the sky.

Otter shifted back before she could stop herself — then checked and drew herself up very tall. "Master Thistle," she said.

Thistle looked over the blue ward with flint-dark eyes. "I think you cast this," she said to Otter.

Otter was silent a moment. What would they do to her, the binder who was not a binder?

Cricket put a hand on her back, strengthening.

"Speak," said Thistle.

Otter spoke: "I cast this ward."

"Can you undo it?"

Otter had not thought about undoing. She had tied her mother's knots, in fear and in wild power, in dream and instinct. Now that she was not caught in fear, she knew that undoing a ward was a binder's hardest task. She had not the first idea how to go about it.

Willow had undone cords with a touch. But Willow was becoming something different: an unbinder. That was not a path Otter could follow. Not one she wanted to.

If the ward were a string figure, one would start with that third twist, and lift — She raised her hand toward the place, to try it.

The ward pulsed.

She froze. The ward sniffed toward her and suddenly she was clench-jawed, trembling, ready to topple forward into the ward, into the shadows, as if pulled by a rope of her own power.

But she had to undo it: She had at least to try.

She slipped one hand into place where the strands crossed.

Otter's fingers were suddenly tangled in yarn. The knots flexed open like tiny mouths and bit. Otter shouted with pain. The knots were like leeches, working their way to the soft places between her fingers, drawing power from her. It went rushing out and left her feeling as if she had stood up too fast. She felt sleepy, she felt stupid.

"Otter!" Kestrel shouted. Cricket wrapped an arm around her waist as if to pull her back.

"Wait —" Otter said, her teeth rattling. If he pulled her now, she might leave her hand behind. She —

If the ward were a string figure, then the finger trapped at that crossing could be freed: tuck, turn, under, pull.

Something was pouring out of her into the ward, something as irreplaceable as blood. The world dimmed. Tuck, turn. Under.

Pull.

Otter sagged backward against Cricket, who caught her, stumbling backward.

"Then you cannot undo it," said Thistle.

"I cannot," said Otter thickly.

Her ward, her power. The moon-count of children behind her. Were they trapped?

They were trapped.

"Fetch me Fawn," said Thistle.

Otter lifted her head.

Fawn. Not Willow. Fawn.

Kestrel looked at Thistle, at Otter and Cricket, back at Thistle. She went.

Kestrel had choked on her words earlier, when Otter had asked for her mother. Words broke out of Otter now: "What happened?"

"It can wait," said Thistle.

"It can't," said Otter. Thistle's staff was lifted, ready in her hand. What kind of woman did not rest the butt of her staff on the ground in such a moment? Otter was unreasonably irritated by that. "Willow —"

"Master Thistle," said Cricket, soft and strong, behind her.

"Rangers' business, Lord Story," said Thistle, making it sound like a very minor title. "Binders' business."

Cricket said: "It is her mother."

"And it is my daughter! Do you think that means nothing to —" Thistle stopped. Her voice dropped into a frightening softness. "Should I say this to my granddaughter with a wild ward between us, and no one to hold her? Should I send dark news into darkness?"

"I'll hold her," said Cricket.

But Thistle stepped sideways and vanished.

Otter could not hear Thistle move. She might be three steps away. She might be gone. The doorway, brighter now behind the dark slashes of the ward, stood empty.

Silence.

"Dead," Otter whispered. "She's dead."

Cricket held her from behind, and didn't answer.

And Otter realized: "Dead is the best of the things she could be."

She felt Cricket breathe deep, his chest pushing against her back. "Yes," he said.

Fawn came.

Otter and Cricket watched her come across snow, the ice of the river shining behind her. She looked so small, as if the weight of the buffalo coat might crush her. She looked, more than she ever had, like a child barely into her sunflower years, a girl not half a moon-count old. But she walked like an old woman. Like someone ready to fall.

She came closer and closer, and stopped almost in reach. Otter's view of her face was streaked like shattered ice by the dark strands of the ward.

Fawn lifted a hand and spread her fingers.

Otter lifted her hand too, as if they might meet palm to palm, like to like. But an arrow's length of charged air stood between them, and neither of them touched the wild ward.

"My mother?" said Otter. She braced her whole body against whatever Fawn would say next. She could hardly breathe, waiting to hear.

But Fawn only said: "I am . . . not sure."

"Is she dead?" said Otter.

"No."

"Touched?"

Otter felt Cricket's body tighten behind her.

"She went out to it," said Fawn. And for a moment, nothing more.

"To the White Hand," said Cricket the storyteller, coaxing. "She went out to the White Hand. . . ."

"She walked out down the ice," said Fawn. "I went behind her, and Master Thistle, and two of the rangers — Kestrel and another. The others were too . . ."

"They were frightened," said Cricket. "And you were frightened."

"It was — it was made of something like ants boiling, ants swarming out of a nest. But it had human hands. White Hands."

"She went out to it," said Cricket.

"She called to it," said Fawn. "She called it Hare — and then Tamarack. And then Mother."

Hare was from the story; Hare, mother of Mad Spider.

"She had a cradle-star lifted," said Fawn. "You have never seen such a casting, Otter — the thing, the dead thing, it was pushed back, just by the lifting of the strings. The strings were a staff-length from it, but they made lines in the stuff of it. Lines like a spoon through porridge. It shrank back and I thought — we all thought —"

"You thought you were saved. Saved by the power of Willow, the greatest binder of the age." Cricket, drawing out the words, making it a story. Cricket the storyteller, who knew the next word was *but*.

Because Cricket was telling it, Otter knew that too. She whispered: "What happened?"

Fawn laughed, then, shrill like a blackbird scolding, an un-funny, hysterical noise. "She slipped!" The little binder swallowed. "She just slipped, Otter. It was icy and she slipped. She fell down and it helped her get up. It took her hand."

For one drumbeat, Otter was not horrified. It was so normal. So human. It helped her get up. It took her hand.

It took her hand.

The White Hand had touched her mother.

"Where is she now?" said Cricket.

"With the Lady Boneset, and a brace of rangers." Fawn looked over her shoulder. "She may lose the arm."

Otter felt Cricket take a jerking breath. The memory of his own pain, she thought. But what he said was: "Would that help?"

Otter felt a jolt of horror and hope: The poison of the White Hand, that went to the mind — did it start in the body? Could its spread be stopped with something as simple as the blow of an axe?

"It is not so, in the stories," said Cricket. "But perhaps it has never been tried."

The three of them stood for a moment in silence, with the ward between them.

In the lodge behind her, Otter could hear the shifting of people trying to be quiet, and the small voices — sharp as fox kits — of the ones who were too young to try. There was a fox-ish smell too: The night pots were full, and someone had dug a hole in the floor for a latrine, but there were thirty people in the lodge. No water anymore, little enough food. They would not last long.

Her mother was dying or transforming into one of the dead. Otter kept picturing the rangers holding her arm straight, the axe coming down. But what she said was: "We need to bring down this ward."

And Fawn said: "Yes."

One of the babies went *huh-a-huh-a-huh* and then started to cry.

"I don't know how," said Otter. She reached toward the ward and again saw its pulse, felt its pull. "I should not have cast it."

"We came very near to needing it," whispered Fawn.

And Otter realized she did not know what had happened after the binder fell. Had the White Hand . . . Had the slip, the gast . . .

But the pinch was standing. The dead must have been unmade, or at least driven back. She looked again at Fawn, whose face was tight and smudged with fatigue, and decided not to ask for the story.

The little binder lifted her hands again, reaching and stooping as she followed the central lines of the ward with her fingers — not quite touching it. The cords twitched and trembled.

The lodge behind then was breath-warm, breath-damp, and it seemed to breathe out of the open doorway: A little wind came from inside and turned to cold, glittering mist around Fawn's fur boot tops and careful fingers.

Otter watched the slow tracing. She felt it, almost, as if the sweeping hands were moving through the fine hairs of her skin, not quite touching her, leaving her shivering.

"There is no weak place in this," said Fawn. "And no navel, either: no knot through which all the power must come."

She did not say quite what she meant, but Cricket guessed at it: "You mean there is no way to bring it down."

"We must bring it down." Fawn met Otter's eyes. "I mean it will not be easy."

She lifted her hand to within a tremble of one of the knots. "We will start here," she said. "Will you help me?"

"I'm not a binder," said Otter. For once, she felt no bitterness, no loss as she said it. It was a warning.

Fawn took it in that spirit: "I know. But it is your ward, and I will not be able to control it."

Control it. From nowhere Otter again saw her mother's arm held down, and the axe swinging. And in another flash she remembered her mother leaning forward at the welcoming fire, entangling Fawn's fingers in knots, her hiss: *You know that this will kill you.*

"I will help you," said Otter. She could say nothing else.

"Good," said Fawn, and she slipped her fingers into the ward.

/\/\/\/\/\

Fawn spread her fingers inside the crossed cords and they lifted and separated. Otter saw where her fingers should go and she slipped them into place, then slid them down into the tighter spots of the ward. She turned her wrist, making the cords shift and open: between her hand and Fawn's hand, a small string figure danced.

The figure danced, and power with it, sliding back and forth down the cords.

Otter felt as if the ward were her heart, and her heart had left her body. She knew they were trying to undo it, and she thought that if she did, her heart would slowly come undone.

She looked through the strings and caught Fawn's eye. The other binder's eyes were round, showing white all around like a rabbit's.

They untwisted the figure between them into three sets of crossed lines — into two — and then it was gone. Fawn gasped aloud.

And they went on.

What else, Otter asked herself later, could they have done?

They went on, while the children cried and the icy mist swirled around their knees. The day at Fawn's back grew stark and blank, a cold day where the very brightness made it hard to see. Fawn would choose a place to put her fingers, opening the ward a chink, and Otter would slip in her hand. Over and over, the wild fear that Otter had built into the ward made their fingers lock and their arms tremble. It poured down their bodies like lightning into the ground. Otter was shaking, Cricket's steady hand on her back. Fawn was alone.

Fawn chose slowly, then more slowly. The ward was down to its most powerful snarls now, and they didn't seem to pulse — they seemed to lunge. Fawn looked at them. She looked at Otter. She was breathing with her mouth open. She picked a snarl, and put in her hand.

She tried to open her fingers.

The cords snapped closed.

And all at once, Fawn was swaying on her feet, sweat springing out on her face.

She put her other hand into the ward, trying to spread the cords.

Otter put her hand in too — and jerked it back. She hadn't thought about pulling away, she'd just done it, her body snatching itself back as if it had touched fire. For the cords were fire now — they were raw power and raw pain and raw hunger. Their hunger was like the hunger of fire, which cannot be satisfied. Their hunger was like the hunger of the dead.

Fawn had both hands caught. She tottered.

Otter felt Cricket tense behind her, as if to reach into the ward, but he didn't, couldn't.

Otter braced herself and put her hand in. It caught fire. She yanked it back, gasped in air, put it in again.

Fawn fell.

She went forward, into the ward.

The weight of her body brought the last few cords down. The jerk of power through Otter's hand brought her down too, and suddenly she was kneeling, Cricket's arms wrapping her and pulling her back, and Fawn was in the dirt at her feet.

The little binder was tangled up. It was impossible that the ward, that handful of cords, should hold her. It was like a spider catching a rabbit. Impossible. Grotesque. It should not hold.

It held.

The cords — as Cricket dragged Otter back, the cords pressed into Fawn. Made lines in her like a spoon through soup.

"Let me go," Otter spat, reaching. "Let me —"

"Don't touch her," said Cricket.

"Why?" cried Otter. "It's my ward, it's my fault, why —" Why shouldn't she touch Fawn? Why shouldn't she throw herself into that fire?

There was one cord across Fawn's throat, the skin bulging around it. There was another slashing slantwise across her face. It had closed one eye and was snarling itself in her hair, pulling the braids.

The other eye was open.

As Otter struggled in Cricket's arms, that eye finished widening. It grew blank as the sky.

"Why?" said Otter, pulling desperately at the hands that wrapped her. "Why didn't you let me go?"

"Because," said Cricket, softly, in her ear, "you are the only binder we have."

Chapter Eleven

THE PRINT OF THE HAND

For a while, Cricket and Otter sat there with Fawn's body. They didn't dare to touch it. They had not the heart to move. The children cried behind them, and no one came.

And then: Willow.

She came walking without a coat over the snow. She was wearing her fine blue shirt, her hair was undone, and she walked tall and easy, the white fringe swaying. To Otter, for just a moment, she was only *Mother*: only love and strength and safety, come to save them.

She was more than that, of course. And they did not know what.

Wordless, Willow knelt in the bright snow, her body a dark shape against the harsh light behind her. She looked at Otter and Cricket. She looked at the body of Fawn.

"Mother," said Otter. Even in her own ears, her voice sounded broken.

Willow looked up, her face sane and sad. "There is no bottom to sorrow, is there?" she said. "No knot can hold it."

She touched the cords around Fawn and they first stirred, and then lifted, curling away from the body like sprouts curling away from the used-up seed. Willow gathered them in one hand like flowers. They wrapped up her arm.

The buffalo robe Otter had clutched around herself when she stumbled to the door that morning was still on the ground behind them. Cricket passed it forward, and Willow lifted the little body onto it and tucked it in, as if tucking a child to sleep. "May her name forgive me. I did warn her. I did."

"She was very brave," said Cricket.

"A fine young woman," said Willow, stroking down the sheared fur of the robe that had become Fawn's shroud. "I was proud to call her daughter." She looked up. "Come here, Otter."

"Mother," said Otter, and shuffled forward on her knees, into Willow's arms, into the light.

Willow hugged Otter against her body, and Otter tucked her head under her mother's chin as if she were an infant. "Mother," she said, "I thought . . . We heard . . ." Against her ear, she could feel her mother's heart, going fast. Her own body grew slowly stiff as the knowledge came to her — what she'd thought, what she'd heard: They might yet be true.

Coldness came to her.

She pulled away, hugging her arms around herself.

"Fawn thought they might take your arm," said Cricket.

Willow lifted her arm. Now that Otter was in the light, she could see more than just the shape of it. She could see that the inside of Willow's hand was white as if dipped in paint. White as bone.

"Thistle wanted to," she said. "Almost I let her. To give her that hope."

"But, not?" said Cricket.

"Little point." And with her white hand, Willow pulled open the deep V of her shirt.

There was a white handprint over her heart.

/\/\/\/\

Otter thought for a moment her own heart would stop.

Then she thought it would deafen her, pounding in her ears. Her throat grew tight.

Willow stood up and reached down to help Otter up — reached down with her white hand. Otter froze.

Cricket, behind her, took her under the armpits and lifted her to her feet.

Willow pretended not to notice. "Let us go," said the binder. "Let us get out of this place."

"Out of . . . Westmost?" said Cricket.

Willow looked up at the blank bright sky, her eyes watering. "Would that we could. Away from this lodge." She rubbed at the skin between her eyes. "If it would burn, I would burn it." She turned to them. "You have a home, do you not? Let us go — get away from the arrows of everyone's eyes."

Otter looked up. Yes. No one was approaching, but people stood here, there, in little knots. And all of them were watching. The arrows of their eyes. Movement caught her eye and she turned. It was Kestrel, coming toward them, leaning on her staff, weary as winter. Silent, she linked her arm with Otter's. Cricket took her other elbow. The three of them went back to their home, and Willow, white-handed, followed them.

Willow sat on the fire bench, in the circle of light cast from the smokehole. No one came too near her.

"You are not mad," said Cricket, cautious.

"Have been and will be," said Willow. She steepled her hands in front of her face. Bone-white fingers laced with human fingers. "Tell me, Lord Story. How long does it take?"

Otter put her back to the wall and tried to breathe. The yarns around her wrists itched and tugged as if they were twisting in the presence of something strong and dead — but when she looked down, they were not moving.

"Lady Binder?" said Cricket.

"The thing that will eat its way out of me," said Willow, her words coming faster. "How long does it take?"

"There are different tales," said Cricket softly.

Willow's look was pure irritation.

"If I had sureness, I would share it," said the storyteller. "I do not." He sighed. "Mad Spider — that is the strongest of the tales. Mad Spider was touched by the Hands on the stone in the middle of the stream. Do you know that story?"

Everyone knew that story.

"It is three times three days in that story," said Cricket.

And Willow said: "Tell it."

Cricket took a slow breath. Then he came and sat beside Willow. "Lady Binder, I will tell you anything you need. But first tell me what is happening to you. Because I think you are going to die. And I think there is a story that should not die with you."

Otter looked at her mother. At her mother, who was alive. It would not last. Could not last. Otter stumbled forward and went to her knees at her mother's feet. She took Willow's unmarked hand.

There was a silence that went on longer than it would take an owl to cross the whole sky. Then Willow said: "I do not know how to start."

Unexpectedly, it was Kestrel who answered her. The young ranger sitting on the sleeping platform, the cords of her staff loose and tattered, her hands shaking. "Tell us about Thistle," she said.

"When I was a child," said Willow. Then she opened her eyes. "Yes. Does it not always start so? When I was a child . . . When I was a child, my mother loved me. I was not alone, Otter — not like you. I had brothers, twins: Moon and Owl. They were trickster children, Red Fox's children: mischief-makers, far-rangers. Older than me, three winters older. Our mother Thistle was a ranger. And I — I was a girl with knots.

"Once in the winter, I tied a line from wattle to wattle inside our lodge — just a drying line, it was to be, just something from which we might hang our coats, because the snow was thick that year. But it was — too strong. It pulled the lodge in."

"The walls fell in?" said Otter.

That was what Mad Spider had done, when touched by the White Hands: She had turned her binding power backward, let it run wild. She'd pulled down the great poles that held up her lodge. She'd buried herself alive.

Willow put her hand on the upright pole beside her. Overhead, something creaked.

"Only in pieces," said Willow, telling the story. "Where the ties were. One bit of wall fell onto my brothers' pillow and they woke up sneezing and filthy with the dust. They were so dusty they looked half-made, like . . . like . . ."

"Like one of the dead," said Cricket. "White Hands."

"So I thought," said Willow. "I had never seen one. For a drumbeat I was so frightened — and then I laughed. May their names forgive me."

Something fell, soft as snow, soft as dust, around Otter's face. She looked up. Above her, a wrist-thick grass rope held the canopy poles in the fork of the upright pole. From that rope bits of grass chaff drifted down, glittering.

May their names forgive me. It was something that was said of the dead.

"Thistle told the pinch it was the weight of the hanging coats that pulled the walls in."

"But there were no coats," said Cricket.

"No. She knew then. My mother knew then. She didn't speak of it, but there were other things: a string game, a lashing on a shirt. I was a girl of knots. Tamarack saw it. I was too young for the cords — only thirteen winters. But Tamarack came to Thistle in quiet, and said she would offer my belt at the great fire. And Thistle — my mother — she said no. 'I am going to lose my boys this year,' she said. 'Let me keep my daughter.'"

"And Tamarack did," said Cricket.

"She did."

"Lady Binder," said Cricket, without looking up, "what is happening to the knots above our head?"

There were bits of chaff falling all around them now, from all four corners of the canopy around which the lodge was built. It drifted down like snow into their hair. It fell into the fire and whirled up again, as brief red feathers of flame, as slow black feathers of ash.

Willow pulled her hand away from the pole, drifted to her feet. She turned her marked palm up, and let chaff fall into it. "It has always been too strong," she said. "Before the Hand touched me, long before. Since I was a child. It has always been too strong."

"What has?" said Otter.

"The binding. The knots." She looked down at Otter with those mad desperate eyes, the ones that had said: *I will never hurt you*. "There's something wrong with the knots. Oh, Otter — I wanted to save you from them. I wanted . . ." She swallowed, her eyes becoming softer. "I wanted you to be safe. I wanted you to be happy."

She reached upward.

Willow was not a tall woman; she could not quite reach the point where the crossed canopy beams were bound in the fork of the upright, could not quite reach the golden, unraveling grass rope. But she had blue yarn wound around her arms: the yarn Otter had used to cast her first ward; the yarn that had killed Fawn. Willow reached up, and the yarn unwound and reached farther, winding upward as if toward the sun. It climbed into the canopy. It wrapped. It tied. It was impossible that yarn no thicker than an earthworm should hold a pole as thick as a thigh. But it held.

The groaning of the lodge stopped, and the last shards of grass fell glittering into the new silence.

"Tell me how long I have to live, Cricket," said Willow.

"Nine days, then," said Cricket, soft as a blessing. Soft as a killing snow. "Nine days by the story."

Otter felt those words fall on her, and fall on her, and fall on her, until she was cold and buried.

Chapter Twelve

BINDING FAWN

For years, Otter had dreamed of the first day her mother would let her tie a binding knot.

She had thought of the summer in which her mother would make a woman's belt for her. She had thought of the fall fires, where her mother would rub red ocher into the part of her hair and say to the folk of Westmost: "My daughter is a daughter of my cord. Otter, a binder for Westmost."

She had dreamed of the winter that would follow: They would sit together in the amber-rich silence of the binder's lodge, Otter and Willow and Tamarack, binders all three. The resinous smell of the glims would wrap them. Otter would learn the knots, and Tamarack would cook a string of dried squashes spiced with meadow garlic and the berries of red cedar. Otter would wear the silver herself someday; she would have a child, a daughter. . . .

"We must dye you a shirt," said Willow, sudden and stark. "Bloodroot for the dye and saxifrage to fix the red. If someone has the fine leather — brain-tanned — I do not — nine days, it's too short to make a shirt."

"Red," said Otter. Red was used only for the binders' funeral wear, and for the shrouds of corpses, and the cords that bound them. Otter suddenly wanted nothing to do with the color. "I don't need a red shirt."

"True enough," said Willow softly. "When the time comes, you can wear mine."

They were alone together in Otter's lodge, just sitting. Fawn, Westmost's little binder, was dead. Kestrel and Cricket had gone to carry messages to Thistle, to arrange the bier and the shroud, the escort and the drum.

It surprised Otter: the bustle that followed the great stillness of death.

So Otter and Willow were alone: Otter could see the heartbeat moving under her mother's skin — it made the white handprint stir and pulse. A White Hand.

Otter just wanted someone to cook them squash.

Nine days, by the story.

Otter had killed someone. And her mother was going to die. "I don't want your shirt," she said.

"Oh, Otter," said Willow, and dropped her head against her hand. "So hard, I tried to keep you from this. But I think we are bound to it. I am going to be bound in a tree and you are going to do it. My daughter, daughter of my cord."

Otter tipped her head down and was silent.

Willow touched her then, cupped both hands around her face and thumbed the tears off her cheekbones. Ran her bone-white hand through the black shine of her daughter's hair. "Otter," she said. "A binder for Westmost."

Fawn had been a binder. There should have been greater honor for her — all the women of the pinch, gathered in quiet, walking in silence, as they had for Tamarack. But somewhere in the dark woods that hemmed the pinch, the White Hand that had touched Willow was still waiting. No one would pass the ward who did not need to pass it. So Fawn's procession was just six: Otter and Willow, a drummer, and three rangers — two to bear the bier, and one to stand against the dead.

Flea, the storyteller, had turned her ankle on the day of Tamarack's binding, so it was Cricket who drummed. Because it was Cricket who drummed, it was Kestrel who came to stand against the dead. The other two rangers were Mink and Apple — twins, three years older than Otter. She did not know them well, and couldn't easily tell them apart. Their faces were painted in the bearers' black — their eyes looked very white against that. The long birch poles came out over their shoulders like extra limbs. They hardly looked human.

Cricket bowed his head, took a breath, and bounced his hand against the heart of the big drum. Then softer, with a fist. *Lum, dum*: a low sound. The heartbeat of the world.

They went out.

It was the height of the day. A clear sunlight made a yellow ribbon out of the river. Everything else was shadow, and stirring: Tall pines tossed and the aspens shivered. Otter's eye was snagged again and again by something in those shadows. When she looked, it was nothing: a blue jay, a boulder, a fallen branch. She could see it better when she didn't look at it: something big and watching, something gray and waiting.

The White Hand. Somewhere, the White Hand. Otter stumbled on the ice, and her breath came faster. By the time they reached the granite slope up to the scaffolding grounds, she was shaking. It seemed to her that even the drum had sped up. Glancing back, she saw Cricket with his face stiff with fear. He played the drum without faltering.

They climbed the shadowy, rocky slope to the scaffolds. They saw nothing. Everywhere Otter looked was nothing. It seemed to fill up her eyes.

Finally they came to the scaffolds, inside the ward. A red ward: a ward of the dead.

Otter had cast a ward herself, since last she had stood here. She had felt the binding power carve through her, making new paths from heart to hand. Those paths stirred and tightened inside her, as if the cords of the red ward pulled on cords inside her body. Plucking her. Tightening in her, like leather drying.

Beside her, she heard her mother make a sound, an outgoing breath that vibrated like a drum, a huff of pain. She glanced.

Willow's hair was floating as if the binder were underwater — as if the strands of her hair were cords boiling in a dye pot: restless, roiling. One of the young rangers bearing Fawn's bier stepped back from her. Otter saw the whole frame lurch, the red bundle on it lurch and roll. It was a very living sort of movement, like a child hiding in a rug.

Cricket played the *pat-pat-pat* of a song ending. A heart stopping.

There was a sudden, thick silence. Otter was almost brought to her knees: the hunger of the ward, the strangeness of her mother's hair. The two bearers staggered to find their balance. For a tight stretch of heartbeats, no one said anything. There was a gust of wind, wrapping Otter's hair around her face. Overhead, the scaffolds rubbed against the stirring trees with high moans and a squealing scream.

"Fawn," said Willow. A sound like a slap in the face. "Fawn!"

It sounded like a summons.

No, thought Otter, *please no*.

But no one moved to touch Willow. The binder's hair was churning, and her face stark. The V at the neck of her red shirt framed the print of the White Hand. Otter could swear she saw those white-print fingers flutter and clench. No one was going to save Willow.

"Mother," she said softly. She touched Willow's elbow.

Willow's head whipped around like a snake's.

Otter jerked back — then swallowed her fear. "Mother," she said, and tried to be gentle, "don't call her."

Willow looked at her for a moment, her eyes flat and hard and wide.

"Don't call her," said Otter. "We have to let her go."

"You killed her," said Willow. "You let her go."

Otter flinched, swallowed, and said: "Show me how."

Willow's eyes, locked on hers, showed white all the way around. But Otter could see her mother in there somewhere. A softness, surfacing. "It's the ward," said Willow. "The knots are clawing at me."

"Show me," said Otter. "Show me how to bind her."

"You didn't want my shirt," said Willow, her voice soft.

"I do not. But there's no one else."

"I did not want this for you," said Willow. Her fingers tugged at the neckline of her shirt — there was something childish about it, like a child hanging on to the hem of her mother's garment. "But I will show you. The binder's secret. Sorrow's knot." She reached for Otter's hands. "Do you have a cord? Here."

Otter had a cord, of course: the yarn bracelets on her wrist, long sinew cords wrapped up her other arm. She unwound one of those, held it out in two hands.

Her mother's hands closed over hers a moment, and then she took the cord. "This should be the last thing you learn. But . . . Watch."

Otter watched. Willow folded a place in the cord double, making a bight in it, and then the intricate, quick one-two-three of a wrap, a tuck. Her white hand seemed to flash. There was a knot there for a moment, a three-fold thing like a strange kind of heart, and then Willow tugged on both ends of the cord and the loop slipped through the turnings, and the turnings unspun themselves, and the knot was gone.

"Did you see it?" said Willow.

Otter said: "Show me again."

And Willow did, slowly. One of the rangers holding Fawn's bier, three steps away, had her eyes closed. The others were turned away, guarding the forest, watching beyond the ward. It was clear that the knot was a deep secret. They would not look. Otter watched the knot, letting her world narrow until it was only the cords crossing. A bend, a wrap that went fast, a tuck . . .

When she looked up again, she met Cricket's eyes. They were open and bright. Willow gave him a smile, as if slipping him a sweet.

"Once more," said Otter.

And Willow did. "Three times," she said. "That's right, because there are three wrappings. But this is the real secret, Otter. Sorrow's knot is not a knot at all. It is a noose. Use it to hold a dead wrist." She held up hers, white as birch bark. "Or to fix the first cord of the ward to the tree. But, by itself . . ." She pulled the ends of the cords, and once more the loop ducked into itself, the wraps turned against themselves, the knot flashed and vanished. "A noose with nothing in it pulls open. It is meant to be a release. And yet we use it to bind. Now that I am going mad, I wonder about that."

Otter looked up at her, startled. Her mother's smile was sweet, her eyes wide and terrified.

"And now for little Fawn," said Willow. "A chance to practice." She turned so fast her coat spun out, whirling. Otter could see the ranger with the poles trying not to flinch away. Willow dropped her coat on the ground and stood there, red as a shroud. She lifted her hands and the red cords wound off her arms. She caught one of them as if catching a snake, holding it by its head and tail. "Come here, Otter."

Otter's heart made a little triple beat, like a song's ending. She breathed in for courage, and went to her mother's side. Willow started with an ankle. "You may have the wrist," she murmured, as if offering a pheasant's drumstick. Otter looked at the little bare foot. Its high arch. Blood pooled purple in the heel. Otter watched her mother make the wrap, the cords biting into the slack flesh. Her ward pressing into Fawn's throat flashed before her. Willow did the wrap, the pull. The ankle moved, stiff against the one of the poles.

The other ankle. Otter was glad of the shroud, glad that she couldn't see the form of the legs, which must have been spread. To tie a young woman so, a small woman, to tie her up . . . It was a terrible thing they were doing. Otter felt that terror run in the new cords inside her body; she felt that terror wrap around her heart.

Willow bared a wrist, pulled it out, held it fixed against the corner of the frame. Willow's back was against the back of one of the rangers holding the frame. The woman was shaking. *How can she do this?* thought Otter. *How can anyone do this?* "Otter," said Willow. She sounded impatient, as if calling Otter in for dinner.

I'm dead, thought Otter. *I must be dead, because no one living could be this frightened.* She looked up and saw her mother's arm stretched out toward her, the hand white, the bracelets twisting and digging into the skin. She stepped forward and took her mother's hand.

And then she bound Fawn's wrist. A loop, three wraps, the twist . . .

"Yes," said Willow.

Otter did not want to throw up on the body of her friend. So she walked around the little binder's body and made the knot again. Then she leapt away, stumbling. Willow stepped back. "Now the words."

"Fa —" Otter stammered, then made her voice ring. "Fawn. You are done with your name."

Her mother's hand was soft on her shoulder. "Your name is done . . ." she corrected, whispering.

"Fawn, your name is done with this world," said Otter, looking down at the red bundle, so small. "Hold fast to your name. Follow it from here and do not return."

I'm a murderer, she thought.

"Raise her," barked Willow. And the rangers began the hard work of casting ropes into the trees, raising the new dead to rest among the old. Fawn's red shroud shone harsh against the black trees, the bare winter sky.

"May the wind take them into the wind," said Willow, when they were done. "May the rain take them into the water. May the wood hold them away from this world. May the ravens fly them far."

I'm sorry, said Otter, in her heart. *I should not have done that to you, Fawn. I'm so, so sorry. I am sorry we bound you here, but please do not come back.*

Chapter Thirteen

STORIES IN THE DARK

"Ah," gasped Cricket, falling onto the bench beside the fire. "So, that is the greater world."

"It is," said Kestrel softly.

The hasty winter sun had been lowering as they came back to Westmost. Shadows had fallen across the frozen river, turning it the color of sage blossoms. The rangers had walked around the other three in an arrowhead, using their staffs to nudge back the boldest of the little dead.

They hurried like the hurrying sun. The round stones at the edges of the stream were wearing little hoods of snow, and their gray bases seemed to spill grayness like a stain onto the ice. Shadows, thicker than shadows should have been: slip.

And then they caught a flash of white, like the flare of a junco's wing. A glimpse, in the dim forest, of something that might have been a lifted hand.

So they had gone quickly.

Back in Westmost, back inside the lodge, Cricket pulled the great funeral drum up into his lap and wiped his hand in circles across the surface, cleaning it of the little flecks of mud and ice. His hand was trembling slightly, just enough to graze stray voices up from the big drum. "The greater world," he said. "You might have told me it was nothing but fear and strangeness. All this time I have been jealous, *okishae*: to go among the trees. New skies. New birds." He fingered the thong that tied his braid. It was strung with beads and a present Kestrel had given him: the feathers of a woodpecker. It was the finest thing he owned, and he had worn it, Otter knew, for Fawn. There were streaks of tears on his face.

Had Otter herself wept? She could not remember. It had been so *wrong*. Even weeping seemed the wrong thing.

"It is beautiful too," said Kestrel. "The world beyond the ward."

"Is it?" said Cricket. "I missed that part."

"Me too," said Otter. Her mother was pacing — throwing herself from side to side of the tiny space like a fish in a box trap. That's what Otter felt like: something trapped. Beautiful? No.

"Once we lived without a ward," said Willow.

Cricket stopped his work — he had begun braiding a sweetgrass smudge, to smoke and bless the drum — and looked at her.

"We did," she insisted. Her voice was like someone stepping on a dry branch: a crack, a breaking.

"Mad Spider made the first ward," said Cricket, carefully.

"That story," she said. "Tell it."

"Lady Binder," said Cricket, covering his eyes, "have mercy and let me find my breath. All day I have been the heartbeat of the world."

"Lord Story," she snapped. "I have eight days left. Tell it."

So Cricket did. His head bent over the drum, he swallowed once, twice, three times. Then he began, softly, to speak. "In Eyrie, then. Warm and gentle Eyrie, where the lake lies dreaming; Eyrie the sunlit; Eyrie the high city. In Eyrie, in the days before the moons were named, in the days of the binder Hare, Eyrie had no ward.

"Gentle work, it must have been, to be a binder in the days of Hare. To bless the knots of *okishae* and tie the rangers' staffs and hunters' arrows. To lay to rest the restful dead. Gentle work; a soft place.

"But the blistering fever can come even into a soft place, and so it came to Eyrie. And so Hare died, and her daughter, Mad Spider, became binder in her turn."

Cricket did not strike the drum. It was the funeral drum of Westmost, and it was not to be played except to walk out the dead. But he leaned close to it, and his breath played it. It echoed him; it thrummed and whispered.

Otter found herself growing very quiet, to hear what the drum might say.

"It was Mad Spider," said Cricket, said the drum, "who made the first ward. She strung it through the birch trees. She strung it through the stones. It was made of rawhide, because there was not enough yarn, but it was blue as the cords of the weaver, blue as the cords of the sky. She wove it through six moons, from shoots to snow. Her hands grew hard and her hands turned blue.

"'Little Spider,' said the people, 'what are you weaving?'

" 'Little Spider,' said the people, 'what do you want to catch in your great big web?'

" 'I am weaving a web to catch the dead,' she said.

"And the people said: 'The shadow ones are a trouble to us, but so are the wolves. Would you weave a web to catch them too?'

"And the people said: 'Come now, Spider, you trap us too. You will make us into fish in a net, if you keep at this.'

"But Spider did not listen, and they called her Mad. Mad Spider, then: She tied and she cast until all of Eyrie was encircled.

"And the people said: 'Take down your web, Mad Spider. We can live with the little dead.'

"And she said: 'There is one who is not little.'

"And the people said: 'It is of no use to keep out the dead. They are both in and out.'

"And she said: 'There is one who is out.'

"And that night, in the dark of the moon, came the White Hand. First of its kind, and cloaked in horror.

"The people fell silent. And they left the ward standing. And if it has not fallen, then it stands there still, through the moons that no story counted, in the hot-spring steam of the lake, in the sunshine and snow, in the silence of Eyrie."

He spoke the last word across the face of the drum, and it stirred and whispered through the lodge. Eyrie, the lost city. Mad Spider's place. The first ward. Otter shivered.

"And does it?" Willow's voice was sharp as a new knife.

The three young people looked at one another.

"Does . . . what?" said Otter.

"The ward. Mad Spider's ward. Does it stand?"

Cricket looked at Kestrel, who said nothing, and then back at Willow. His voice was careful again, the certainty of his story gone. "That is the end of the tale."

"Boy," said Willow, "that is the beginning."

And she snapped around and went out into the snow.

That became the pattern of it. Willow: restless, breathless, angry. She fell on stories as if she were starved for them.

Cricket told stories until his voice began to rasp, until a dry cough came to him even in his sleep. Mad Spider — that was what Willow wanted.

Cricket told her the smallest things, the silliest things. "Mad Spider and the Stuck Sheep," about the bighorn caught by that first ward. "Mad Spider and the Men," on how the Water Walkers had found a White Hand for the first time and tried to kill it with sticks. Willow ate the tales of the great binder as if they were things that could drip from her jaws.

And when she was full of them, she would turn and walk away.

Otter let her go, even if it was deep dark. What could touch her that had not touched her already? If she slipped in the snow, if the gast had her . . .

She had eight days. What did it matter?

But it did matter, because sometimes she was tender. With seven days to live she spent an hour brushing Otter's hair.

136

And it did matter, because Otter was to be Westmost's only binder. And Willow was the only one who could teach her.

So: It was six days before the Hand would hatch. Cricket was telling a story. Willow and Otter sat side by side on the sleeping platform, mother and child, warm together, a cold winter day. The knots in Otter's hands, Willow's murmuring voice, her slipping fingers. The secrets of the binder's cord, whispering between them. It was everything Otter had dreamed of.

It was a nightmare. The whiteness spread in streaks up Willow's arms like the streaks of blood infection. It spread from her heart, up her neck, like reaching branches.

And the way the cords moved under their own power, twitching against the soft places between Otter's fingers: nightmare, purely. She knew what they could do. She knew they could pull the life out of the living. The deadness out of things that should be dead. They could do it — they wanted to do it. They had killed Fawn. The knots were powerful. They were willful.

They were mad.

And Otter could feel them, as if they were part of her. As if she held her own skin stretched and twisted into rawhide while still living, between her hands.

I've always wanted this, she thought.

And now she was trapped. Willow was dying. The binder dying.

Her mother, dying.

And Fawn, dead.

And she was trapped.

I've always wanted this, she thought. *And I was wrong.*

/\/\/\/\

Five days left. Cricket was running out of safe, soft tales. His voice was rough and low.

Otter was hardly listening to him, but suddenly she heard him say: ". . . and so she became full binder, while her hair was still fully black."

Mad Spider, she thought. It was the secret story, the story of the first White Hand.

Too young and too frightened, she thought. *Mad Spider. My mother. Me.*

Cricket coughed, then: a dry cough that shook him from teeth to hands. Kestrel was already sitting beside him on the sleeping platform, her hand rubbing circles between his shoulders. Now she braced him as he began to fold up. The turtle-shell rattle in his hand shook and clattered. Kestrel pounded on his back, as if to knock the air into him.

As the story stopped, Willow froze.

She and Otter had a cast spread between them: the scaffold, caught halfway to becoming the sky. Willow jerked to a stop halfway through a twist and the yarns moved so fast they burned against Otter's fingers.

Willow stood up.

The casting tore upward on Otter's fingers. It felt like something was being pulled out of the center of her, pulled out by the roots. She gagged as it moved out of her — and then it was gone, leaving her head filled with lights and echoes. She fell back, panting.

Willow loomed over her. The sky was spread between the binder's fingers — her human-colored fingers, her white fingers. The blue cords seemed to glow in the dim light. Cricket, still coughing, lifted his head, his eyes wide. Kestrel reached sideways and put her hand on her staff.

"More," said Willow. Her voice was hollow, like the moan and hiss of the wind across the smokehole. It was not her voice. "More. Don't stop."

"B-binder —" Cricket sputtered. "I —"

Willow — the thing that was Willow — pulled her fingers slowly apart. The yarn stretched — Otter felt it stretch — and then the crossings and tucks of the pattern came undone all at once. The sky pattern burst open.

Around the lodge, the old, dry blessing knots popped off the wattle.

Pop, plink, tick — they fell one by one, like the first fat raindrops that herald a storm.

Willow took one step forward.

"Stop," said Kestrel. Her voice was quiet. Her hand was on her staff. "Stop."

Willow did not stop.

"Willow," said Cricket. "Willow, tell me a story."

And that, of all things, worked. The rain of knots stopped.

"Story," said the thing, in that hollowed voice. And then Willow said: "What story?"

Cricket — sweating and shivering, his voice broken — straightened up. "'Thistle said to Tamarack: I am going to lose my boys this year. Let me keep my daughter.'"

"And she did," said Willow. "But the boys, she gave away. Moon and Owl. My brothers."

And then she shouted — she screamed: "Thistle! Thistle!"

Thistle came.

Otter did not wonder at it at the time. Willow's voice was like a hook in the heart. It pulled at her. She would have come. What wonder that Thistle came? Only later did she ask herself how long the ranger captain had waited, standing in the snow, slipping through the darkness, waiting for her daughter to scream her name.

"They never came back," screamed Willow.

Thistle dropped the curtain and smoothed it before she turned: "Who?"

"My brothers," said Willow. Her voice was softer, suddenly. "Oh, Mother: Moon and Owl. They never came back."

"I know," said Thistle.

"They went with the Walkers, and those Walkers —"

"I know," said Thistle.

"What happened?" asked Cricket.

"When we send our boys away, they do not come back," said Thistle. She did not look at Cricket. She did not look at Otter. She was looking at Willow. The wild hair. The white streaks reaching like little hands up the neck. "But we have news of them, stories — sometimes our granddaughters come. But those Walkers — they did not return to the prairies. They did not return to Westmost. They never came back."

Willow reached with her white hand and smoothed her snaking hair. "Did you ever wonder why?"

"They died," said Thistle sharply. "The dead had them."

"But why did they not come back? I know you wished for them. You called their names."

Thistle's staff was in her hand, its butt off the ground, held light, held ready — but her voice was stiff: "Any mother would, Willow. You should know that, now."

"But I called Tamarack and she came back," said Willow, mad and reasonable. "She was bound and she came back. But the unbound dead — is that better then, not to bind them?"

"If we did not bind them, we'd be buried in them," said Thistle.

"Do you think so?" said Willow. "But it feels . . . it feels . . ." Her hair was stirring by itself, and Otter could see the white fingers growing thinner, longer. "The ones I bound *are* buried, Mother. They are buried in snow. They are dried like meat — stretched out — drying —"

"Willow." Thistle's voice was soft. "Is it time?"

She tipped the staff toward Willow — and Otter leapt forward.

It was not a staff. It was a spear.

That was why. That was why Thistle had been near, near enough to scream for. She was waiting for the moment in which she had to kill her daughter. Standing in the darkness. Slipping through the snow. She must have trailed Willow like a wolf trailing a wounded dear.

Willow was bent up with shaking, her arms wrapped around herself. Against the ordinary suede of her shirt, the white hand looked strange — white as birch twigs, talon-tipped. "Not yet," she said, her teeth clattering. "Not yet . . ."

Thistle, very slowly, lowered the spear until it was pointing at Willow's heart.

"No!" Otter pushed herself between her mother and the spear.

"Otter . . ." Willow's voice was not quite her own. It slipped into Otter's ear like a drop of water.

"I said *no*," Otter snapped. At her back she could feel something cold — radiating, bone-deep cold. A hand put itself on her arm — a white and twiggy hand. Otter whipped around and caught her mother in her arms. "Come back, Mother. Please come back." She felt the hands on her back, one warm and one cold.

"Otter. I . . ." Willow leaned her forehead into Otter's forehead. "I only wanted to protect you. Do not follow me. Do not be a binder."

Thistle said: "She does not have a choice."

"Of course she has a choice," said Cricket. Otter had almost forgotten about him — his quiet manner and face that looked foolish whether in delight or surprise. But he was still there, of course, his voice hoarse and his eyes tired, standing with a storyteller's rattle in his hand. "We are the free people of the forest. We do not take slaves. She has a choice."

Thistle ignored him. "We must have a binder."

Willow glared. "When I wanted to take up the cords you would not have it. You said you would never again call me daughter." She stepped forward — and there was something alien in the movement, something snake-like and fluid. "And now you would give Otter to the knots."

"I was wrong then," said Thistle. "It is so dangerous, to be a binder. I loved you, and you were all I had left."

"You should kill me," said Willow, her voice fierce. "You should kill me while I am willing." On her shoulder, the sinew that stitched closed her shirt was coming out of the holes, one by one, making a small slithering noise. "You're going to kill me, so kill me."

Thistle paused. A long moment.

Then the ranger knelt down and laid her spear at Willow's feet. "Not yet," she said.

Willow closed her eyes, her face for a moment sane and aged with fear. "Mother," she whispered. "Don't make Otter do it. Promise me. Promise me it will be you."

Thistle stood, paused. Then she leaned forward, tangling her hands in Willow's hair and kissed the closed eyes. "Daughter. I promise."

From that day Thistle stayed with them, with the spear in her hand.

/\\/\\/\\/\\

Down and down went Willow.

Her tongue thickened and sometimes she could not speak, or spoke nonsense. Her hand turned white all over. It changed from moment to moment — sometimes withered and woody, sometimes pure human in its shape, fat as a baby's hand, with clear fingernails.

"Otter," she said, "you will need a red shirt."

"I don't want your shirt," said Otter.

And Willow answered: "I'm cold. I'm so cold. Tell me a story."

On the other sleeping platform, Cricket drew breath and coughed. He'd been telling tales every waking hour for four days. His voice was rough, the power stripped from it. "I can't," he said.

"Mad Spider," said Willow. She was curling her fingernails down her neck as if trying to get them under a noose. Long red scratches joined the white streaks. "Mad Spider — what happened to her? What's happening?"

Slowly, Thistle stood up. Slowly she walked to her daughter. Knelt at her feet, the spear in her hand.

"What's happening?" said Willow, again. A child's voice, a child's question.

Thistle reached out with her free hand and took Willow's wrist — the one that still looked human. "Daughter. Don't hurt yourself."

"Mad Spider," said Willow. "Mad Spider. What happened to her?"

Otter saw Thistle shift, her hand tightening on the spear. The lodge grew breathlessly still.

But Thistle did not strike. She knelt with Willow's wrist jerking in her grip. "Long she lived," said the ranger captain. "Mad Spider: She lived a long time, and she kept her people safe. She unmade many of the White Hands. She was a great binder, and we will always remember her."

Willow lifted her chin. Her face was all white now. Her

eyes were a strange white-blue, like blindness, like frozen water.

There was nothing in that face that Otter knew.

"We remember her," said Thistle, again. "We — I — I hope she was happy."

"But the story." The words came out of Willow's mouth, but not in her voice. The words were as hollow as if Willow were nothing more than a hole the wind moved across. "Tell the story."

"Daughter," said Thistle.

But Willow was gone. She had become a door through which something was entering.

"Tell it," said the thing.

"It helps her," said Otter. It was a whisper — almost she was begging. *Not yet. More time.* Her eyes were on the spear-point. It was obsidian, glossy as hair. It caught a flash of Willow's white reflection. "It brings her back. She listens."

"Long she lived," said Thistle, again. She had a ranger's endless woodcraft, endless dead craft. But she spoke awkwardly, as if she'd never told a story. Perhaps she hadn't. "Long she lived. She grew strong in a strong place. In Eyrie, the high city, before the moons were named. She was binder until her hair was fully gray, a woman of power.

"And then one day — three children went straying. As children do. And a sudden flood swept them out of the pinch and into the forest. Into the hands of the forest. Mad Spider went out to find them, and she found them on a stone in the middle of a stream.

"And there were three Hands that had found them too.

"So Mad Spider, all alone, called to the Hands. She was the first binder to face the White Hands, and she was the best. She was not afraid. She called to them."

It was a famous story, and Thistle had the rhythm of it now, had the words. "Like frostbite they came," she said. "Like snow they came. Mad Spider was quick; she danced like a rabbit; she sprang like a deer. She caught them in her cord. But she was touched."

"She came too close," said Willow. Her voice was softer, a thing of breath and blood again. "And she was touched. Eye and eye and cheek and hand, she was touched. And this she did to save the children."

"Daughter," said Thistle.

"Tell the end," said Willow.

"Willow . . ." said Thistle.

"Tell it," said the thing.

"She died," said Thistle, no longer like a storyteller, but like a woman who had heard brutal news, and had no way to soften it. "Mad Spider died. She stayed six days, but then she could stay no longer. She pulled her lodge down on her own head, and buried herself alive. And three days later, the Hand hatched from her. And that is the end of it. That is the fall of Eyrie."

"To save the children," said Willow, in her human voice, and then —

And then the white hand struck out, fast as a branch whipping, snatching Thistle's spear-hand.

Thistle screamed and staggered back, clutching her wrist.

In Willow's white hand, the spear bent like a sapling. It creaked. The knots all around it came raveling loose, fast as if they were caught in fire.

"To save the children," said the thing.

"Mother!" shouted Otter.

The thing twisted its head like an owl. It stared at her. Otter froze.

"Lady Binder," wheezed Cricket. "Willow."

Kestrel had caught the staggering Thistle, dragged her out of the thing's range. If it had a range. Cricket was standing alone. "Willow," he said in his raspy voice. "Would you like to hear a story?"

He lifted one hand. The thing mirrored him, lifting its human hand, the last human part of it. Cricket swallowed, loud enough to hear. Then he took one step forward and wove his fingers through Willow's fingers.

"Where does it start?" said Willow, humanity drifting back into her voice. "Where does it start?"

"A long time ago," said Cricket, his voice ruined, shaking. "A long time ago, before the moons were named, there was a binder named Birch. And she had a daughter, a binder named Silver. And she had a daughter, a binder named Hare. And she had a daughter, a binder named Spider, who later was Mad Spider, and that is as far as the memory goes."

Willow sank down, sitting on a sleeping platform. Her movement was too smooth, as if her legs had joints like a spider's. Cricket, his hand entangled, sat with her.

"So," he said. "So. Mad Spider was not much more than a sunflower when her mother died in the blistering fever. She was too young. She was too frightened. She did not want to let her mother go."

Otter swallowed. Across the lodge, Thistle was folded up on the other platform, the hand Willow had touched pushed hard against her chest. Otter could hear her breathing.

"Mad Spider was strong," said Cricket. "It is said she could tie a knot in living bone: She had that much power. What she bound stayed bound. And so she bound her mother high in the scaffolds, under the pale sky. But the wind did not take Hare. The rain did not take Hare. The ravens did not fly her far. She was bound there, with her bones knotted, and she stayed bound."

"Storyteller," hissed Thistle, around a mouthful of pain, "what are you doing?"

Cricket lifted his chin, met Thistle's eyes.

His chin was proud, defiant. His eyes were wide with fear. This story: This was a secret story. Otter had grown so used to sharing the secrets of other cords that it seemed like nothing. But it wasn't nothing.

Cricket turned back to Willow.

"Mad Spider felt the pull on her knots," he said. Willow leaned her head against his shoulder like a sleepy child. Their joined hands rested on her knee. "The knots tugged her and the knots troubled her. One night she went out to the scaffolds. And when the moon rose she saw it: hands that opened and closed. That begged and beckoned."

Softly, Cricket shifted, slid a hand around Willow's shoulders, lowered her onto the bed. His voice shifted, singing a lullaby. "Mad Spider bound her mother too tightly. She was caught there, neither living nor dead." He freed his hand, carefully. "And that was the beginning of them," he said, beckoning to Otter. "The Ones with White Hands."

Otter went to the bed. The thing lying there was white as birch bark, strange-eyed. But it looked at her as a mother looks at a child. "I have to show you," said the thing, "how to let them go. The Ones with White Hands."

"Show me," said Otter, her voice shaking.

She knew it was the last thing she had to learn.

She put a cord into her mother's hands.

"This," said Willow. She lifted the cord. Doubled it back on itself, wrapped it. Her mismatched hands fumbled over the knot-making. Twiggy fingers snagged the yarn. But as Otter watched, the knot took shape. It was a knot she'd seen before: It was sorrow's knot, which began the wards and bound the dead. It was a noose.

"This." Willow had made it big — big enough to go around a whole body. "Tie them like this. Then pull —" Her voice became hollow again. "Closed."

A noose with nothing in it pulls open. Willow had said that when Otter had first tied this knot, the day they'd bound Fawn. It was meant to be a release. A noose with nothing in it . . .

Willow drew the noose slowly closed. But not all the way. She stopped when it was still large enough to slip around the neck.

Her drifting eyes sought Otter's. They had changed, but there was still something in them that hooked right into Otter's eyes, into her heart.

And in that moment, Otter knew exactly what that noose was for.

"Mother." She choked on the word.

"Let me go . . ." said the hollowed voice.

It was what Tamarack had said, dying.

"I love you," said Otter.

"Always," answered Willow — answered the last of Willow. "Now. Go."

Otter hugged her mother — what was left of her mother. Felt the heat of her and the coldness, the movement of her ribs. The fierceness of her returned hug. And Otter did the bravest thing she'd ever done. She let her mother go.

Chapter Fourteen

WHAT THE NOOSE WAS FOR

Otter burst from the earthlodge, where her mother was dying, and bolted into the cold. She spun away from the clutch of lodges and ran across the top of the snow — a handful of heartbeats, another handful — then the snow crust broke under her and she staggered, tumbled.

Ice bit her hands. She was panting, gulping. Not yet crying. The light shot rainbows into her eyes. A cold wind whipped her hair everywhere. It howled in her ears like a lost thing.

She knew exactly what the noose was for.

It wasn't something she could run from, but as she knelt in the snow her body jerked and jerked as if it needed to run. "Belt of the Spider." The words seemed to come through her from somewhere else. "Belt of the Spider. By the potter and the weaver — by . . . Mother."

She felt a hand on her shoulder. Kestrel, crouching by her, balanced on top of the wind-sculpted drifts of the snow. Cricket was there too, though the snow wouldn't hold him. He kept breaking through it, stumbling, loud as a buffalo.

"Better she choose her time," said Kestrel. "Better her own noose than a spear to the heart."

"There's something wrong with the knots —" said Otter. She knew, even as she said it, that she was not making sense.

"Otter?" said Cricket.

She pushed herself up. "Where's Thistle?"

Kestrel stepped forward and caught Otter in a hug. She held on ferociously.

Otter struggled loose. "Where's Thistle?"

For five drumbeats no one answered her. "She's . . . helping," said Kestrel. "Willow . . . would need help."

"I hate her," said Otter. "I hate her."

A howling silence. Then Cricket said: "Thistle does this so that you don't have to."

"I hate her," said Otter again, shivering — and started, at last, to cry.

"She loved you," said Cricket, not meaning Thistle.

The three of them held on to one another, shivering and crying, shin-deep in the broken snow.

/\/\/\/\

Thistle, as rangers do, took care of things.

Took care, perhaps, of too much.

When Otter and the bonesetter, Newt, went back inside the lodge, they found Willow's body already cut down from its noose, already wrapped up — as Fawn had been — in a buffalo robe. Otter was left to imagine her mother's hands — one white, one human — curled up on the chest. She was left to imagine the scorch of the noose on her mother's throat.

She could see a bit of hair escaping from the top of the shroud. She could see toes.

It did not seem real.

Willow. Her mother. Dead. Right in front of her.

Surely, it could not be real.

Thistle sat, as still as a hunting heron, one hand cradled against her breastbone. Her eyes looked blank and she wasn't crying. Otter could just see her shoulders twitch as she breathed.

Newt was brought up short by the figure in the shroud, but she blinked and turned. "Lady Thistle," she said briskly, "let me see your hand."

"The body is knots," said Thistle. "Willow used to say that."

Then she held out her hand.

It was not marked white, as it would have been if the dead had taken it. But otherwise it was a dead-thing touch-wound: The hand was slack were it should not be slack, swollen like spider bites. Unmade. The sudden strike of Willow's white hand had unmade it.

Otter swallowed down bile.

She looked at her mother's hair again. It was still now, no longer moving as if made of snakes. A little wind lifted three strands. Otter turned and saw the curtains were still hooked open. She went back into the cold, back to her friends.

∧∧∧∧∧

Newt came out sometime later and spoke to the women clustered in the open space of the palm. "This has happened," she would be telling them. "The binder has killed herself so that the White Hand will not hatch from her. You do not need to be afraid."

Newt always did like to be first with the news.

"Willow has killed herself. Don't be afraid."

Or would she blame Thistle? Give Thistle the credit? "The woman so strong she could kill her own daughter. Thistle, she has defended us."

Thistle, she is broken.

Otter didn't even know which story was true. Which one she wanted to be true.

There was no story in which her mother wasn't dead.

No story in which Otter would not have to put on a red shirt and walk into the forest. Bind her mother as Fawn had been bound. As the mother of Mad Spider had been bound. There were eyes on her, glances coming from the palm.

She would have to wear red.

◊◊◊◊◊

The sun had rolled halfway along the rim of the world before Otter saw Thistle again.

She and Cricket and Kestrel had gone to the only place they could think of, though it was the last place they wanted to be: the binder's lodge. The place where Otter had grown up. Where Tamarack had died. Where the children had huddled in fear of the White Hand. Where Otter had cast her first ward — her only ward. The ward that had killed Fawn.

"It smells like Red Fox's den in here," said Kestrel. And then she said: "Sorry."

The lodge stank with urine and fear and worse. It had only been five days.

Hanging on the wall hooks were blue cords for casting a ward. Red cords for binding the dead.

Sitting at the foot of Otter's old sleeping platform, folded neatly, was a red shirt. A white belt with silver disks. And a knife with a handle of human bone.

A binder's funeral gear.

Otter stood and stared at it and shivered, shivered. "Can you sleep?" said Kestrel, her hand on Otter's shoulder.

Otter shook her head. Not there. Never. She would never sleep again.

"It may yet be a long day," said Kestrel.

Cricket snorted. "I think the sun might be lost, this day has been so long already. And of course she can't sleep here." He looked at Otter. "Could you drink something? A broth? A tea?"

She didn't answer him. The shivering was bad.

"Something hot," he murmured. She could hear the damage in his voice, the price of four days telling stories. The fire pit was gray and cold. Cricket frowned over it.

"Never mind," said Kestrel.

Cricket said: "No, I'll go," and went to borrow an ember from someone else's fire. Otter wondered if he'd go back to their home — their had-been sweet, cheerful home — that held the body of Willow and the silence of Thistle. She didn't ask him. She sat down beside the red shirt.

Cricket didn't come back, and didn't come back.

Otter raised her fist up to measure the movement of the sun — but her eyes hit only earth and darkness. Of course they were inside.

But surely, it had been two fists of sun. Maybe three. Strange. Too long.

But Cricket didn't come.

Thistle did.

For a heartbeat, Otter didn't recognize her. She'd aged a moon-count of years. She leaned on her staff — the spear-point gone, the ranger's knots burned away by the strike of Willow's white hand — and came to them almost shuffling.

But her voice was strong. "We must bind Willow," she said. "Kestrel: Will you go to guard?"

Kestrel shook herself as if trying to wake up. Then she tipped her head and covered her eyes to the master of her cord. "Of course."

"Good," said Thistle. "I will ask Cress and Feather to bear the body. And send for Flea, to be the drum."

"Flea?" said Kestrel. Flea, not Cricket?

"Flea is first storyteller," said Thistle.

Otter's gaze snagged on Thistle's hand — not the one that gripped the staff, knuckles yellow, but the one that hung, half-hidden, in the folds of Thistle's long shirt. It was elaborately splinted, bound in many small red cords. She could barely imagine how much that must hurt.

"That will do, then," said Thistle. "The fewer, the better. Otter: Put on your shirt."

"The fewer . . ." said Otter. It sounded in her ears like *I hate her*. "No. No. She was the binder of Westmost. We should all go."

"She was a White Hand," said Thistle. "And we will not."

The whole pinch had walked out for Tamarack. And Willow — she'd been better than Tamarack. She'd been stronger. *She'd been* — Otter thought — *she'd been everything*.

"She wasn't," said Otter. "She wasn't a White Hand. Not yet, and now she won't ever be."

Thistle's ruined hand stirred. "You don't know that. And it is dangerous to leave the pinch. The White Hand that touched her — it was never undone."

The shivering came back to Otter.

"Otter." Thistle lowered her voice. Otter thought she might be trying to be kind. *I hate her*, she thought. *I hate her*.

"Otter: I must keep us safe. Sometimes it is hard. Willow — Willow knew that. You know that."

It was not kindness, it was pleading. *Forgive me*, that was what Thistle was saying.

Otter didn't.

"We must keep to our ways, and we must be strong," said Thistle. "You must be strong, Otter, Granddaughter, Lady Binder. Put on your shirt."

So Otter put on her red shirt.

She went with Kestrel.

And for the third time in her life, she went out to the scaffolds, to bind a binder. Tamarack. Fawn. Willow.

And now me, Otter thought. *Me in a red shirt.*

Cricket's voice came back to her: *She was too young. She was too frightened. She did not want to let her mother go.*

They went beside the river because the ice would not hold them. They hurried because the sun was sinking and because somewhere in the forest was the White Hand that had killed Willow.

Otter went silently, stumbling. Her body was so numb she felt as if she were drifting. As if her feet were frozen. But the embroidered rib cage on her red shirt prickled her own rib cage, as if she were wearing needles. She didn't cry.

Later she would remember how Kestrel looked hard at Flea, looked long back into the pinch. Cricket never had turned up with the tea. But at the time, Otter went drifting, silent. Her head and her heart were full of knots. She followed the bearers, and the body of her mother, and thought about nothing at all.

They reached the scaffolding grounds later than they should have, long after the shadows swung east. In the ordinary way of things, they would not have set out at all. But things were not ordinary. They were not quite sure that Willow's body — white-bleached, changed, strange — wasn't dangerous. It needed to be bound. It needed to be bound right away.

We must keep to our ways, and we must be strong, Thistle had said.

Thistle had stood beside the ward, in the river gap, and watched them go. She was leaning on her staff. Her face was almost green. *Pain,* Otter thought. *Something hurts.*

Then she remembered that her mother was dead.

We must keep to our ways, and we must be strong. Sometimes it is hard.

It was very hard. Very hard. The knots on her mother's wrists. Her one remaining human hand. Her bare and dusty toes.

She did not want to let her mother go.

It was very hard. The knots were hard. Her hands shook. The cord burned them. The knots fought her, as if the noose did not want to be made, as if her hands did not want to make it. They writhed and snapped as she tried to pull them closed on her mother's wrists, as if they wanted to take her too.

So. High above Westmost, in a grove of pines overlooking a black lake, on a cold day late in the winter, there stood a binder named Otter. And she had a mother, a binder named Willow. Who was dead. And that was as far as Otter could go.

She bound her mother to the frame and then she just stood there.

There was a blessing to say, but Otter was past all blessing. She stood and she stood. The trees creaked around her. There was — faintly, for it was cold — the smell of death. Fawn, surely.

It was cold. It would take a while for that rope to rot.

I'm sorry, Fawn, thought Otter.

I'm sorry.

I'm so sorry.

Finally, Kestrel came and embraced her, whispered to her. "The words, Otter . . ."

Otter only shook her head.

"We need to go," Kestrel coaxed. "We will lose the light."

Cress, one of the rangers Thistle had picked to carry the body, held out her hand at arm's length and measured the distance of the sun above the horizon. "We've already lost it. Six fingers till sunset, or I'm no ranger." She was a gray-shot woman, Thistle's second, powerful, blunt as an old knife. The black paint on her face was just a streak across the cheekbones. They'd been that hasty. Even as Otter looked at her, she smeared it away with the back of one hand.

Flea said: "You think, Cress, the shadows will trap us?"

"They have trapped us already. The riverbed will be shadowed now. Full darkness will catch us if we go back. There is a ward here, a strong one. Better to stay."

That suited Otter. To stay there, to stay lost, to stay with the dead. But Kestrel was shifting foot to foot, looking back toward Westmost.

Flea caught the look: "Is it better to stay, Kestrel?"

"We will stay here," said Cress.

Flea was still looking at Kestrel. But Kestrel did not contradict, and Flea lowered the drum slowly, and covered her eyes. "As you say, then. Though if it were a story, 'Five Women and the Dead' " — the old storyteller eased herself down on a fallen log, stretching out her stiff ankle — "that does not have a happy sound."

And the other ranger, the young one whose name Otter couldn't remember — the other ranger said: "We do this —

rangers do this: Live outside the pinch. We have here a ward; we have here a binder. We have wood and ember. We can live here, one night."

"Come here, little Otter," said Flea. Something in her voice made Otter remember that Flea was Cricket's friend and teacher, master of his cord. She wished it were Cricket: wished it desperately. *That's strange*, she thought. She went over and Flea put out her arms, pulled her in. *That's strange. I think I love him too.*

"Should I say the words, then, little binder?" said Flea, touching Otter's face.

Otter could not speak. She nodded.

Flea paused and gathered herself, and when she spoke, her voice was not loud, but her words were right as spring coming, right as anything in the world. "Willow," she said, "your name is done with the world. . . ."

When Flea said it, it sounded true. As if Willow were not tied like a knot in living bone. As if she would not be coming back.

"Now, child," said Flea, warm, like a mother, like a grandmother, like a memory, "I think you should cry."

And Otter crumpled as if an axe had hit her. She wept, and wept, and wept.

PART THREE

Chapter Fifteen

LOST

Five women and the dead. Otter and Kestrel, Flea the story-teller, the two rangers — one old and one young, and the bones all around them. High above Westmost they stayed, with a fire burning, inside the red ward with the dead creaking overhead.

Night fell. They waited, watched. Only Otter slept — wept herself into sleep and drowsed with her head on Flea's knee.

Otter expected — she had not really thought about it, but numbly and distantly she expected to die, in the darkness, among the restless dead. She expected the slip to boil up over them like ants. Expected the White Hand that had touched Willow to walk through the ward as if it were a spiderweb.

But none of these things happened. The five women spent the night among the dead, and they did not die.

The dawn woke Otter.

Wood smoke. Cold. Too bright. She had not slept outside in winter before, and for a moment she was dazzled, not sure where she was. What was the square thing above her, caught in the trees, dark against the sky? Too square and too big to belong in a tree. A human thing, a — She saw the red-wrapped bundle. She remembered.

Otter felt Flea put a hand in her hair, motherly. "We lived," said the old woman. "The storyteller in me is almost disappointed."

Ah, yes, this would be Cricket's teacher.

Otter stood up, and refused to look at the square blots against the lightening sky.

The others gathered themselves. The rangers tightened ties and brushed snow from mittens. The light grew stronger and stronger and stronger as they went down from the scaffolds to the river path, and finally, finally, stumbled back into Westmost.

Cricket was not there to greet them.

/\/\/\/\/\

Cricket did not come to the river gate to see Otter and Kestrel safely in.

He was not in their lodge.

But then, he was the pinch's second storyteller. He did have work and learning. He did have secrets.

Still, the two girls stopped inside the curtain of their lodge. Looked at its emptiness. Caught at each other's hands. "*Okishae?*" called Kestrel. Her voice trembled.

Otter's heart trembled too. A complicated kind of tremble.

The lodge looked different. The platform where Willow had slept was bare. Someone had taken the grass pillow to burn: a small and practical kindness. Cricket? The buffalo robes were rolled up and tucked at the platform's foot. Willow's spare shirt, the one that laced across the top of the arms, the one she could not wear, still hung on the wall. Willow's body had worn the blue one. Otter was wearing the red.

She broke away from Kestrel, suddenly desperate to take off the red shirt. She dropped the belt and the binder's knife onto the bare wood of the platform — her mother's platform, her mother's things. She was yanking the shirt over her head, caught inside its darkness, when Kestrel said: "Otter."

The frozen voice stopped Otter. She pulled the shirt back down.

"His things," said Kestrel. "Some of his things —"

Otter did not instantly see what Kestrel saw. They had made of their home a cheerful jumble. And Cricket was not tidy as Kestrel was — a matter over which they sometimes fought. There were no bare hooks that made Otter think: *This is gone, and this.*

"His coat," said Kestrel. "His second shirt. His carry bag and mittens." She ran her hands over the walls, touching the things still there, seeking the missing ones. "Some food."

"Food?" said Otter.

The pinch was small enough for an owl to cross in one glide. It was impossible for someone to go far enough from home to need to take food.

Kestrel bolted for the door. Otter grabbed up her coat and ran after.

Cress, the blunt-knife ranger who had carried Willow's body, met them at their door.

"Thistle's in the palm," she said. "She would speak to you."

Otter's heart skipped a beat.

They hurried to the edge of the open space at the heart of the pinch. Otter almost stopped: There was a single figure in that empty snow. Lonely as the dead. Her hand bound in red cords. Her face gray. Waiting for them.

"Where is he?" said Kestrel. "What did you do?"

Thistle was her cord master and the most powerful woman in Westmost. But Kestrel did not cover her eyes. "Daughter of my cord," began Thistle.

And Kestrel shouted: "Where is he?!"

Thistle stood up straight as a lodgepole pine. "He is gone into the West, under the eyes of all the dead."

Kestrel screamed. Wordlessly screamed, like a hawk, and struck out. Cress stopped her. The ranger second-in-command caught the wild swing easily, and in a blink had Kestrel's arm pinned and twisted behind her back. "Do *not*," she said into the girl's ear. She pushed Kestrel free.

Kestrel staggered. Fell to her knees in the blank snow.

"*Why?*" said Otter. "Why did you do this? Have we not lost *enough*?"

"It is because we have lost that we must hold fast to what we have," said Thistle, and not unkindly. "We must keep to our ways. You know what he did."

Cricket had betrayed the secrets of his cord. First for Otter, on the day Tamarack was bound. And then for Willow.

Otter remembered how Thistle's gaze had fastened on the storyteller. How Cricket had lifted his chin to meet her eyes.

"He was kind," said Otter. "To your *daughter*—he was kind!"

But it was more than that. He'd done something *important*. That story . . .

"Yesterday you did this? Or today?" Kestrel's broken voice came up from the snow. "Just today?"

Thistle nodded, spoke softly. "He walked out well. He was brave."

"Always," said Otter, her voice cracking.

Kestrel stood up. "Then he is alive. I am going after him."

She did not look back even once as she stalked away.

In the silence of the pinch, a sound rose: a single wail. Flea, getting the news.

Thistle flinched from the noise. She followed Kestrel with her eyes as the young ranger went back to her lodge. "Lady Binder," she said softly, and for a moment Otter did not realize that Thistle was talking to *her*. "Can you stop her?"

"Stop her?" said Otter. "I am going with her."

Kestrel was stiff and fast as she pulled food from hooks and put bundles in bags. Otter watched her for a moment, trying to catch her eye, to ask one question. But Kestrel did not turn around. She worked, her shoulder blades jerking.

"He would stay to the river, at first," she said. "But it is midwinter. One cannot walk that water for long. After that" — she stopped in the middle of rolling cords into a pouch — "he will not know where to go, Otter. He did not even take yarns —"

"Ch'hhh," said Otter. "I will take them, then. I am better with them anyway."

Kestrel turned around.

"I am coming with you," said Otter. And as Kestrel gaped at her, she added: "Don't argue with me."

Looking in Kestrel's face, Otter found she did not need to ask her question after all. Kestrel knew: They likely would not find him. At least not alive. And Otter knew: They had to try.

At the river gap, the rangers had gathered: the sisters of Kestrel's cord, steady women dressed in green and gray. Otter looked at them and wondered: *Will they try to stop Kestrel and me? Will we have to fight? We cannot win such a fight.*

And she looked at them and wondered: *Did they gather for Cricket? Or did they send him out alone?*

Kestrel's gaze was fixed on the frozen path of the river. She did not meet her sisters' eyes.

"Kestrel," said Thistle.

Kestrel said nothing.

They were almost to the ward. The high sun cast the shadows of the blue cords: blue gashes on the snow.

"Lady Binder," said Thistle.

Otter swallowed hard on the title, like swallowing fury. She spun on Thistle. "Would you stop us?" she said. "We are not slave-takers. We are the free women of the forest, and we are leaving this *pinch*." The word came like spit from her lips.

Thistle did not even lift a hand. But she said: "Lady Binder, there are children here. A moon-count of children."

The children she'd tried to save, the night Fawn had died. The smell came back to her: the fox-ish stink of trapped fear.

"There are five moons of people, all counted," said Thistle softly, "but you are the only binder. You leave us defenseless."

None of the others said anything. No one ordered. No one begged. *They should*, Otter thought fiercely. *They put my mother between them and death and they never even asked. They should beg.*

"We are going to fetch my *okishae*," said Kestrel. "He will not have gone far. We will not be long."

Thistle said: "And if you are?"

Rangers, even rangers, were lost in the forest. Kestrel's own mother had gone out and never come back.

Kestrel said: "In Little Rushes, the binder has two sisters and three daughters: a cord of six. Send to them." She looked hard at Thistle. "Will you stop us?"

"If I could, daughter of my cord." Thistle closed her hand around her own wrist — a gesture children made, seeking the comfort of their bracelets. "Granddaughter," she said. Then she stepped aside, and opened her arm toward the gap in the ward. "Go safely, and come back soon."

So they went out.

As the forest closed around them, a drum began to play. *Lum dum, lum dum*: the heartbeat of the world, the drum that was played only when the dead were walked out.

Otter's breath caught — and the drum caught too, and began again, its beat backward: *dum lum, dum lum. Come back*, said that drumbeat. *Children of Westmost. Come back safely. Come back soon.*

The funeral drum was a secret of the storyteller's cord. Flea. Cricket's cord mother and master, his teacher and friend.

Find him, said the drumbeat. *Come back.*

"Flea," said Kestrel, who knew this too. Otter nodded. And then they went on without speaking, and the drum went with them, softening slowly, staying a long time. Otter listened to it even as it became faint, and sometimes lost, like the sound of someone breathing on the other side of a lodge.

The day was windy. The trees were shaking off their coats of snow, shaking themselves clean like dogs. Still, the snow had — as snow often does — made it warmer. The still and shattering cold that had frozen the Spearfish and laid the pinch open to the White Hand was gone. The river was thawing, from the bottom up. The ice that had been blinding white on the day of the White Hand was dark now, blue. They could see the water push bubbles of air across its thinning underside. In places it was thin as a sheet of mica. In places it was gone.

It would not hold their weight.

They went beside the river, down its fringe of grasses, down the path in the snow they had broken earlier, coming home from the scaffolds. Kestrel had her staff lifted in her hand. Otter had her bracelets loose. They were not defenseless.

Cricket had been defenseless.

They could see his footprints, sometimes on the path, sometimes dodging onto the ice of the river. There, sometimes, breaking through: dark holes in the ice, water bubbling in them and freezing white around the sharp edges.

What had he been dodging?

On the riverside path, their own footprints, returning to Westmost, overlaid his, going out. They had walked past this. Walked past him. They had not known.

Otter watched Kestrel's face grow tight.

Otter shifted the pack on her back: the unfamiliar weight. Kestrel had, with haste, shown her how to pack a ranger's travel bag: cornmeal and sunflower meal, pemmican and dried saskatoons. She'd shown her how to strap an axe to her hip. How to wrap a live ember in birch bark and a bit of tube cut from the horn of a mountain ram. Some of those things were probably secrets of the rangers' cord. Otter did not care.

The drum was gone now. Either Flea had stopped beating it or it had vanished into the slough and rush of the wind in the trees.

They went past the path up to the scaffolds, beyond the edge of the world that Otter knew. And following them, it seemed to her, came patches of shadow, shifting from branch to branch in the black pines like crows.

She began to be afraid.

They had ranger's gear — wolf-fur hoods and mittens, boot coverings made from the sacs that hold the hearts of buffalo, which could hold out water. As they slipped past the path up to the scaffolds, Kestrel pulled her hood down, to track better. Otter pulled her mittens off, to free her fingers for the yarns. There were still footprints in front of them: only one set now. Deepest at the toes. Cricket. Running.

Running, with nowhere to go.

The footprints were always on the fringe now, not the ice. His feet must have been wet, cold — the kind of cold that blazes. It was like the touch of a gast, that cold. Even without the dead, it could kill him quickly enough.

The prints went slower. They were no longer deeper at the toe. They were unevenly spaced. The wind picked up, swirling the snow across the river. If it covered the prints then how would they . . .

Otter put her mittens back on. Kestrel put hers on too, and slung her staff down her back. It was reckless to put away their defense, but their hands were freezing. They needed speed more than safety. They went faster — as much as they could — knowing the day was short, and that they had only the day. They nibbled balls of sunflower meal to keep their strength. They chewed juniper berries against the fear that dried their mouths.

And all the while, the wind scoured away the footprints they were following, and the ones they'd left behind.

Otter would never have found Cricket. But Kestrel was a ranger. A hunter, among other things. She could track a deer, spot a rabbit run, and tell the best place to set a snare. She could follow a wild sheep up a rock face.

She found the place where the footprints left the river. The river wore a skirt of snow-covered grass, hemmed with aspens. Under the trees, raspberry cane stuck up through the snow in half hoops. Kestrel spotted a place where the tops of the raspberry wore no snow. Where one of the hoops had been wrenched free of the ground and now wandered half-upright in the air, like one of Willow's yarns.

"Here," she said.

The sun was low by then: pink where it shone down the river, catching the breaking, jumbled sheets of ice with gold. Under the trees, it was blue and purple, thick as if coming through smoke. Slanting in here and there in yellow beams, solid-looking as the trunks of birch.

"He would have . . ." said Kestrel, and then: "He needs a fire."

Otter peered past the smooth gray trunks of the aspen. Under the pine trees, little grew. Indeed, there was very little snow. The slopes were covered in pine needles, smooth where the ground was smooth, drifted next to boulders: long fallen needles the color of a dead woman's skin. There was nothing in those shadowy woods: nothing at all. Nothing looked at her. She could feel its eyes.

To go into the woods — Cricket must have had some

urgent need. For instance, fire. He could only have been driven in by the coming darkness. The same darkness in which they now stood. "It cannot have been long ago," she said.

"Quickly," said Kestrel, pulling her staff into her hands. "Let's go."

It was louder under the trees: The branches rustled and murmured above as if talking to one another. Otter had lived all her life in sight of this forest, but she had not stood in it before, not in a trackless place, not alone, not like this. The thick light shifted and coiled as the high branches moved. The trees spoke. And the dead: Otter's bracelets stirred and twisted.

Otter pulled the yarns free and cast a cradle-star between her fingers: a knot to detect and repel. The loops burrowed like leeches toward the soft places between her fingers. The crossed strings pulsed and tugged. But there was no direction to that tug. It was as if something was . . . everywhere.

She lifted the cradle-star as if it were a torch.

There was nothing near enough to see.

But the pulsing strings, her prickling skin, told her differently. If the cradle had been a torch, it would have cast a circle of light. And right outside that circle, the cords told her, there would be something watching.

Kestrel had stooped. There were footprints again: places where the needles had slipped under a foot, making little curls of bare earth. Kestrel's eyes were on the ground, but her staff was lifted. They crept forward. The needles gave way under their feet too. The darkness rose up out of the earth and began to swallow them.

But before it did, before it quite did, they found him.

First it was a stick, and then two. And then, as the track cut upward toward a huge nest of boulders, each twice a woman's height, Otter found a bundle of fallen sticks. Fallen pine branches, all aligned, but sliding over one another. Firewood. Dropped firewood. She met Kestrel's eyes. Raised her cradle-star, so that the ranger could see how the strings were pulsing.

Kestrel ran her hand down the knots of her staff, making the little silver charms wink in the last of the light. She nodded. They edged forward.

The trees surged and roared in a gust of wind, and then suddenly dropped into utter quiet.

And in that quiet, something drifted to them from behind the gray stones. A voice. Warm and weak, beloved and afraid. "Now," it was saying, "even Red Fox had to sleep sometime."

Kestrel hefted her staff and sprang around the flank of the standing stone, and Otter lifted her casting and charged after.

Cricket was sitting on the slope above them, his back to a boulder, his head in a streak of twilight, his legs so deep in shadow they could hardly be seen.

Not just sitting, Otter thought: He looked as if he'd been thrown there, like a jointed doll. His head was leaning back, his braids splayed over the stone, glossy hair catching on the rough places.

He heaved a huge breath when he saw them, and his voice jerked. "Hello," he said, and swallowed once, twice, three times, "I was just telling it a story."

The strings on Otter's fingers jerked sideways. She whipped around. Standing beside her was the White Hand.

Chapter Sixteen

FOUND

Otter raised her cradle against the White Hand. It flowed backward — not far. Mostly as if it wanted a better look at her. A handful of strings suddenly seemed like a flimsy thing against the rising darkness, and the strongest of the dead.

"It hasn't touched me," said Cricket, uneven — almost laughing with fear. He did not get up. "I don't want it — can you stop it? I don't want it to touch me."

Otter took a step backward, to get away from the Hand, to be closer to him — and Cricket said: "Stop." A gulp of a word. "Stop, Otter."

She spread the cradle taut, and risked a look backward.

Cricket — the stuff around his legs wasn't shadow. It was slip.

They had gathered around him like leaves, drifting into the corner where he lay. He was up to his waist in them. He had one hand in them. The other was held up, straight out from the shoulder, the elbow bent, the arm shaking. He turned his head against the stone to look at Otter, but didn't lift it. "Mind your step," he said, and tried to smile.

The stuff around him eddied sluggishly, like boiling soup.

Kestrel was there, using her staff — prying at the edges of the stuff, pulling off fists and clots of shadow, unmaking each. But Otter could do nothing. She couldn't even watch, not with the Hand right there. She felt the yarns shift against her fingers, and she turned back around.

The White Hand. She could hardly see it in the purpling light. It did not hold its shape, but drifted and billowed, swarmed and bulged. Only its hands were clear: white as peeled roots, five-fingered human but twig skinny, bone skinny. You could have taken them for a birch twig, if you were just glancing — but then your hair would rise in warning and you would turn slowly back and look again.

It was just — what? Watching. Waiting. "Tamarack?" whispered Otter.

It jerked at the name. Stretched taller, thinner. Its top stretched out and then bent down toward her like a wasp flexing to sting. Otter shouted with pure fear and swung the cradle-star upward.

The sting stopped. It hovered over her head, and horror seemed to drip off it like venom.

And Cricket, behind her, said, in a strange, wet voice: "Now, even Red Fox had to sleep sometime." The flexed shape in the darkness seemed to soften. "But he knew that as soon as he closed his eyes, Old Mother Wolf would drop from the tree like a bolt of lightning. *Snap!* So much for clever foxes!"

An old tale, a children's tale, a trickster's tale. But the White Hand softened into itself as if listening.

"Otter," whispered Kestrel, "can you cast us a ward?"

Again, Otter glanced around. The slip were gone now. Cricket was still leaning into the stone, his hand that had been lifted was curled into a fist in his lap; the other fell at his side, limp as if frost-blasted. He did not get up. His eyes were closed. But he was still telling the story.

Otter looked at the White Hand.

It was still listening. Otter lowered her cradle-star slowly. The Hand did not move.

"I'll get the firewood," Kestrel whispered.

The place where Cricket had fallen was sheltered by two trees. A digger pine grew from a crag on top of the boulder to his side. Those three points could hold up a ward — no longer than a lodge, and much narrower, but enough, perhaps. Especially if they had light: a fire. Enough.

So as Kestrel drew out her tinder bundle and coaxed up a fire, and Cricket told a trickster's tale in a voice that kept wandering off into weakness, Otter cast her second ward. She knew more this time: to fix each section with a knot that Fawn had called the navel and Willow had called the child. To twist the cords in twos to make the knot called mother. To bind each cord to the tree with a constricting noose, the too-known knot that made her heart shake: sorrow's knot. It looked thin, the ward: a handful of cords cast up against the huge and muttering darkness. But she could feel the wind making it sing. The song hummed in her blood and she knew the ward would hold.

"And if she hasn't come down," said Cricket, "Old Mother Wolf is up there still. And that is why . . ." He sighed, then pulled hard for air, pulling his voice back up from the strange place it was sinking to. "That is . . . That is why the trees will sometimes howl."

Overhead, the trees howled.

Cricket slumped sideways.

"Cricket!" said Kestrel. She had been facing down the White Hand — lifting her lopsided cradle-star, just in case. But the whole time Cricket was telling his story, it hadn't moved. It moved now, drifting forward, as if to see what was wrong. Kestrel dove away from it, and was just in time to catch Cricket as he slid into the pine needles.

Otter watched the Hand three breaths more. It pressed toward them — and she could see the lines forming in the stuff of its body. Lines that had the same pattern as the cords of the ward. They would hold. The cords would hold.

She closed her eyes and shuddered with pure fear and release of fear. And then she turned to help Cricket.

/\/\/\/\

Kestrel had him laid out on the pine needles, his head near the fire. The orange light leapt over his face, caught in the twisted gloss of his braids. "Thank you," he said, lifting his one hand, reaching. Kestrel caught it. "Thank you."

"Cricket." Otter picked up the other hand: the one that had been in the pool of slip. It was limp, cold. Softer than it should have been, like meat going bad.

"I didn't want to die," he said. "I didn't want the Hand to — I wanted to stay myself. I wanted to die still Cricket."

"You're not going to die," said Kestrel.

Cricket opened his eyes. "You've never lied to me, Kestrel. I beg you: Don't start."

The fire cracked and popped; the trees howled. Then Kestrel said: "I won't. I swear."

She stroked the hair out of his face, tucked braids behind his ears.

"I was afraid you'd come," he said. "But I hoped too — dreamed it . . ."

"Of course we came," said Otter. "And we'll take you home, Cricket. We'll get you home."

"Oh, good," he said. "Because in my dream you did not have wings."

"We cannot carry him such a distance, Otter," said Kestrel.

Cricket coughed raggedly: a wet sound.

The touch of many slip was a mud to drown in.

The cough went on. Cricket turned his head away from Kestrel, rolled away, his shoulders pulling in, his back shaking.

Very gently, Kestrel pulled on his shoulder and turned him back. "Don't go before you go," she said. "Stay with me."

He closed his eyes a moment, and swallowed so hard Otter could see it, a shuddering that ran all the way down him. "Lie down with me, *okishae*. Hold on to me. I don't —" his voice cracked. "I don't want to die."

In answer, Kestrel reached for her pack. Otter put down Cricket's already-dead hand to help her. They pulled out what soft, fine things they had. Their wolf hoods. Otter folded them into pillows. One buffalo robe between them.

They spread it out next to the fire. They eased Cricket onto it.

"Like Fawn," he whispered, and closed his eyes again. He lay panting a moment, then reached out, blindly, for Otter's hand. She squeezed it. "Don't take my body back," he said. "Don't even try. You'll be killed, trying. Don't even try."

Otter choked back her "But —"

Kestrel lay down beside Cricket, slipping her arm under his head, pressing the length of her body to his.

Around Otter's fingers, Cricket's hand suddenly tightened. The cough came into him. Kestrel held him. He shook and shook.

"I've got you," said Kestrel. "Cricket, I've got you. I'm not leaving you."

But what Cricket said was: "Don't bind me."

Even Kestrel said: "What?"

"Mad Spider," he said, "bound her mother too tightly. That's where it started. That's why the story —" His words were coming in bursts. He coughed again, but just once. "That's why the story is a secret," he said. "I was going there, if I could — I knew I couldn't, but if I could. I was going to Eyrie. To Mad Spider's place. Eyrie. *Is the ward still standing?* Willow asked: She was right to ask. The story" — he gasped — "ends where it begins." He swallowed, another hard, shuddering swallow. "Don't bind me."

"Cricket —" objected Otter.

But Kestrel said: "We won't."

"I'm so frightened," he said, his eyes closing, his voice going high as a child's. "I've always been so frightened. Don't let me go, Kestrel. Not yet."

"I have hold of you," she said, breathing into his ear, wrapping a leg over his, stroking his hair.

"I can't feel it," he said. "Hold on to me."

Kestrel lifted his head and pulled him against her. And then she kissed him, fearsomely, fearlessly, until his eyes opened again. "Feel that?"

"Past the edge of the world, I would feel that."

Then he coughed again, helplessly, horribly, endlessly, while Kestrel held him and Otter pushed both hands over her own mouth so she wouldn't scream. But it didn't kill him. He fought back into his breath, and said: "I'm so sorry, Kestrel."

She dug her fingers into his hair, leaned her forehead into his, their noses touching. "I am not sorry."

"Good enough." He sighed, letting go of fear.

Otter's hands were wet where the tears ran over them.

There was a huge gust of wind: The trees loosed a prickling fall of snow onto them. The fire sent up a whirl of sparks.

Cricket gasped, pulling air in deep. He took three hard breaths. Paused. Took three more. It went on. He seemed to be climbing. Resting. Climbing.

His eyes floated open. "I saw a new kind of bird today," he said.

And then he died.

Kestrel held Cricket's body through the night, kissing him softly sometimes. Talking to him. Otter tended the small fire, carefully: There had not been that much wood in Cricket's dropped bundle. The world shrank to the size of the firelight: the little ward, the one robe, the two lovers pressed close. Otter wept and kept watch. Sometimes she drifted into sleep, but when her head jerked back up, the world was still small inside a big darkness, and Cricket was still dead.

Willow. And Cricket.

The fuel was gone when the sun came up, and the fire was sinking into embers. Otter stood and walked, just two steps, to the ward. She stood there, and was still standing when Kestrel came up behind her. "There's cord enough," said Otter. "There's no scaffold, and no way to raise it, but —"

"We won't bind him," said Kestrel.

Otter looked at her. The ranger's face was still and blank. Her eyes were swollen from tears but the rest of her was just . . . washed away. "I won't lie to him," she said.

Otter's heart seemed to spin between grief and fear. The dead: They must be bound. They must be kept safe. Her fingers still hurt from pulling the knots shut on her mother's ankles. The binding was all of her history, all of her training, her whole life.

"I *won't*," said Kestrel, snapping like thunder, loud and sudden.

"Ch'hhh," said Otter. "We — we won't, then." She turned and caught Kestrel in her arms. The ranger was rigid, braced against the loss that had already ruined her. She did not melt.

"He died," Kestrel said. "He died still Cricket. The White Hand didn't touch him. He's not coming back." A shake went through her tight body. "He's not coming back."

"We won't bind him," said Otter again. It was wildly foolish. But it was the only comfort she could offer.

"He was *Cricket*," said Kestrel.

Otter nodded, her face moving against Kestrel's hair. "Yes. He was." Cricket had never been more Cricket than in the moment he'd died.

Kestrel folded up then, as if she'd been struck across the back of the knees, went down so completely and so suddenly that she slipped through Otter's arms. Otter lurched and caught her and lowered her into the pine needles. "What can we do?" sobbed Kestrel. "What can we do for him?"

"Let's make it softer," said Otter. "Let's make it warm."

So they took off their mittens and gathered pine needles handful by handful: dry ones, drifted in the nooks of rocks, the roots of trees. They were piercing to gather — their hands were quickly all pricked — but soft when piled. They piled them, handful by handful, into a bed. Handful by handful, it took a long time.

They lifted Cricket's body by knees and armpits, and laid him in the piled needles. He sank a little, as they'd hoped he would: The bed was soft. They helped him curl onto his side, tuck his knees up. Kestrel took his hair from its braids and ran her fingers through it, over and over, long past the point where it was smooth.

Otter nested his carry bag by his feet.

Thinking twice, she opened it. His storyteller's rattle was there: red and black, and collared in black feathers. She put it in his hand.

The smell of the needles was sharp and sweet.

She sat down beside Kestrel and pulled the ranger's hands into her hands, away from Cricket's hair. The death blessing caught in Otter's throat — *may the wind take him, may the rain, may the ravens.* She knew they were coming. She did not want to call them.

"Cricket," she said, "you told wonderful stories. You were braver than you think. You were kind."

Kestrel said nothing. Her hands shook in Otter's hands.

"Cricket," said Otter, "I think you saved me, that day Tamarack died. Did I thank you for that?"

"You didn't," said Kestrel.

"Well," said Otter, "thank you for that."

Kestrel wiped the cuff of her mitten across her nose.

"Cricket," said Otter. Her voice caught. "You snored. No one who wanted to be Red Fox should have snored like that. We never had the heart to tell you, but you were very loud. Also, not as good at hoop-and-lance as you thought you were."

"That was sweet, though," said Kestrel. "I liked to watch you try."

"Not me: I was always afraid the lance would go through someone's foot."

"Or maybe a wall." Kestrel laughed, hiccupped, choked on tears. "Belt of the Spider," she hissed. "I will never forgive this. I will never forget it."

"I know," said Otter.

"It is not fair."

"I know," said Otter.

"*Okishae*," said Kestrel, and started to weep. "Half my heart, my other half."

The sun — in that season rolling close to the southern rim of the world — was as high as it would get. The light under the pine trees was pollen thick, full of slant and dapple. The wind had fallen away. They could hear the little creaks of the individual trees, the wings of the chickadees that darted around them, watching them with cocks of their bright-dark heads. They could hear a woodpecker nearby, its resonating *thk-thk-thk*.

Cricket, though, was silent.

Otter got up. By herself she pulled the fallen pine branches she'd gathered. The bare ones she used to build up the fire, to keep Cricket company in his first time alone. The ones still soft with green needles she piled over him. They would keep him warm. Keep him safe, for a little while, from those things she was supposed to call: from the ravens, from the wind.

Chapter Seventeen

WEST

Midday, the day after the night when Cricket had died, Otter and Kestrel paused side by side by the river. Behind them, the raspberry canes, which had been pulled loose by a terrified boy, were waving aimlessly in the winter breeze. Otter looked back toward Westmost. Their tracks were gone now: The snow curled and eddied as if no one had ever come this way at all.

"I am going to —" said Otter. "I am going to kill Thistle. I am going to push her into the ward. I am going to put an arrow through her open mouth."

Kestrel paused. Swiped tears away with the back of her mittens, and said: "Hmmmm. It seems a waste to do both."

It was exactly what Cricket would have said, and just Cricket's manner too: the soft thoughtfulness that was itself the joke. The recognition brought a scorching ache to Otter's throat.

She turned and saw Kestrel with her face uptilted into the light — looking west. "I am not going back," said the ranger.

"What?" said Otter.

Kestrel was looking upstream. Upstream, where the rivers ran smaller, and then ran out. There was no path to safety, and no safety to reach. Upstream, not far, was the back-bone of the continent, which was impossible for the living to cross.

But Kestrel kept looking: "I am not going back."

"Kestrel . . . there's nothing —"

"Mad Spider's place," said Kestrel. "Eyrie. The place where Cricket was going . . . It is two days west."

Otter's heart spun. She felt caught in a hoop of stories and histories and memories — and the hoop was turning. Mad Spider's place. Was it really a place that could be walked to? It seemed to her that such a place should be past the edge of the world.

She shook her head, bewildered. "How do you know?"

"The rangers go there sometimes," said Kestrel. "There's a holdfast — a lodge and a ward in one thing, that is: a stick frame bound in yarn." She pointed upstream. The finger rocks rose nearby — slants of bare granite, like the fingers of the potter who made the earth, reaching up to the weaver who made the sky. Beyond the finger rocks there rose the black bulk of the first of the true mountains. "Up there," Kestrel said. "Two days, or perhaps three: Our start is late. And the snow."

She turned then, and grasped Otter by both her upper arms. The girls leaned their foreheads together, their breath warm on each other's faces, steaming in the cold day. "Oh, Otter," Kestrel whispered.

Otter squeezed Kestrel's strong arms. "I have hold of you, Kestrel." Too late she realized it was what Kestrel had said to Cricket. Still, it was what needed saying. "I have hold of you."

"Don't kill Thistle. It would hurt your heart."

"As if I could kill her." Grandmother she might be, but Thistle was strong as flint, and fast as a striking hawk. And the rangers would protect her. Otter remembered how Cress had spun Kestrel around, had her helpless in a heartbeat, with a twist of the arm.

"From a distance, maybe," said Kestrel. "With an arrow."

"I cannot shoot," said Otter. "And anyway, I'm going with you."

Kestrel pulled away, still clinging to Otter's arms but staring now. "Otter."

"Are you going there to die?" said Otter.

Kestrel did not answer. Her face was tight. Otter could hear the water running under the ice, and the ice creaking and crackling.

"Are you going up there to die?" said Otter. "As if Cricket —"

"Do not tell me what he wants!" Kestrel let go of Otter's arms and took a deep breath — a shuddering breath, like Cricket had taken, dying. She took three of them, and paused. Three more.

The roof of Otter's mouth ached: fear, grief, the work of not shedding tears. She had to save Kestrel — she had not saved Fawn, she had not saved Willow, she had not saved Cricket, but she was going to save Kestrel. She would save Kestrel, before she cried again.

Kestrel's breath went climbing, as Cricket's had done. Then she whispered: "No. I don't want to die. But I cannot go back to Westmost. And I would go — I would see what Cricket wanted to see. The beginning and the ending. Mad Spider."

"The start of the story," said Otter. The tale the storytellers knew and the binders did not. The story that Cricket had died to share: Mad Spider bound her mother too tightly. It meant something that a binder knew that story now. "Kestrel, I am going with you."

"It is a secret place," said the ranger seriously.

"It was a secret story," said Otter. "And I would see it too."

"Come with me, then," said Kestrel. "Enough of secrets."

"Tsha," swore Otter. *"Enough."*

And so they went into the West, along the river, over the untracked snow.

/\/\/\/\/\

They went slowly.

There was no reason to go quickly. Cricket was dead. They were exhausted, hungry, heavy with grief. So they went slowly.

Kestrel's face was drawn; she was nearly silent. But her eyes were open: She stopped and pointed out the haw apples, stooped and brushed the snow from a crack in a fallen tree trunk to reveal a line of fawn-colored mushrooms, leathery with winter. They picked the haws and cut the fragrant drifts of mushrooms, and Otter began to feel they might not starve.

They stopped early and chopped off a few aspen poles to thrust into the soft ground near the river. Otter strung a ward. Kestrel built a fire bowl of stone and gathered tinder. They had a thin meal of corn porridge and wild mushroom, and spread their one robe on the cold ground. They huddled together on the robe where Cricket had died, with the ice of the river creaking and snapping like a wolf at their ears. They were so tired they were nearly sick with it. They did not keep watch, and they did not dream.

By the morning, the slip had found them.

Otter woke to them: a pair of dark things the size of crows, moving with stiff slowness, pushing close against the loose ward. Otter blinked twice and yawned before she realized that they were not crows, not the shadows of crows, not the shadows of anything at all — simply shadows. Stirring, hungry shadows. She rolled up with a shout, reaching for her bracelets — and Kestrel dropped a hand on her shoulder. "Don't," said the ranger. "You'll only draw more."

Otter felt as if she were still dreaming, an old nightmare — caught in a small space with the dead pressing in. And as in a dream, she was the only one frightened, and could not speak her fear: Kestrel was still blank-faced, silently feeding branches into the sleepy fire.

"Have you ever watched them?" Kestrel asked. "Sometimes I think they are as much longing as hungry. Cricket had a story — do you know it? — about the lost woman who was starving, and wished that everything she touched would turn to meat? And then she found her children. . . ."

Otter shuddered. "How do we unmake them?"

"The rangers' way." Kestrel picked up her staff. "Quietly." She edged the staff through the woven cords some distance from the slip and made its end flutter and brush in the pine needles, like a mother quail drawing off a fox. The slip nearest bulged and twisted, until its swinging nose faced the quivering knots. Slow as a leech it flowed in that direction. When it was close enough, Kestrel lifted the staff, raised her elbow, and struck the thing through from above. For a moment the shadow stuff clotted and squeezed around the staff, then one of the knots there gave way — and the slip was gone. Kestrel turned to the other slip and did the whole thing again.

When she was finished, she passed the staff to Otter and gave her attention, still blankly, to making a tinder bundle — dampening a bit of grass and tough wood-ear fungus, setting it to smolder, wrapping it tightly in birch paper. She was dry-eyed that morning, though her face had aged by winters and winters.

Otter sat watching by the fire with the staff across her knees, as she had done in Westmost. This — this was how the rangers' knots came to be unraveled. This simple, quiet unmaking of little spirits, the rangers' way of dealing with the dead. All the time she had worked in secret on Kestrel's staff, risking her status, risking Kestrel's . . . risking their very lives, for they, like Cricket, could have been sent west.

All that time she had thought there would be more to the unmaking of those knots: more of a story.

A story. Cricket.

Otter retied the knots. She undid the ward and reclaimed its cords, wrapping a few up her arms and putting the rest in a pouch outside her coat. By then it was full morning, and time to move on.

/\/\/\/\

It was warmer that day. The last snow was melting away. The river ate at its fringe of ice.

They went without trouble, though there was the creeping sense of eyes on them, of rustle in the forest, though the day was very still and nothing was rustling.

When the sun began to sink and turn golden, they stopped in a meadow at the foot of a waterfall. Ahead of them, the Spearfish came tumbling over boulders. The spires of the finger rocks rose, bare granite, showing like black hands against the brightness of the western sky.

At the edge of the waterfall pool was a single, huge willow, its roots undercut and arching toward the water. Between two of the leg-thick roots Otter cast a small ward — not much bigger around than a pair of beds.

This time, Otter did not sleep easily. Past the scanty cords of her ward she could see the twilight shadows thickening, and tried to guess which of those shadows would clump and stir: which was not a shadow at all, but a little piece of the hunger.

"There will be fewer," said Kestrel, rolling over on her side and tugging her coat around her. She watched Otter watching. "As we go away from Westmost, we should see less of the little dead."

"They are not — everywhere?" It was a startling thought.

"They are everywhere. They are always. But they are drawn to the human, and to power, and to fear. There will be less."

Otter looked again. The waterfall meadow must have flooded in the last spring: The little birches and dogwood scrabble were undercut, standing tiptoe on their own roots. Under those roots were balls of shadow. She could see them, curled up like rabbits asleep. Stirring. Breathing.

Like the thing in the corn, the thing that had first hurt Cricket, first exposed her own power.

Drawn to the human, or power, or fear . . .

Otter reached out from her bed and put her hand on the cord of the ward. Her fourth ward. Already it was not a wild thing, like the ward that had killed Fawn. It was more dog than wolf. The knots on either side slid toward her, until her hand was like a bead among smaller beads. She closed her eyes and eventually fell asleep.

The little dead were all around them. But Otter's ward held them all night, and Kestrel's staff undid them in the morning, and the girls walked on.

The third day was hard going.

Past the waterfall, the way cut into the hill. It was rocky, steep, and narrow. Snowy in the shadows. Icy in places. They needed their hands to grab onto the rough bark of digger pines and pull themselves along. They went up slowly, panting.

All the time the river grew smaller. They met its tributaries: little creeks and less than creeks, shooting out of slots in the rock to join the main stream, or spilling over the lip of a boulder in waterfalls small enough to catch in one hand.

Otter thought they were like squirrels going out to the end of a branch. Eventually the stream would grow too thin to protect them. It would be two strides across, it would be one. It would be the sort of stream that ran dry now and again, or iced over, and the dead would cross it in one slide. This was why there was nothing west of Westmost: The rivers gave out.

They stumbled on and the Spearfish grew smaller. The land kept sloping up and the stream, small as it now was, kept carving down, until they were in a canyon, shoulder high, rocky, overhung with dark pines. They had to walk in the water and it was cold enough to make their feet shoot with pain, cold enough to make a woman clumsy. The current was fast, and in places it had carved hollows. In the hollows, the water was deep, and it pushed at them. Otter fell once, but Kestrel — who had not been sleeping, whose eyes were hollow with grief — fell over and over again.

The third time Kestrel fell, she fell badly, catching herself on one hand, with a *snap* that pulled a cry from her.

"Let me look," said Otter, as Kestrel tucked her hand against her belly and folded up. "Kestrel, let me look."

Kestrel held out her hand, her teeth set.

There was little enough to see: a scrape that was bleeding sluggishly, the mottling that came with deep cold. Otter took the hand carefully, and tried to rotate Kestrel's wrist.

The ranger cried out and pulled her hand away.

"Broken, do you think?" said Otter.

Kestrel answered through her teeth: "Does it matter?"

They were standing in cold water. They could not stop there.

Otter made a sling from some of her cords, tied Kestrel's arm against her body. They went on.

Where she could, Otter walked beside her friend, and steadied her. But often the canyon was too narrow, and the way too steep: It was less a walk now than a scramble, a clamber over boulders and a creep along thin sloping margins of scree. So Kestrel fell and scraped her other hand to bleeding, fell and had her breath knocked out. And at last she fell into the river and did not get up again.

Otter knelt beside her, lifting her from the water. The canyon was now only a stride across; its wall brushed her shoulder. The cold of the water was of the kind called bitter, because it was a flavor, a poison. Otter was shivering convulsively. Kestrel was no longer shivering at all.

"We must leave the water," said Otter, realizing it as she said it, and fearing that she might have realized it too late. "We must go into the forest and make a fire. Now."

What would come over those skin-colored needles — her heart lurched at the memory of Cricket fallen into the sludge of shadows. But what would come would come. Like Cricket, they did not have a choice.

But Kestrel mumbled: "... No ... We're almost ... It opens ..." She got up, took three staggering steps forward, and fell again. Otter clambered to her, splashing on her hands and feet through the water. The teeth and knives of the water.

But, quite suddenly, the stream was gone. It had become a marshy slope — and at the top of the slope was clear sunlight and sky. Otter heaved Kestrel up and together they went stumbling toward the light. They topped the rise. In front of them, the land slanted down. The sun lay on the west-facing slope like a warm hand.

They went a few more steps out of mad habit, and then Kestrel stumbled and knelt, and Otter knelt down with her and held on to her, shaking. The forest was a bow-shot behind them. The slope was part of the rim of a crater, a caldera. It was huge — two days' walk across, maybe more — and nearly as round as a dish. No trees grew in it, and there was no snow: It was a bowl of sunlight and grass, and in the center was a great black lake — a lake four times bigger than the whole pinch of Westmost. Open water — no ice — steamed and stirred. In the center of the lake, like a stone in a cupped hand, was a rocky, wooded island. There was warmth coming from somewhere, and a smell Otter did not know. She huddled into Kestrel.

They slept then, on the western slope of their world, their strength used up and their hopes forgotten. They slept shivering all afternoon, as the kind sun dried them, and they woke only as the light began to swing down toward evening. It was a wind that woke them, picking up as the day changed, sending its fingers through the last damp spots of their coats. Otter got up and helped Kestrel up, both of them stiff and still tired, but alive in the evening light.

And that is how they came to Mad Spider's place, to the ruin of Eyrie, the city of dreams.

Chapter Eighteen

THE HOLDFAST

The day was ending in a sunset of orange feathers. At the edge of the sky was a line of mountains. They were taller and younger than the mountains that were the home of the Shadowed People, and their rocky peaks were white with snow.

Kestrel and Otter paused to watch the distant mountains become a hem of flame. They were huge and beautiful. *So,* thought Otter, *this is the greater world.* "Does nothing come from there?" she asked. "From the West?"

Kestrel was leaning on her ranger's staff, weary, unbalanced by her bound-up arm. "Nothing human. Deer. Elk. Mountain sheep. Bears, when the blueberries are ripe. But the streams run a different way from here. And there's no river deep enough to make a road."

A gust blew across Otter's ears; it filled them with a sound like wings beating, and for a moment she could hear nothing else. The wind was cold, but the air, when still, was not. "Where is the warmth coming from?" said Otter. It was a strange place, the caldera. It seemed held in a different season, as if winter could not quite reach it.

"From the potter's fires," said Kestrel. "From under the earth."

Otter knew that it was a potter who made the earth and a weaver who made the sky. But she'd never expected to feel the heat of the pot-firing coals, however faintly. Eyrie, place of stories. Eyrie, where things began.

"Come," said Kestrel, setting off down the slope toward the lake. "We're losing the light." As evening came, the shadows would spread like spilled water, would cover the whole of the world. Otter put her hand on Kestrel's arm, and the cords in the injured ranger's sling edged toward her fingers. The knots were awake. Otter's power was awake.

There might be anything in the shadows.

They went down the slope as quickly as they could.

Despite their hurry, it was fully dark by the time they reached the shore of the lake. The stars came out, thicker and thicker, and the band of small stars and fainter things that they called the Weaver's Tears spilled itself across the sky.

Otter had never walked in darkness, not away from Westmost. Not in a place where she could see no firelight, smell no cooking, hear no laughter or song or babies crying. The darkness seemed to make them more alone. It made the wind louder, it made a heart-stopping noise of a rabbit bolting out from under their feet. Otter's heart beat faster. She slipped her fingers under her bracelets, making sure they were loose. She saw that Kestrel — though limping — was not leaning on her staff. She had it lifted in her single uninjured hand. She too was ready.

. And yet, as they walked and walked, in thicker and thicker darkness, nothing happened. The slope bottomed out, changing from grasses and yucca to a low meadow of cushion moss and frost-black speedwell, wires of spiderwort curling upward, the red stems of saxifrage spilling from the cracks of the rocks. The soil had a give underfoot. It was not wet, but Otter thought there might be wetness, not far down — the moss underfoot felt like a deer hide over a mud puddle. The strange smell was heavier. It stirred around them.

When something loomed up, shaped like a bear in the darkness, Otter was afraid. But Kestrel said "At last," and strode toward it.

"What is that?" said Otter, hurrying after. In the starlight she could just see it. A structure: birch poles thrust into the earth in a ring and bent together at the top. It was wound around with blue cords.

"The holdfast." Kestrel lowered her staff and leaned on it. "A place where the rangers may stand a day or two, and sleep safely."

"They come this far?" Otter was awed.

"This far and no farther," Kestrel said. "Late in the summer, this whole bowl is filled with blue lupines. The rangers come here and pick them by the basketful, and pack them into bags for the dyers. This is where blue comes from. This is the true edge of the world."

Otter walked around the holdfast, touching the cords. There were many: The lowest part of the holdfast was thickly wound as a bird's nest. And there were many knots. It was not a ward — no one but a binder could have tied a ward, and no binder's hand had made this. It was . . . The rangers had wrapped their holdfast as if it were one of their staffs. They'd used many cords, tied many rangers' knots, small and sure. The knots stirred as Otter touched them, but nothing made to pounce. The power of the place was as faded and fuzzed as old yarn.

It was comfortable. Old. It had protected the blue-gatherers for years, perhaps generations. It would keep back the slip, she was sure.

But somewhere, still in the world, was a White Hand. *Drawn to the human, or to power, or to fear.* Otter could not shake the sense that it might have followed them.

Even if it had, they could do little about it. Still alive, and at the very edge of the world, they went inside.

/\\/\\/\\/\\

It was darker inside the holdfast, though not much: The white-barked poles were open as a rib cage against the sky; light and wind came through them with barely a waver. But for all that, the darkness was a sheltering one. There was a floor of woven willow that held them above the damp of the earth. There were piles of dried ferns to make sleeping places; there was wood stacked high; there was tinder already laid in the fire bowl. The holdfast wrapped its soft power around them.

"The ember is gone," said Kestrel. There was something broken in her voice. She was bent over the nest of grass and dried tinder, and Otter could not see her face. The ranger was holding a contraption of stick and sinew, a fire drill that spun a bit of flint against dry wood. Otter recognized it but only vaguely: The fires of Westmost never went out. Still, she saw at once that it could not be used one-handed.

"Here," she said, and took the drill. She set the tip in the tinder and fumbled with the cord and bow that made the fire bit spin.

Kestrel turned aside and took off her coat. Beneath it, her shirt was still damp: The leather was dark under the pale quills. She opened her pack and pulled out a new shirt. As the shirt caught starlight, Otter saw that it was yellow. New yellow leather, dyed with prickly poppies, the shirt Otter herself had stitched and Cricket and Kestrel had laughed and laughed over. The pair of them, each surprising the other with yellow. Cricket's *okishae*-pledge shirt. He had taken it with him when he went out of Westmost, and Kestrel had taken it from his travel bag, after he died. Otter kept the drill spinning — she had to — and Kestrel turned aside and folded the leather shirt around her face.

A moaning wind began: constant, and longing as a voice.

Kestrel was shivering. Otter realized she could probably not take off her damp shirt, not with her arm tied up in binder's knots. "I will help you with that," she said. "A moment. I think the fire —"

It was smoldering now, a single eye of orange looking out of the knot of grass and smoke.

"Did we do right?" asked Kestrel. "We did not bind him. What if . . ."

What if. Otter knew that *what if.* She had not been able to stop thinking about that *what if.* The dead were bound to keep them away from the world. To keep their bodies from moving while their names were leaving.

What if Cricket's body moved, though his name was gone?

What kind of creature would he become?

The fire needed her. Otter leaned in and blew softly on the orange spark, feeding it splinters of bark, one by one.

"What if —" said Kestrel. And then suddenly, her voice cracked. "No, he's not coming back. He died and he's gone." Otter, tending the fire, could not even touch Kestrel as her shoulders shook and her grief sounds fell into the leather.

Otter fed the infant fire twigs, then small branches. And she finally found something to say: "He was Cricket."

Kestrel looked up. There was silence for a long moment. Otter could see her eyes shining in the darkness — turning to the stars. Otter looked up too, picking out the band of light the Shadowed People called Weaver's Tears, and in them, the seven faint stars called the Cricket.

"There it is," she said.

"Little stars," Kestrel said, "for a storyteller. They are not much honored."

"I would name the moon after him," said Otter.

"The moon and the *sun*," said Kestrel.

"The moon and the sun," said Otter.

And then Kestrel made dinner.

The little holdfast boasted a cooking pot, small sacks of sage and serviceberry for flavor, dried milkweed blossom for thickening stews, forage foods — biscuit-root, wild onion, dried mushrooms — and even dried meat in a stone-lined cache hole.

Otter and Kestrel had only been three days walking, struggling to cook with a walker's pot — a tough pouch made from the heart-sac of a buffalo. Still, they had been long days, numb days. The two of them had, in their different ways, lost everything. The stew Kestrel made, with the last of their cornmeal, seemed like a feast, and after the feast, a kindly tiredness fell on them. They sat by the fire, talking little. Otter was sleepy, but the name of the place hung unseen all around them. Eyrie: Mad Spider's place. Eyrie: where Mad Spider had bound her mother too tightly.

They had seen nothing of the city. Nothing human. But even so, Mad Spider's story hung close. Her story, and the *what if* of not binding Cricket.

And somewhere in the darkness, the White Hand.

The one who had been Tamarack, beloved grandmother, sneaker of sweets.

Kestrel and Otter lay close together in the dry ferns. Warm and fed, exhausted and terrified, they slept.

That night, Otter dreamed of a cord tied around a birch tree — a ward fragment, but not one yearly renewed: It was ancient. The tree had grown around it. The woody flesh bulged. The crackling white bark closed over it like dead lips. Then suddenly, she saw that some of the birch branches were bones.

Otter rolled over, the fronds around her crackling. And she dreamed that bound tree was not a birch, but a willow.

And then she saw that it was not a tree, but her mother's wrist — the swollen skin lipping over the cord. The hand — the hand she had tied shut — was uncoiling like a fern. Even in the dream she reeled back, and thought: *Her hand is only falling slack.* Then she saw the gray fingers fist and flex.

Otter slept badly and woke stiff. Kestrel slept like the dead, and woke pinned under her stiffness as if under a rockfall. She could hardly rise. Her eyes were hollow and her wrist was swollen.

But here, at last, the world was kind to them. As Kestrel lay resting, the day dawned bright and grew warm, then warmer. In Westmost, it would have been the ragged end of winter, the end of the Hunger Moon, coming toward the Moon of Sap-Running. The sun might have been warm once in a while, but the wind would have been raw. In the high caldera, by the steaming lake, the wind was as playful as a butterfly. It plucked at their hair.

And then, day after day, that weather held. It thawed their fear; it softened their hearts.

Their third day in the holdfast, Kestrel sat on a stone in the mild sun and tried to help Otter find the dried feather-flowers of prairie smoke, whose root could be crushed and used as a liniment for pain.

"This?" called Otter.

"That's a thistle," said Kestrel.

Otter brought a pod of something over in one hand to show the ranger. "This?"

"That's milkweed. Binder's daughter, you've led a sheltered life if you don't know milkweed."

"Oh, but I do," said Otter, and brought the other hand from behind her back, releasing milkweed seeds in a puff into Kestrel's face.

"Tsha! Otter!" The ranger batted the downy, floating, clinging things away.

"Make wishes," said Otter. "Make a skyful of wishes."

"But there is only one thing I want." Dressed in Cricket's yellow shirt, Kestrel looked little as Fawn, little as a child.

Otter stiffened. "I'm sorry."

"Ch'hhh. You didn't remind me, because I hadn't forgotten. I'll just wish for him a skyful of times."

Otter was silent a moment, putting her hand on Kestrel's shoulder.

"Prairie-smoke root?" Kestrel prompted.

Otter turned, searched. After a while, called: "This?"

"There are squirrels who are better at this than you."

She found it eventually, and milk vetch too, the root of which is a chew for muscle pains, and soon Kestrel was moving — walking in that sunny, strange place.

Their days in the caldera were a sunflower girl of a time, an idyll between one thing and another. They taught each other. Before the Hunger Moon was dark, Kestrel could tie the simplest of binder's knots, make a small, one-strand ward. Before the next moon opened, Otter could bait a fishhook, set a snare, gather rosehips without scratching her hands.

And the lake. They swam. Westmost's drought pool was cold, even in midsummer. This lake was warm — nearly hot.

The water had a metal tang, like blood, that made it strange to drink, but the minerals held them floating and the heat pulled the pain and fear from them. When they came out, their bare skins steamed and they were not cold.

Nor were they hungry. There were not many fish in the strange lake, and the rabbits Otter tried to snare seemed smarter than she was, but there were geese. The lake was thick with geese: brown-bodied, black-necked, fat as fall pumpkins. They had missed their migration and stayed the winter on the open water.

"Oh, for a bow," said Kestrel one day, lounging and watching them. "A bow and a big roasting pit."

Otter put down her digging stick: She'd been uprooting cattails, whose roots could be baked — a good food, though dull. "Could we snare them?"

"Maybe. I've never snared for a water beast."

"Could we just catch them?"

Kestrel stood up. "Oh, let's try."

It wasn't even hard.

The first few times Otter tried, it turned out badly, with splash and crash and honking. Kestrel laughed and laughed. "You do it, then, Lady Ranger," Otter said, using a pinkie to scoop mud out of her ears. On the lake, the goose she'd been trying to catch reared up on beating wings, snaked out its black neck, and hissed at her. "Don't argue with me," Otter told it.

"Try it a ranger's way," said Kestrel. "Try it quietly."

She crumbled the roast biscuit-root she'd been eating and tossed the crumbs toward the geese.

The hissing one stopped hissing. It looked at the crumbs.

Kestrel made a clucking, coaxing noise. Otter backed off. Kestrel threw more crumbs. More geese looked. They swam toward her. She threw crumbs. They waddled ashore. With a few more handfuls of biscuit-root, with a few easy steps, Kestrel was up to her waist in eddying, eating geese. She sorted through them with her eyes, picked a fat one, and fell sideways on it.

The little flock exploded into wings and indignation, but it was too late. Kestrel stood up with her arms full of struggling goose. A twist of the ranger's capable hand — and a flinch from Otter — and it was over. It was, in fact, dinner.

Incredibly, it worked the next day too. And the next. They had, for the first time in their lives, more meat than they could eat.

"They are dumb as rocks," said Otter, when it worked a fourth time.

Kestrel flicked her sore wrist — breaking a goose neck was near the limit of what she could do. "Well," she said, "these are the ones that got lost."

"Oh," said Otter. "Oh, tell it!"

"'The Geese that Got Lost Going South,'" said Kestrel.

It had been one of Cricket's favorite stories.

"'The Geese that Got Lost Going South,'" she said again.

And — finally, finally — Kestrel started to cry.

They cried until they couldn't cry anymore. And then Otter told the story, and they laughed.

Cricket. They laughed over his memory, they cried over it. They were warm and fed, and nothing came at them in the darkness. They thought themselves as safe as they had ever been. They forgot, almost, what they had come to do: that they had come to find something, to find Eyrie, to find the living root of the stories about the dead. They did not notice that, apart from the holdfast itself, they had found nothing human at all. In that warm, sunlit place, the perfect place for humans to live — nothing human at all.

Then, one day, they swam out to the island.

Chapter Nineteen

THE ISLAND

They had not meant to go. Why would they? Where most of the caldera was a soft curve of soil, the island was rock: young and ragged. Where the meadow was moss and grasses, the island was trees. Its black pines shocked the eye. It was shadowed.

But one day they were swimming, and they found something curious. There was a place in the meadow where the ground bumped up as if over a huge tree root. Where it met the lake, the bump made a finger of land, pointing straight out toward the island. Off the tip of it, the girls discovered a line of submerged boulders. Their tops were hidden an arrow's length under the dark, restless surface of the lake. Stepping stones, if you were a giant. Diving stones, otherwise.

Otter dove like her namesake, twisting and flashing into the dark water. Kestrel sat on the edge of one of the stones, up to her collarbone in the water, her bare shoulders shining like copper. Otter dove deep, pushing against the lifting force of the thick water. She felt the darkness and the heat that rose under her. She felt the power of her kick, the strength of her body, and the smoothness of bare skin slipping through the water. When she surfaced and turned, Kestrel was still sitting, twisting droplets from the dark rope of her hair. She was half-smiling, but a deep and silent sadness was sitting beside her.

Otter, though only one winter past her girlhood, knew sorrow. But she had fought it, run from it, bound it tight with her power. She knew nothing of sitting with it. And she was named, after all, for an otter: a spirit of strong play. She was a girl who could aim a snowball. Sneak a peeled acorn into a stew pot, just to surprise someone with the bitter bite. She dove again, and this time stayed under until she found Kestrel's foot. She pulled the ranger in.

When they came up, Kestrel was spluttering: "Tsha! Otter! I am going to —"

"You'll have to catch me first," said Otter, and dove.

But Kestrel did catch her, and then Otter splashed her, and then Kestrel dove — and before they knew it they had collapsed, laughing, on the shingled fringe of the island's shore.

◇◇◇◇◇

They both lay panting, half in the hot water, half in the cool air. It occurred to Otter that she'd nearly lost track of the moon: Sap-Running, she thought, but what phase? Kestrel sat up, fingering the tangles out of her hair. Otter's eye caught on an old arrowhead lying half in the water. The lap of the lake had dulled the glass-black of its obsidian. But though it was old, it was a human thing, a made thing.

The sight made Otter a little uneasy. She was not sure why. But before she could decide, she heard, very faintly, the throb of a drum.

At first she thought, *Oh, a drum*, and then a jolt went through her whole body. She held up a hand, making the ranger's gesture for quiet. Kestrel snapped into silence. She held still as a startled deer.

Yes, there, under the murmur of the trees, was a drumbeat. A small drum, by the sound of it, like Cricket's fireside drum. It kept making a few heartbeat beats, and then stumbling and lurching. If a dying man was playing a drum, he'd play it like that.

Otter and Kestrel silently climbed to their feet, looking at each other. They did not dare say his name.

His name that was done with the world. His body that they'd left unbound. What if . . .

Otter looked around. There was water, right there at their feet. Water was safety. The dead could not cross water.

But if that were true, then how had he — how had Cricket — how had the drummer come to the island? She did not think it could be a human drummer, here at the edge of the world. But what manner of dead thing could play a drum?

The breeze shifted, and suddenly the drumbeats came clearer. And under them — did she fool herself or could she really hear it? — under them came a voice. It came weaving through the drumbeats: light, male. They could make out no words at such a distance, but the cadence was a storyteller's.

Horror bloomed in Otter's heart. Cricket. They'd doomed him, they'd made him into something. She turned to Kestrel, not knowing what she would say. She turned just in time to see the flash of recognition on Kestrel's face, the spring of tears. The ranger bolted for the heart of the island, for the shadows, for the voice.

Otter dove after. She caught Kestrel by the arm, and when that didn't work, she threw herself on top of her friend's body. They went crashing together into the rushes, loud as bears. "Wait," hissed Otter, as they rolled apart. Kestrel met her eyes, and stopped moving. "If it's Cricket," Otter whispered, "if it's Cricket, it's not Cricket. We can't — go to him like this."

It seemed to occur to Kestrel, quite suddenly, that she was naked. She folded her arms around herself. They were both naked, of course, and neither of them cared — but the gesture made Kestrel look small. She looked cold. She looked vulnerable. "If it's Cricket . . ." she said.

The wind shifted again, and the voice was lost. The drumbeat vanished under the pounding in Otter's ears. "We could swim to shore," she said. "They can't cross the water."

"We can't leave him," said Kestrel.

If they had made a dead thing, a horror thing, of beloved Cricket, then they had to unmake it. They did not know how to unmake it. But they had to try.

Otter tried to think like Kestrel, since Kestrel clearly could not think. She tried to be calm, practical. So: They could not confront any kind of dead thing, naked. Nor in wet clothes, not during the last turn of winter. "Those diving stones," she said. "They make a path." As she said it, she realized it was true. And what if they were a path: not a thrust of the land, but something human-built? Or if not human, at least *built*. An island, surrounded by stirring water, surrounded by sunshine. It should be the safest place in the world. And yet humans had lived there — and they had *left*.

Otter's breath was coming fast and faster. But she managed: "Give me your bracelets. Any cord you have. Go and fetch our gear." It should be possible to carry their clothes and coats, her cords and Kestrel's staff, in a bundle above the head, above the water, dry. Otter could have done it, but she wanted to stay between Kestrel and the voice that might, at any moment, whisper her name.

Okishae. That was a word that would carry: a word you could blow through a flute made of bone.

Kestrel's eyes were round and wet. But she nodded. She handed over her bracelets silently. And she went.

Otter wrapped the extra cord up her arms. If something came at her, out of the forest, the cord would give her a chance: She might be able to cast a loop around it. Sorrow's knot: Pull it closed. Meanwhile, she cast her own bracelets into the cradle-star. She waded out a little way into the water, for warmth, for safety, to be back in the place where she'd just felt herself strong. Then she turned to watch the dark, ragged forest. It loomed over her. And faintly, faintly, came the drum.

The water lapped ceaselessly around Otter's waist, and her shadow shifted slowly across the dark-bright surface as she waited for Kestrel to come back. Sometimes she could hear the drum, and sometimes she could not. The voice did not return. Her shoulders began to ache from holding up her cradle-star against the blank face of the island. She let the strings lower. Nothing happened, and nothing happened.

The sun shifted one fist across the sky.

And Kestrel came back.

Together, silently, they pulled on leggings, shrugged into coats, laced up boots.

Together, silently, Kestrel with her staff and Otter with her strings, they went toward the wood.

The island shore rose sharply at first, not high but steep: almost a little cliff. The stones had strange colors, rimed by the mineral breath of the lake. They had a strange smell. They had strange shapes.

Otter and Kestrel found a huge rock that had feathered out from the cliff face and scrambled up the tight, scree-choked gap behind it. They went on all fours through the clicky, stony space. It was not a long climb — Kestrel with her damaged wrist could not have managed a long climb — but it was like climbing into another world.

They reached the top. The ground leveled and the forest began. Boulders of obsidian lay like gleaming eggs under the dark trees. Ferns grew everywhere, green as summer, though away from the lake it was colder. They stopped in that green space, breathing fog, and listened.

When Otter had been waiting in the water, the drum had seemed to be everywhere and nowhere. Now it was — that way. She glanced at Kestrel, who pointed in the same direction with her staff, silently.

The voice came back to them, wavering.

Otter made the ranger's sign: *Let's go.*

Hurry, Kestrel signed back. And they ran.

Otter thought that Kestrel ran like a wolf — like something fearless and forest-born. Almost silent through the thick fern. Leaping from stone to ground to stone, leaping over branches, quick as dreaming. Otter was no forest thing. The ferns tore at her leggings. Hidden branches tripped her. The drum and the voice rose like dread to block her throat.

Otter did not want to find out what they had made of Cricket, if it was Cricket. But she thought if she were not with Kestrel then the ranger might simply throw herself into dead arms. *No*, thought Otter. They had to find him. *But let it not be him. Let it not be.*

Closer. The drum grew louder, the voice clearer. They could have made out words in it, if they had not been running, if they had stopped to listen.

And then —

Otter almost crashed into Kestrel as the ranger came to a stop.

They were on the edge of a small open space, like a dry pool made of stones. It would have been full of sunlight at midday, but it was not big enough to keep such sunlight long. There was only a crescent rim of light now. The light lay a quarter turn around the meadow from them, perhaps a tree's height away.

In that fragile, shrinking light stood — someone. A living someone, it seemed to be. Huddled up in a coat that was like folds of shadow, with a drum in one hand, a human woman — no. A boy, a man.

And just in front of him, making the edge of the shadow bulge like a hand lifting wet leather, was —

"Tsha!" shouted Kestrel. "Leave him alone!"

The dead thing spun. Its focus snapped toward Kestrel, its stuff twisting like a snarl. It was coming at them before Otter was even sure what it was.

It came over the ground, fast, fast. It came flattened out like a badger. The substance of it was like the black powder mold that grew on corn. An arm shot out: elbow bent backward from human. But the hand. The hand was perfectly human, and bone white.

Otter had already had her cords in her hands, but she'd had nothing cast. You couldn't run with something cast: It would be like running with your hands tied. Her breath tore up her throat and her body shook as she moved her fingers: turn, flip, under, loop, under — all in four heartbeats as the thing came at them. Its arm hooked forward and the dead thing rushed at them face-first, hook and side.

Otter was shouting with horror, wordlessly, hardly even knowing she was shouting. She could feel her power burning from her heart to her hands, her heartbeat trying to pound its way out of her ears. Turn and under — and she had her star. She thrust it out at the thing.

It reared up, towered over her, so close she braced herself to feel its breath — but it had no breath. It had nothing at all.

The thing was stopped against her cradle-star like a bear stopped on the end of a spear. But it was big. It kept flowing around the edges of her protection, trying to reach over it, around it. She saw the white hand slash toward her eyes.

Kestrel was pressed close behind her. The ranger blocked the blow with her staff and the thing bubbled away on that side, bulging upward. Kestrel reached past Otter and swatted at its edges: up, left, right, right, up — driving it back. Otter could see the cords breaking free from Kestrel's staff as if fire were eating through them. The dead thing flowed backward a single step.

"To the light!" said the ranger.

They edged sideways. Otter did not dare look away from the dead thing. It bulked large against the sky, pouching and squeezing. One of the white hands was still reaching toward her.

Otter was shaking, begging herself not to stumble. The loose stones rolled underfoot. The stones clicked. The dead thing was silent.

Otter and Kestrel went crabwise, step by step. The thing, though it had no face, swung its blunt side as if watching them. Otter felt the sunlight touch her temple. Then it hit her eyes. Then they were full in sunlight, beside the cowering, shivering drummer.

The stranger tucked his face away from them, lifting his hand as if against a blow, curving his body protectively around the drum in his other hand. "Once —" he said. His fingers skittered against the drum, and he choked out a few words. His voice was ragged, hoarse, wild with fear. He swallowed and spoke again: "Once, when the world was new . . ."

Then he looked up. A young face, a stranger's face. A boy their own age. Black eyes wide. Darkness whirling strangely across jaw and cheekbones.

Not Cricket.

No one they knew.

"Who —" said Kestrel.

Otter kept her cords lifted, her eyes fixed on the dead thing. It had not followed them, or at least not with its terrifying, snake-strike speed. It was leaning toward her, like slimy waterweed streaming in a current.

Three of the stretching strands seemed to thicken together, and the white hand appeared at the end of them. An arm. A finger. It was pointing at them.

No, not at them: at her. At Otter.

Binder, curled the whisper in her brain.

Her own heartbeat sounded like a drum in her ears. She was not sure the whisper was real.

"Tell it," said the boy. "I have told it — everything. All my tales. Tell it. Tell it a story."

Chapter Twenty

THE BOY IN THE BOWL OF STONES

"Tell it a story," the boy rasped. "I can't, I —" His voice cracked, then broke. He asked: "Do you have water?"

"At my hip," said Kestrel. She had both her hands on her lifted staff, and she did not spare the stranger so much as a glance. "Take it."

"*Xashi*," he murmured, a word they didn't know. The tone of it was gratitude — desperate, broken gratitude. Otter heard his fumbling to pull Kestrel's waterskin free, and then she heard him swallow. It was very quiet in that bowl of stone. The White Hand made no sound at all — it was like a hole in sound. It was a hole in the world: a rotten softness hidden inside wood.

"*Cu xashi*," said the boy. He shook, then coughed. His voice was rough as if he'd been caught in smoke. "Thank. I mean, thanks. Thanks to you. I have been spinning tales — I don't know. Two days. This is the third, and almost over."

"That . . ." began Otter, and did not know what else to say. No one could have stood against a White Hand for days — and least of all someone powerless, someone male. But there was no time to sort it out. The sun was slipping, the shadow lapping at their toes. The White Hand oozed forward, and Otter and Kestrel, moving together like dancers, each took a step back.

"We are losing this light," said Kestrel.

And again the White Hand advanced.

Otter spread her cords. Careful not to let a moment's slack enter the pattern, she turned the cradle-star into the tree. A more powerful casting. Harder to hold. The Hand stopped. It was still a pole's length away, but Otter felt its press against her cords. Her pattern was raising no answering pattern in it — no marks in its stuff. It was not falling back.

"I do not know . . ." she said, and swallowed. Her fingers were already cramping. "I do not know if I can hold it, without the sun."

Three heartbeats of silence. Then Kestrel answered: "What, then?"

"You must . . ." the boy wheezed. "*Tomteka*, stories — tell it a story."

From the corner of her eye, Otter saw Kestrel's staff jerk, as if she'd turn and strike the stranger. "Stop talking about stories."

"Cricket told a story to the White Hand," said Otter. "And it listened."

"Cricket *died*."

But not of this, thought Otter. The Hand had listened.

But this White Hand . . . this one was different. The Hand that had once been Tamarack had helped Willow to her feet. That one was loss, was sadness. This one — this one was ravening and madness. Still: "Kestrel, it must work." Otter pointed with her elbow at the strange boy. "It worked for him . . ."

"Orca," he said in that smoke-dried voice — a voice that had been talking down death for three days. "My name: Orca."

Another word neither of them knew.

"We don't know what he did," snapped Kestrel.

"What do you think, then?" said the boy, Orca. "That I gave it sweets and hoped?"

"It's a *White Hand*," said Kestrel. "It doesn't *listen*."

"I don't know what it is," said Orca. "It is every horror I ever heard of; it is something new. But I say: It listens." His rasp broke then into a shattering, bloody cough. Otter thought of Cricket, coughing, drowning from the inside. Kestrel must have thought of Cricket too — she looked around at the boy.

The White Hand seeped forward, into the gap of her attention.

"Tsha!" Otter shouted it down, pulling her casting taut and putting all her power into it.

The thing stopped again.

The cords between Otter's hands were as alive as lightning, shooting through her. She locked her arms, set her teeth, felt herself become rigid as the second day of death.

Orca coughed and coughed, folding up on himself, then sinking to his knees. He was still alert, though, still watching the Hand, still keeping his hand on his drum in the shrinking light. "I can't," he said. "I can't keep talking."

"Kestrel," said Otter, "it has to be you." The shadow was at their feet again. Otter stepped backward. This time it was a moment before Kestrel stepped backward too. It would be their last step: They were out of light. "Kestrel," said Otter, almost begging, "tell it 'The Goose Who Got Lost' — tell it anything."

In answer, Kestrel took a deep, shuddering breath. Then two more, as Cricket had, dying. And she said: "One day, Red Fox was out hunting when along flew a raven as big as the moon. And the raven —"

And she stopped, startled, because the White Hand had — no, not backed off, but settled in. Its shape eased toward something human.

"Don't stop," gasped Orca, even as, in the silence, the Hand changed again, its forward edge sharpening like an axe. Kestrel started talking again, so quickly she tripped over the words: "And the — the raven swooped down and landed on one of the finger rocks, which are like mountains made of one stone. So big — so big was the raven that the stone looked like an egg."

The Hand's knife-edge softened again. It was listening. The rabid, liquid thing. Truly listening.

Kestrel lowered her staff, slowly, experimenting. " 'Well,' said Red Fox. 'This is something new.' "

"And Red Fox called up to the raven . . ."

Otter slid in close beside Kestrel as the ranger lowered her staff. Orca fell in behind them, and all at once Otter remembered the day that Tamarack had died, how she and Kestrel and Cricket had slid into an arrowhead of three, becoming one thing without a word between them.

Otter and Kestrel and Orca stood pressed close together. The White Hand stood still, as if looking at them.

Otter let a little slack into her casting, and shuddered. She'd been holding the cords too tightly: so tightly, giving them so much power out of her own body that she herself had no slack to breathe. She found herself gasping.

Kestrel shot her a glance, but kept talking: "'What do the humans need to talk for?' said the raven to Red Fox. 'They are silly enough.'"

Otter lowered her cords. They had no lifted ranger's staff now, no lifted casting. Still the White Hand did not move. Behind her she felt Orca shift, and then came the sound of the drum. It rose under Kestrel's story, wove through it, gave it steadiness and strength. Otter found her breath falling into the rhythm of the drumbeat.

As Kestrel told "How Red Fox Stole the Words," the sunlight slipped away from the bowl of stones. The ferns beyond, under the trees, faded to black as shadows gathered. Soon they could not be seen at all: only the mass of them, the movement. Thickness and stir. Like Cricket up to his waist in the little dead.

Otter tried to stop shaking, tried to think. What were they going to do? They could not tell stories forever. But they could not run. The forest was nothing but shadows, and in those shadows might be anything. Even if they found nothing more than a tree branch to trip over, it would be too much. The Hand — it had been so fast, so fast.

The light was purple now, thickening. Twilight. In darkness — would they even be able to see the Hand, in darkness? The stuff of it was nothing more than darkness clotted up. If they could not see it . . . might it not creep closer, if they could not see it? Might it not slip around?

Might its hand not fall on her skin from the side? From behind? From anywhere?

Kestrel told "How Red Fox Stole the Words" as the Hand faded from view. By the time she'd given the trickster fox his last word it was — gone? Otter was sure it was not. Its nearness crawled like ants over her skin. Kestrel's breath snagged at the end of the story, broke for an instant into — was it grief? — and silence.

Orca's drum, which had flourished up under the ending, was silent for a beat too. And in that beat of silence . . .

Otter had almost no warning. She felt the yarns jerk on her fingers; she saw something pale hurtle toward her face. She yelled and brought her hands up, casting, cowering. And the Hand stopped. She could see it now, because it was so close. In easy reach. The darkness in front of her was knotting and working like a mouth.

"Keep talking," gasped Otter. "Keep talking, keep talking —"

Kestrel said: "Once —" and "Now —" Otter heard her muffle a sob. Kestrel was crying. Swallowing it down, trying for control, but crying. She could get no words out. Behind them Orca's drum hesitated, looking for the beat. Otter pushed her casting out and spread her hands wide. The web of yarn between them bulged inward, toward Otter's face: once, twice, three times. The Hand. Right there. Pushing.

And then, suddenly, Orca found his beat. He struck the rim of the drum with a *crack*, and then the center, and suddenly he was playing something fast and four-fold, like the knots of a pounding heart. *Lum dum*, *dum lum* — fast. "Now," Otter heard herself say, "in the days before the sky was finished, the Weaver worked at her loom. She was happy with her silver bracelet flashing in the blue cords, and she was lonely as one stone, and she worked singing. . . ."

Orca's drum shifted under her story. The pressure on Otter's fingers eased. She told "How the Moon Began," and as she did, the real moon — Sap-Running, waning half — rose up. Silvered light flooded over the round stones. The light made another moon of Orca's mottled drum. The light caught on the still, human hands of the thing that stood listening. It was an arrow's length away, less.

Near the end of her story, a thought smashed into Otter, sudden as a thundercrack. The reason for Kestrel's sobbing: Cricket. If this worked; if a story could hold back the dead . . . If this worked, then Cricket could have been safe.

Should have been safe.

Should have been cherished. Honored.

Should have lived.

He should have lived.

Her voice skipped with the grief and waste of it — and in the skip, the White Hand tightened. Otter felt it tighten and shot forward in the story: "And then the Weaver's bracelet fell, and went tumbling into the sky," she said. So Otter created the moon while the White Hand listened. And Cricket stayed dead.

Otter would not have believed it was possible, with the Hand standing there, to sleep. But the strange boy, Orca, had been standing for three days, and as the moon swung up the sky, his drumming faltered. She remembered how she'd heard it from the water: coming in bursts and silences.

Kestrel was telling the story just then, and Orca and Otter were behind her, pressed shoulder to shoulder. Otter felt Orca lean against her, heavier and heavier, and his head nodded down then jerked up.

"Sit," said Otter gently. "Stay behind me."

"My . . ." he said. "My drum?"

"I'll hold it." She would never have asked a storyteller for his drum, but this storyteller held his in hands that were bone-thin and shaking. "Only to keep it safe," she told him. "I can tell a story without it. If you fall over, you will break the tale. So sit."

In the moonlight, she could the see whites rims of his widened, desperate eyes. At last he nodded, and passed over his drum. He sat. And Kestrel told a story. Then Otter told two. Then Kestrel. It was more than either one of them could have done alone, facing down the White Hand. *Though*, Otter thought, *Orca did it*. If he was to be believed. He'd done it, and it had broken him. Asleep — or passed out — he lay curled up on the stones like a dead coyote.

When it was her turn to rest, she sat beside him. Her legs were trembling, her throat was dry. She was not going to fall over, but it was no wisdom to stand until that point came close. So she sat, carefully near Kestrel, where she could be kicked awake when the ranger's voice weakened. Orca lay at her right hand, as still as if his body had been abandoned.

The moon was high now, and Otter had light and time to notice that he was thin — more than thin, starve-haunted. What she'd first glimpsed as a whirl of darkness across his face was actually a pattern of ink set into the skin. Creatures swam on each of his jawbones. They were arch-backed like trout leaping, rising from the swirl of waves that crested along his jaw from chin to ear. Their backs strengthened his high cheekbones, their dorsal fins pointed toward the corner in his eyes, from which tears sprung. Tears: He had been crying. His face was dirty enough to show the tear streaks, even in the moonlight. His hair was knife-hacked, short as a child's. But his coat was a very fine thing: silvered gray, mottled with black and pale, the fur short and soft.

Otter touched Orca's coat shyly. It was sleek as a baby's hair. An animal she didn't know had given its pelt for this coat. An animal she didn't know.

A White Hand, listening.

The world was bigger than she'd thought.

Kestrel was telling, at last, "The Goose Who Got Lost." Otter suspected that the ranger did not know many more stories, or she would not tell that one. She shivered, watching the stillness of the pale hands floating so near she could have reached out for them. But still: It was a comfortable sound, a comfortable thing, falling asleep to the pulse and ebb of that story.

That long, silly story.

The horror of the White Hand, breathed in and out.

And Orca sleeping, his hands curled loosely on the river stones.

River stones.

A river . . .

It began to rain, softly. A cold drop that fell here, fell there. Clouds were coming up, thickening around them, covering the moon and stars. Darkness was taking their view of the Hand away. A drop here. A drop there.

Otter drowsed, tucking her chin against the rain, bending her body protectively over Orca's drum. The story touched her here, touched her there. She drowsed, not knowing if she would ever wake.

/\\/\\/\\/\\

It was near dawn when Kestrel nudged Otter awake with the side of her foot. The light was gray and murky. Otter had never been more than half asleep; now she struggled to come more than half awake. She squeezed her eyes closed and then stretched them wide. A story — she needed a story. She was not sure how many more she knew. Kestrel's voice, coming from above, was growing hoarse and flat.

They could not keep doing this.

The light was coming up. The Hand was visible in it, even through the slow rain. It made the half-darkness clump the way blood clumps.

Kestrel's voice was hoarse, her story coming to its final twist.

Otter got to her feet.

They had to think of something else.

But first, she had to think of a story.

All the stories in her mind were told in Cricket's voice. Her coat was wet through and hung heavy on her. It was still raining.

Kestrel's story was coming to its end. Otter, without thinking, struck the drum in her hand three times, as story-tellers did in her country to close a tale, or a life. At her feet, Orca shifted in his uneasy sleep, stones rattling.

She struck the drum again, *lum, dum* to begin, and said: "A long time ago, before the moons were named, there was a binder named Birch. And she had a daughter, a binder named Silver. And she had a daughter, a binder named Hare. And she had a daughter, a binder named Spider, who later was Mad Spi — Oh!"

Because in front of her, the Hand did not stand as it had all night. It was not soft and listening. It was tightening itself, twisting itself like cords being twisted into rope.

Otter caught herself before she was silent more than a heartbeat. "And that is as far as the memory goes. Now, it was said of Mad Spider that she could tie a knot in living bone. *Kestrel, take the drum; I want my cords.* Mad Spider had that much power. What she bound stayed bound."

Kestrel took the drum. Otter felt her move, heard her say: "Wake up, boy! Wake up!"

"Am I a dog?" muttered Orca. "Stop kicking: I wake."

Otter could feel them move; hear Orca getting to his feet behind her, but she didn't turn. The Hand was taut in front of her, twisting, reaching. She saw its white hands splay into claws and flex. Her breath coming faster, her fingers fumbling with the wet yarn of her bracelets, Otter kept talking: "So. Mad Spider was not much more than a sunflower when a blistering fever came, and her mother died. And her mother's second died. And she was left the binder and she was very frightened. She did not want to let her mother go."

The Hand was all knot now, drawn back like a wolf's snarl. Otter kept talking as she lifted her yarns, trying to keep the thread of the story and the dance of her casting moving at the same time, even though she was beginning to shake. "She was frightened, but she had to do it anyway. She had to bind her mother in a tree. . . ."

The White Hand wasn't moving and it wasn't making a sound, but it was howling at them. The howl made Otter's teeth chatter, her hands shake. "Tell it something else," said Kestrel.

But Otter was as caught in the story as she was in her casting. Neither of them could be dropped without consequence, without a beat of silence in which the Hand would surely strike. "So she went out to the scaffolds, under the gray winter sky," Otter said. She made the last turn and twist to finish the cradle-star, and lifted it against the Hand.

The Hand did not fall back. Slowly, slowly, its own hands — grown longer than any human's, grown thin past even the thinness of bone — its hands lifted. Its claw tips were just a sparrow-hop away from Otter's fingertips. It spread its fingers as if it too were holding a star.

"And —" said Otter, her voice trembling. "And —" It was no time for silence. "And she bound her mother there. She put knots in her bones."

The Hand struck.

Otter screamed and sprang backward. She came down on the round stones and stumbled, her hands still lifted in front of her, the casting taut between them. Orca and Kestrel caught her and dragged her backward to the edge of the fern.

Otter stood panting. The cords between her fingers seemed to be made of living fire. They blazed into her. She could not hold them, not long, she could not hold them. Kestrel and Orca were holding her up, each with a hand on her.

Then Orca, in her ear, said: "I hear water."

Water.

They had their backs to the forest, and the Hand was writhing and snarling right in front of them and Otter could not hold it long. They had to do something and it could not be *run* — not in the murky twilight, not into the entangling forest, not with the Hand that was faster than any of them.

But water. The dead could not cross water.

"I hear it too," said Kestrel. She had her staff lifted in both hands, lowering it at the Hand like a spear. With a jerk of her chin she pointed diagonally across the bowl of stones. "That way. Not far."

Otter tried to think. She had had this thought, drifting into sleep: river. These stones were round. River stones. Or, not a river, but a dry wash — a river that ran only when it rained.

It was raining.

Her hands were on fire. Her voice came out in a rush of air and pain: "Hurry."

"There," said Orca, pointing across the stone bowl with two fingers.

"I don't see it," said Kestrel. The light was still poor.

"Trust," said Orca. "My eyes are sharp."

"Hurry," gasped Otter, again. The shaking of her body was beginning to lock, making her once again as rigid as someone freshly dead. She was not sure she could run.

"Get ready, then," said Kestrel, hefting her staff.

And before Otter could ask *For what?* Kestrel had struck past her with her staff.

The staff, with its wrapping of rangers' knots, went into the heart of the White Hand. A gap opened in its stuff, and for a moment Otter could see right through the middle of it, like seeing blue sky through clouds. Then it twisted itself closed and grew arms and things that reached and slashed. Kestrel's hip pushed against Otter's as she leaned out and struck the Hand's side — neck — shoulder — it had none of those things. Cords were springing free from Kestrel's staff. A little silver charm came loose and flew across the stones like a tooth flying.

Kestrel struck again, her side pressing against Otter's side.

She was pivoting, Otter realized: pivoting the whole battle. Knocking the White Hand to one side and turning sideways to face it. She struck and struck and struck. They hadn't moved; the Hand hadn't let them go. It hadn't given them so much as a step. But, where, before, their backs had been to the dark forest, now they were side-on to the forest, and at their backs was a clear space of stones.

"Ready?" said Kestrel.

"Yes," gasped Otter and, "*Uneh*," said Orca —

They turned and ran.

Chapter Twenty-One

BURIED THINGS

Otter, Kestrel, and Orca pelted across the field of stones. They did not dare look back. They could not even think about where to set their feet. They dashed like panicked deer, and stones rolled and clicked and shot backward from their feet. They should have fallen — especially Otter, whose arm muscles were locked, whose hands were still caught in a web of yarn. But they did not fall. Otter stumbled once, and Orca — he was taller than her, and for one dazzling instant she was surprised by that — grabbed her under the armpit and yanked her forward, bruisingly hard.

And then there was water.

They tumbled down the bank of the wash and staggered forward into the rush and toss of the running water. Orca fell in; Kestrel heaved him out; they all ran. Otter could feel the Hand close behind them. Power reached out of it. Loss and madness reached out of it. Wrongness radiated from it, like the cold that comes off a coat.

They hit the far bank of the wash and scrambled up and kept going, tearing through the ferns into the woods, until Otter gasped: "Stop, stop!" She staggered to a stop, folding forward, hands on her knees. "We have to —" she panted. "We have to see —"

They had to know if it had followed them. They had to know if they were safe, or if they needed more. *There was no more*, Otter thought. *Let us not need more.*

The three of them moved close together, their breath loud in one another's ears, and looked back at the water rushing in its channel of stone. Beyond it was . . .

Nothing.

Of the Hand, there was no trace at all.

"It can't cross that," said Kestrel. Without confidence.

They looked again at the stream. Nothing. Nothing. A shivering, prickling nothing. But nothing.

"It could not," said Kestrel. "Nothing dead could cross that."

"What was it?" said Orca, even as Otter turned to him and asked: "Who are you?"

Kestrel made a sharp slash between them with her staff. "Not here." She used the staff to point. "Look, there's light." The forest around them was dim. Rain fell with *plinks* and *plops* from the pine needles to the bowed backs of the ferns. But the forest did not get dimmer as it got deeper: The distance was bright. Otter had no forest craft, and did not know what this meant. But Orca said: "The trees end. Sunlight."

Kestrel made the ranger's sign *Let's go*, which made Orca blink at her. Otter said it aloud: "Let's go, then." The Hand might not be the only dead thing, and the woods were thick with stirring ferns, stirring shadows. They ran.

The sun was just rising as Otter, Kestrel, and Orca stumbled out of ferns and forest, into the high and rocky meadow at the heart of the island. It was still raining — a cold, slow wintery rain; a miserable rain that had saved their lives — but the clouds were torn-edged and moving fast. The ragged sky was visible here and there. Orca collapsed against one of the hillocks that dotted the space. He sprawled there with his mouth open to catch the rain. Otter took a moment to arrange her bracelets and cords. Then she wrapped her arms around herself and shivered.

Kestrel simply stood. Otter knew why. Cricket was still dead — and he didn't have to be.

Anger came off Kestrel the way wrongness had come off the White Hand. Even Otter was afraid to talk to her. Cricket could have — but that thought, Otter swallowed down. It stuck in her throat.

"Mother Cedar," said Orca. His voice was not so ravaged as it had been, and they could hear now that he had an accent, flowing and strange. "Mother Cedar: What was that thing?"

"A White Hand," said Otter.

Orca raked his fingers back through his hair — short and unbraided, it stood up into spikes, like a grouse's crest. "Three days I stood there, telling it stories. It broke my voice and nearly my mind. Then you came and held it back with a bit of string. How did you do that?"

"I am a binder."

"Binder?" he said. "What is a binder?"

How could he not know?

"What are you?" said Kestrel. "How did you keep back that Hand?"

Orca gave her a puzzled frown. "As I said. As you did. *Cu tomtekan* — I told it stories." He had snatched up his drum to run, kept hold of it even as he dragged at Otter, crashed through the stream. Now he bent his head to it. Water was beaded on the face of the drum, and here and there droplets soaked in and made the skin mottled and dark. Orca wiped his hand dry on the inner surface of his coat and ran it in circles over the drumhead. It made a *hish* and *hiss*. "If it comes back, we will need more stories. Tell me your stories. That one you were beginning — tell me that."

Kestrel and Otter looked at each other. The story Otter had begun, of the first White Hand — she was not supposed to know it. The gift of that story had cost Cricket his life. To be asked to hand it over, like a spare pair of mittens . . .

The drum was as dry as Orca could make it. He slipped it carefully into a padded bag at his hip. They watched him, silent, and he frowned at them, baffled. "Well, names then. Kestrel and . . ."

"Otter," said Otter.

"You are angry, Kestrel?" he said. "Here, I'll make you a trade — a gift. I am Orca, son of Three Oars, of the Salmon Running People. *Tomteka-xi*: a storyteller."

Kestrel looked at him, tight and silent. Otter was afraid that when that silence broke it would lash out like a cut cord. To forestall the moment, she asked: "What's an orca?"

"This." Orca lifted a hand, sweeping fingertips from jaw to cheekbone, over the twisting tattoo of wave and eye and fin. "Like a fish, but bigger than a man, and a breather of air. Great hunters of the western sea." He opened his arm toward the wall of black pine — toward the West.

"There are mountains to the west," Otter said slowly.

"And beyond them, a sea."

"Nothing!" Kestrel snapped. "Nothing comes from over the mountains."

Orca put up an eyebrow. "Strange news. That would be strange news to the people of the abalone, the people of the cinnabar, to the Great Sea itself. Help me off this terrible island, and I will make you a map."

"Why should we?" Kestrel had grown dangerously quiet. "Why should we help you?"

"Kestrel!" said Otter, shocked.

"I am human," said Orca, with great dignity. "That thing is not."

Kestrel struck out, hitting the storyteller in the chest with the heel of her hand, her arm stiff behind the blow. Orca cried out and fell over, sprawling against the strange little hillock, and Kestrel spun her staff after him, pressing the butt against his breastbone. "If I have to pin you to the ground and put a knife to your throat to get truth out of you, I will do it."

Orca didn't fight. He lay flat under the push of the staff, his long arms and legs splayed. He looked fragile as a daddy longlegs, though his face was fierce. "Kestrel . . ." Otter began.

The ranger shot her a flinty look. "Think, Otter! What manner of thing comes from over the mountains? Nothing helpless! Nothing harmless! No" — in fury, she fumbled for a word — "No storyteller!"

"Storytellers —" Orca snapped. And then he dropped his voice: It hissed and thrummed like his hand rubbing across a drum. "A storyteller can spin a web that will hold the dead listening until they dry up like stranded eels. A storyteller can change men's minds. Tell their futures. Compel their help. Create their love. With a little work and time, Kestrel, this storyteller could drive you quite mad."

His voice had become stronger and faster as he spoke, picking up like a drumbeat. Otter found herself breathing in time to it. Kestrel let her staff drift out of line: She stood holding it as if halfway into a dream.

Then Orca stopped and gave himself a little shake. "I can do those things," he said plainly, the power gone from his voice. "My father could do them, and he taught me." He dropped his gaze away from them, and for a moment he looked haunted and strange. Then he turned back. "I am not helpless, and I am not harmless," he said. "But then, I did not claim to be."

Otter swallowed. For a moment, there, he had held her — held the rhythm of her breath, her heartbeat, her thoughts themselves — held her as tightly as if his words were a binder's cords. Power. A boy, and yet he had power.

Orca stood and swung up his pack. "It does not matter what you think of me. The rain will stop soon. We must go. I will help you, and you will help me, because we are human. We will leave this island, and then I will leave you, if you want that."

Kestrel looked at him, fiery — and finally nodded. Just once. Sharp like an axe swinging.

"Do you know this place?" asked Orca. "Which way?"

"We don't know it," said Otter. They had not come far inland, so the nearest shore was probably the way they'd come, across the wash. Only a fool would go that way, back past the White Hand. She looked around. The meadow was not narrow — it was nearly as wide as the whole pinch of Westmost — but still, it was longer than it was wide, and it sloped strongly. There were black trees at the top of the slope, to the west, and birch and jumbled stone at the bottom, to the east.

"Water runs downhill," said Kestrel, pointing eastward with her staff, toward the stones.

"Then so will we," said Orca.

He straightened up and put his hand on the bag that hung on his hip. Otter recognized the meaning of the motion, though not the motion itself. He was checking his drum in the same way she checked her cords.

"We should fill our waterskins," said Kestrel. "But it would mean going back to the wash."

"Oh," said Otter, channeling Cricket. "Let's not."

Orca laughed. "*Uneh*: Let's not indeed. There will be other streams."

Kestrel nodded.

They went quickly, the beaded grass shaking droplets as they cut through it, soaking the knees of their swinging coats.

"Kestrel," said Orca then, "who is Cricket?"

"Don't say his name," said Kestrel. "Say his name again and I will break your leg and leave you here."

"Will you indeed?" Orca walked along a little, before he added: "And you said you had no stories."

∧∧∧∧∧

They picked their way among the boulders and the winter-bronze grass, down the meadow, in the cold rain. A cold rain that was slowly giving out. There were gusts in it now, splattering bursts followed by long gray moments.

If it stopped raining, how long would it take the wash to run dry? How far was the shore?

They didn't know.

Midway down the meadow, they found themselves among a cluster of hillocks. Where they'd first stumbled in, the hillocks had been scattered: Here they were gathered like eggs in a nest. They were shapeless slumps of earth, nearly woman-tall, grass-grown. They looked like muskrat houses or prairie-dog towns, like something animals might build — but bigger, and older. Otter trailed her fingers over the flank of one mound as they hurried past. Something answered her touch. Made her bracelets shiver and twist. Without stopping, she slipped them loose, holding them looped around the fingers of one hand, ready.

Kestrel said, "Otter?"

Orca slipped his hand into the bag that held his drum.

"I'm not sure." In the center of the mounds, Otter paused and cast a cradle-star, quick as thinking. She pulled it taut and held it steady. It did not twist.

But something in her heart twisted. Something shivered. "Something and nothing," she said. "Nothing dead."

And at that moment, the sun came out.

It was low, not long past its rising, and it threw long spears of light along the ground. In that light, the hillocks each wore a gold mask and a cape of shadow. It made them look bigger — and it showed the pattern of them. They were no random humps, no jumbled eggs, no muskrat buildings. They were arranged: They stood in two rings, one inside the other.

"Lodges," said Otter.

And at the same time, Kestrel breathed: "Eyrie."

The two girls looked at each other, and looked around themselves, eyes wide. Earthlodges. Eyrie.

Where all stories began.

Orca had his drum out, his fingers wrapped around the laces that twisted and tied across the back of the frame. *"Tveh,"* he breathed. "I think this is not good news?"

"We came here to find this," said Otter. "We came here to see it. The lost city."

Orca raised his free hand to the sky, as if imploring. "No stories, they said. And here: a lost city." The wind curled around them and the sun vanished again. "What happened here?"

Otter answered him: "A White Hand killed this city. So goes the story."

"One?" said Orca, shivering.

"One," said Kestrel.

It had been Mad Spider herself who destroyed Eyrie. She'd been touched by a White Hand, touched as Willow had been. In madness and despair, with the last piece of her that was human, she'd tried to end herself. She had unbound the poles and unbound the wattle. She had pulled down her own earthlodge on her head.

Otter knew why. She had meant to die, as Willow had, while she was still herself. But it hadn't worked. The story did not say why, but standing in that place, Otter suddenly understood: The falling earth had not killed Mad Spider. She must have been trapped, pinned, but still alive. Alive and buried while the Hand ate its way out of her.

Three days later, said the story, the White Hand had clawed its way out of the ruin. *Which one?* thought Otter. *Which mound was it?* This is what they'd come to see: the spring from which the story welled up. But now that they were there — it was bottomless, dark. A dragging, whirling, drowning darkness. Deep in her mind, Otter heard something howling. She found herself backing away.

"Let's . . ." said Kestrel, lifting her staff, keeping pace with Otter as they inched backward. Otter could hear the struggle in her friend's voice. They'd come here to see this, and they should — should . . . "Let's go," said Kestrel.

Orca backed up too. "Yes. Let's go."

A swinging wind slapped them and the rain started again. Rain. Let the streams fill up and run fast. Let there be stream after stream to jump over. They turned their backs on the quiet mounds, and they ran.

The three of them rushed down the meadow, loping like wolves, like humans who must hurry but do not know how far. The rain fell on them, and stopped. Fell on them, and stopped. By the time they'd reached the rocks and birches at the meadow's foot, the sun was breaking free.

The rocks were big, bigger than earthlodges, some nearly as big as trees. There were gaps between them. Some of the gaps were wide as buffalo runs, grassy and easy. Some of them were narrower, twisting with stone on either side, scree and saxifrage underfoot. Some of them held pockets of birch wood. Some of them ended in walls of stone.

It was a maze.

Otter, Kestrel, and Orca went more slowly now, trying to pick their way. They tried to keep heading downhill. The island, seen from the shore, had looked like one hump. If that was so, then heading downhill would lead them to the shore. If it was not so . . .

They had no way to know.

Something came behind them that was howling and hollow and wrong. It was not wind.

They went down a slot between two stones and found their way blocked. They had to backtrack. Sun hit their eyes as they turned west, back toward Eyrie. They turned back to the east at the next gap they found.

It was one of the wide gaps, a little river of grass between the gray walls of the stones. They hurried down it, the howling at their backs. The rain had been gone for some time now.

"If it dead-ends again, we may have to climb," said Orca.

Otter glanced at Kestrel. The last time they had climbed, up the mountain and into the caldera, the ranger had fallen hard enough to make something inside her arm snap. It was less than a moon since then.

"My wrist is weak," said Kestrel to Orca, reluctantly. "I doubt I can."

He looked at her in turn, and they met each other's eyes sidelong, both hurrying, side by side. "Then we won't," Orca said.

The river of grass went tumbling over some boulders in front of them. They scrambled down, went around a sharp corner, and there —

Otter's hair rose and her skin tightened.

"What is that?" said Orca.

"Don't touch it!" Kestrel hissed.

A pole's length in front of them stood a ward.

/\/\/\/\

Otter had dreamed it, and there it stood. An ancient ward.

It forced itself into her eyes as if she were still dreaming. There was a cord tied around a birch tree — the woody fleshy bulging around the cord. The tree was dead. Long dead, by the look of it. But ancient beyond the life of trees, the ward still stood.

There was another cord, and another. The trees that held them had grown around them and then died and then kept standing, in that sheltered place.

"How can this be here?" said Kestrel. "The gardens are gone, the wind poles, the clay palm — the lodges themselves are nearly gone. How can this be here?"

But Otter understood it. She found herself saying, almost with Cricket's voice: "Mad Spider bound her mother too tightly."

Too tightly. The power of that ward. She could feel it, as surely as Fawn once had. As surely as if it were wrapped around her throat. The first ward. Mad Spider's ward.

In other places, it must have blown down, washed away. Wind could touch it. Rain could touch it. But time alone? Death? No, this ward was too tight for that. It was *standing*.

"This is why there are no little dead," said Orca. "Like a smudge, a mosquito smudge. This thing keeps them back."

Kestrel nodded, reflecting. "I have seen neither slip nor gast on this island — few enough on the shore."

Orca was flexing and unflexing his fingers, as if trying to limber them against cold. "This is . . . wrong. This is dangerous."

Otter felt the ward reaching, wrapping itself around her. Pulling her in. And then she saw it. She took one step forward, and then — because it was the only way to stop herself — sat down. She went into the grass as if someone had struck her.

"Otter!" Kestrel lunged to catch her, too late. Otter sat there, panting, with Kestrel crouched beside her. Orca shifted to guard their backs.

"Look." The word clicked out of Otter; she pointed to the ward. "Look."

The ward was full of bones.

They were human.

They were nearly hidden by the grass and bramble at the ward's base, by the shadows that seemed to climb out of the earth and wind up the ward like creeping vines. But they were, once seen, unmistakably human. Femurs. Ribs. The empty eyes of skulls. They were white with age, yellow with age. They should not have been there at all — time should have taken them.

"May the wind take them." Words poured themselves out of Otter before she could stop herself. "May the rain take them." She started to shake. "They ran," she said, understanding — shaking and sick with understanding. "When the White Hand clawed its way out of Mad Spider's place — they ran. But it was *inside. It was inside the ward*. They ran and they were trapped. They ran and the ward caught them."

The people of Eryie had been caught in their own protection. Right here it had happened. Right here was the true end of Eyrie.

"Then it is alone here," said Orca. "That mad thing."

"Mad . . ." said Otter. Because of course it was. The Hand that they'd faced down was the Hand that had been Mad Spider. It had been trapped by the perfect safety of the island, as the people of Eyrie had been trapped by the perfect safety of the ward.

The Hand that had been Mad Spider — death and time could not touch such a thing. Like the ward, it was still here.

It had been trapped here a long time. It had been alone.

It was mad, and it was hungry.

Chapter Twenty-Two

TRAPPED

"We're trapped," said Otter.

She could feel the ward — the mad ward, the too-tight ward. It was as if the cords of it went into her, through her palms, through her heart. She could feel them sliding inside her, as if the ward were pulling them like a needle. An impossible thing.

This ward was an impossible thing. An inescapable thing.

"They were trapped," said Otter. The skulls were looking at her and she was almost crying. "We are trapped."

For a moment, there was only tight silence. Then Kestrel said: "The ward stands here. But it does not stand everywhere. We can still . . ." The ranger swallowed. "There must be a way out."

"Why *must*?" said Orca.

For a moment, Kestrel found no answer. Then she said: "If the ward were whole, it would encircle the ruin. We would have seen the other side of it. We did not, so it is not whole. It stands only in hidden places. In —"

"Dead ends," said Orca.

Kestrel's voice oozed anger: "It's no time for *puns*."

"I cannot think of a better time for puns," said Orca, mild as the Moon of Ease. Then Otter felt his hand wrap around her arm, not bruising this time but careful and steady. "Come, Kestrel. Your friend: This magic sickens her. I think we must help her pull away."

So Kestrel took Otter's other arm, and the three of them together backed away from Mad Spider's ward, from the bones that were all that was left of the people of Eyrie.

They scrambled back over the boulder-step, back into the sunlit slot between the stones. It was a narrow way, and the wind made a noise in it. The howling — it seemed to Otter — was now both in front of them and behind. Trapped. She didn't know if it was true, but it felt true. It felt true as a noose around the neck. She felt sure the White Hand would be standing at the opening of their little canyon. Impossibly across the wash, impossibly across the sunlight. It was impossible that it was real at all, so why should it not be. They came to the opening —

Right there.

But the mouth of the slot was empty.

It spit them out and they went scurrying sideways along the rocks. By unspoken agreement they were going back toward the side of the meadow where the wash ran. Water would know its way through those rocks. Water would cut a short path down to the shore.

Yet they knew the wash was all that separated them from the White Hand.

Otter could feel the Hand waiting. They were getting closer to it with every step.

At the bottom of the open space that had once been Eyrie, the wash divided the meadow from the forest as sharply as a knife wound. On the side where the three humans stood, there was grass and rock. Then the slash of the wash — it had cut itself a gully — and on the far side, a sudden rise of black pines, black ferns, shadows.

Standing in those shadows was the White Hand.

"Good," said Orca, looking down into the stream bed, "the water still runs. Can we go alongside it? Or must we go in?"

"In," said Kestrel, pointing with her staff at where the gully cut like a door tunnel into the wall of rock. She looked down into the wash and her nose wrinkled at the cold, tumbling water. "In, but perhaps not for long."

"Through the rocks, and then . . ." said Orca.

Otter was not listening. She was looking at the White Hand. Kestrel and Orca had not seen it. But Otter could see nothing else.

The Hand was made of congealed shadow, and it blended into the dark space under the pine trees like a quail into fallen leaves. It was standing quite still. One of its hands was lifted and wrapped around a branch. Most of it could barely be seen, but those human fingers — that easy grip, that stillness — it looked like a mother leaning out of a door frame, watching her children leave.

Otter could see its fingernails.

She could hardly breathe.

Daughter, came the whisper into her mind. *Here.*

Otter reached sideways, fumbling, clumsy with fear as if with cold. She caught Kestrel's sleeve. The ranger looked at her, falling carefully still, her eyebrows asking a question. But Otter could not even point. She looked back at the White Hand. Kestrel followed her eyes.

"Orca," whispered Kestrel. She angled her staff a fraction, but her body was still as a rabbit's when the wolves are passing.

Orca too followed the small tip of the staff, the girls' locked gaze. "Oh," he said.

Here, said the thing in Otter's mind. *Here*.

"I can hear it," she told them. "Like the wind talking. It's saying something."

"That's impossible," said Kestrel. She did not sound sure.

"How close can it come to the water?" said Orca.

"I don't know," said Kestrel.

They would be waist-deep in water and penned in the narrow channel. If the White Hand could come into the gully, to the water's edge — they would be in easy reach.

They stood looking at the White Hand, all of them breathing tight.

"While the water runs . . ." said Kestrel. "The day goes. We cannot wait here."

There was no time to find another option.

Orca answered with a Red Fox drawl: "Oh, delight."

Otter was still looking at the White Hand. Her bracelets were crawling round and round her wrists. Those yarn loops had long ago polished a numbness into her skin — but even so, she could feel their small movements, like holding ants. "I cannot both cast and climb," she said. She could not protect them in the water. The water itself would need to protect them — or not.

Orca's hand was on the lip of his drum bag. He tore his eyes away from the White Hand and said to Kestrel: "Will you keep front with that stick of yours?"

"*Staff*," said Kestrel. "Yes. I can guard you."

"Let's go," said Otter.

Kestrel nodded sharply, then slipped into the gully. She leaned backward, picking her way down the steep slope. Stones tumbled under her feet and fell into the water. She put one hand — her good hand — behind her and braced herself, keeping her staff out with her other hand.

Otter stepped forward to follow. And the White Hand stepped forward too. It let go of the branch, and peeled away from the edge of the forest. The light there was dappled: leaves of sunlight, leaves of shadows, rippling.

The White Hand eased and oozed into that light — and stopped. It drew itself smaller, tighter. Otter could see it bubble where the light hit it. She could feel —

"It's burning," she whispered.

Orca had his hand on her back. He was steadying her, not pushing — and yet she could feel him want to, feel him shake. "We *go*," he said fiercely. And they went, sliding down the gully, into the shock and push of cold, bright water.

The water was waist-deep, fast, cold. It swirled around them, tugging at their legs as they hurried through the cut it had made in the rock wall.

"Does it follow?" gasped Kestrel.

Otter looked inside herself for an answer. Her bracelets were wet and still as if they'd shrunk. The hollow feeling that was the Hand nearby — she'd lost it. Was it gone, or could she simply not feel it? "I do not know," she said.

They went fast and tried to keep breathing. Orca was holding his drum up above the water. Kestrel had her staff lifted in both hands. Above them, the stones gave way to higher ground: first birch and sunlight, then dark pine. It was far above them — a tree's height up.

"Out?" said Orca.

Kestrel measured the climb with her eyes. "On."

So they went on — running, stumbling, shaking with wet chill — cutting deeper and deeper into the stones below the forest. The strength of the stream began to give out, the dry wash becoming dry once more. They lost the light: the sky became a ribbon overhead. It came to Otter that they were trapped again, without the water — trapped in a narrow, helpless place. But then, quite suddenly, the gully opened into a pool of stone, with a gap of bright light on the far side. They bolted across the bowl, squeezed through the stony doorway, and found themselves on the shingle of the island's eastern shore.

There on the beach, the White Hand was waiting for them.

The beach was strewn with boulders, big as earthlodges, some so big they were topped with trees. They cast paths and pools of deep shadows, and in one of them, the Hand stood, a dullness against the obsidian gleam of the stone. Its white hands were reaching for them.

"Mother Cedar," breathed Orca. "It waits — it *thinks*."

The Hand came drifting toward them.

"Get behind me," gasped Otter. The wet bracelets were caught on her wrists. Her hands shook as she tried to peel them free. Light: They needed light. But the beach faced east, and the lowering sun cast the shadow of the forest across it. Two pole-lengths out into the water, the light fell, gleaming blackly off the stirring surface of the lake. The beach itself was three pole-lengths wide. The very best light on it was mere dapple and streak.

It was too dark.

It was too far.

Otter's fingers felt both numb and blazing as she lifted her star. Behind her she heard Orca trying to raise a beat from his drum. It must have been damp: It made a flat, lost sound.

The Hand came forward, swelling wider. Otter's cords pulsed.

They backed up against the little cliff.

"I can't do this again," said Orca. He did not sound frightened, but merely as if he were giving them a part of a tale that they needed to know. "We must reach the water."

"Too far," said Kestrel.

"Have you a better plan?"

"Back," said Kestrel, and they edged backward, toward the gap in the cliff where the dry stream opened.

Otter could hear them, but she could not answer. Her mind was full of sound. Like the wind across a smokehole, the White Hand raised a howling in her. Sometimes it was wordless and moaning, and sometimes it sounded like a voice. Sometimes it sang.

Daughter, it sang. *Daughter.*

"Mad Spider had no children," she told it.

It hissed and surged. Otter yelped and yanked her casting taut.

The Hand stopped.

It was close now. Otter could easily have stepped forward into its arms. "Mother," she said.

"What?" Kestrel and Orca spoke together, a voice in each of her ears. Otter fought down the dizziness.

"It's lonely; it's trapped," she said. "We have to let it go."

"It speaks to you," Orca whispered. That a Hand should speak was impossible. But there was no doubt at all in Orca's voice.

"Let it go," said Kestrel. "You mean unmake it?"

Did she? Otter shook her head to clear it and tried to keep her hands steady. A tremor was beginning, running in shudders from her shoulders to her wrists. "Unmake it," she said.

Otter could hear Orca struggle with his drum, his finger-pads striking here and there, looking for a spot that would still sing. "How do we do this thing, this unmaking?"

"We must wrap a cord around the Hand," said Kestrel.

"There is a knot that Otter can tie — and then, pull the noose closed."

"There is cord at my left hip," said Otter.

"*Tveh,*" swore Orca. "Sooner I would rope a grizzly." But she heard the shuffling behind her, and then felt the tug as the pouch at her hip was opened. There was binder's cord in there: four or five pole-lengths, coiled tight and well, ready to unwind. It must have been Orca who took out the cord: The world seemed very silent without his drum. She could feel all three of them breathing, harsh as deer blowing.

"There is no room for such work," said Orca.

This was true. In their panic, they had backed the way they'd come, into the mouth of the wash. They stood now in a little bowl of stones, with cliff faces all around them — the cut of the wash behind, the slot of the way to the beach in front. It had been long since the rain stopped, and the water was only trickling now, running in little channels that looped together like the veins in a wrist. It was clearly not enough water to stop the White Hand. It had followed them as far as the slot. It was a small slot, narrow as a door. The White Hand filled it, like the buffalo trying to enter the earthlodge in the Red Fox story. Like a wolf scrabbling at the entrance of a rabbit burrow.

There was no way to get a loop around it. No gap between it and the rock wall.

Otter could feel Orca at her back, tall and strange. Kestrel at her side, like the sun.

"Let it in," she whispered, and stepped backward, as if in welcome.

Like mud between the toes, the dark stuff of the White Hand squeezed through the gap, and into the pool of stones.

/\/\/\/\

For no longer than it would take one leaf to burn, they all stood frozen. The three living people made an arrowhead, with Otter and her cords at its point. The dark thing had seeped in feetfirst, and then bent itself three times, like the leg of a spider, and twitched its way through the gap. It put its hand above its head and grasped an outcropping, as anyone might do when ducking under a doorway. That gesture was the only human thing about it. The gesture, and the hand, white as birch bark, but human. A White Hand.

"Mad Spider." Otter said the name without meaning to, without thinking. She said it breath-soft. But behind her the name came back as a larger, warmer sound: one drumbeat.

In that drumbeat, the White Hand paused.

"Spider." Orca's voice. He added to it a long hiss, rubbing his hand over the drumhead. And then he started to play, very slow and very soft, a two-beat of edge sound and center sound: a heartbeat. The White Hand seemed to breathe in time to it, to pause there, caught in its human gesture, listening. Orca turned the drumbeat into a name: "Spider, Spider," he murmured.

Little echoes fluttered back from the stone walls like butterflies.

Otter's breath was slowing toward the drum. The star spread across her fingers pulsed to the beat. She folded it away. Still the Hand stood, listening. Moving slowly, as if trying not to startle a rabbit, Otter turned to take the cord from Orca.

The cord was looped around the hand that was holding the drum. It was delicate work, freeing the cord from Orca's hand without disturbing his grip. They had to do it finger by finger, without speaking, because Orca was still murmuring the single word of his song.

Spider, Spider.

Little Spider, before she was Mad.

Otter found herself looking into Orca's eyes. She had not noticed before — it had been hidden by the more obvious strangeness of his tattoos — but his eyes were a different shape than any eyes she had ever seen before. They were wide and tight with fear, but there was something deep in them — something for her. A softness. A smile.

She pulled the cord free from his pinkie, and turned.

The spider leg that was the White Hand unfolded. The joints straightened until it was standing narrow as a lodge-pole, tall as the cliff. Its white, perfect hands were at eye level, a spear's length away. The edge that faced Otter was sharp, like a flint knife. It did not have eyes, but she could feel the tightness of its watching as Kestrel took one end of the cord from her hand. It leaned toward them, over them. Otter remembered the other Hand, in the place where Cricket had died. It had reared up like a scorpion's sting. Orca did not step back; he struck the drum faster, deeper.

The drum seemed to pull words out of Otter. "Little Spider," she said, "what are you weaving?"

Kestrel, the cord end in one hand, edged forward — and

like a snake the White Hand snapped around, turning its blade edge toward her. Kestrel froze. The drum faltered.

Orca struck the drum harder: a hard, sure sound, and caught again the heartbeat rhythm, faster than before. It swung up through Otter. A story. A story.

Orca's drum. The pattern of his voice, that was like Cricket's voice. All at once the words came back to her, the secret story that Cricket had told her. The story Cricket had died to tell her.

She told it.

"The first Hand was made in Eyrie, in the days before the moons were named," said Otter, and her cadence was pure Cricket. "Always there have been the dead, and always the shadows have been hungry, but this was new. Little Spider knew the little dead. She had knotted them away from her home; she had knotted them out of the world. But never before had one beckoned to her. Never before had she seen One with White Hands. One that once had a name, though the name was done with the world. One that had once been her mother."

The impossibly tall, impossibly thin form of the White Hand seemed to shrink, gather itself into something smaller and rounder. It was caught between the twin pulses of Otter's voice and Orca's drum. It was held and poured into a shape that was almost human: a human shadow with no human to cast it. When Otter stopped telling, the edges of that shadow wavered, spreading toward them like a puddle. Kestrel turned side-on to the thing, the cord ready in her hand, her weight coming onto her back foot. She was ready to spring, to rush past the Hand and around it and wrap it in the cord, though surely she would never do it without being touched. She was ready. As Kestrel shifted her weight, Orca lifted his drum. He struck the heart of it with stiffened fingers, and the many voices of the drum rang out at once. He tapped loose the edge voice, and started the heartbeat rhythm, coaxing something dark and fast from the moon-bright skin.

They were ready, Otter realized. Kestrel and Orca. She had asked them to unmake the thing and they would. But the space was too small. The White Hand was going to touch them. They were going to die.

She'd been silent too long. The Hand was stirring, tightening, oozing upward. Otter could hear Orca's ragged breathing grow harsher as he tried to find his own voice, tried to speak. But he did not know this story. Cricket's story. The secret story.

The story of where the White Hands come from. "And she called to it," said Otter. "She said: 'Mother.'" At that word, Otter's own voice cracked. "She said, 'Mother! Why are you up a tree in the moonlight? Why are you in the living world?'"

The Hand was reaching for her. It looked — lost. Like a child who wanted someone to hold her hand.

"She was there because you bound her," said Otter. "You did this. *I did this.* I bound my mother."

Orca's drum swelled up under her. Kestrel's heat was steady at her side. They made her strong. Strong enough to make a plan. A way to save Kestrel and Orca. A way to find the truth.

"There was once a binder," she said, not stopping to think what she was saying, "the greatest of the age. The greatest since Mad Spider. There was once a binder named Willow. She made a ward, as Mad Spider taught us. And like Mad Spider, she was touched —" And suddenly the story came apart around her. "But even before that. Even before that, she knew: *There is something wrong with the knots.*"

The last sentence broke out of her, fast and strange. Like a lightning crack that makes the rain pour, it broke her open, and suddenly she was crying and words were pouring out of her. She held up the cord end in her hand. The knot of undoing was there, half-made. "You started this," she said to the Hand. "I started this. We bound them too tightly. Too tightly! How do we let them go?" She dropped the cord and stepped forward, her hands outstretched.

"Otter!" Kestrel shouted.

Otter gave her one glance, and Kestrel's eyes widened, shocked as if she'd been struck by an arrow.

"Both of you," said Otter. "Run."

And she stepped forward into the embrace of the White Hand.

PART FOUR

Chapter Twenty-Three

ACROSS THE WATER

Otter sat huddled up on the stone beach. She sat with her arms wrapped around her knees, her coat tucked up. She sat all night. The moon came up late, a half moon, looking as if someone had sliced it in two. The air — except where it blew now and then off the steaming lake — was cold. But it had lost the power to make her cold. She was as cold as she could ever be.

Touched. The White Hand had touched her. She had let it. She had taken both its hands. It had embraced her; its hands on her back. It had run its hands through her hair.

And then — Otter had wrapped the Hand in the noose of sorrow's knot like a mother giving a daughter her first belt. She had pulled it to her, and for a moment they had been one thing, and it had been — grateful. It had left the world. Grateful.

Left Otter behind.

And now she sat, a stone among the round stones. Across the lake a fire burned, like a piece of sunrise. But on and on the night went, and sunrise didn't come.

That fire. Her friends.

They would never have left her. She understood, dimly, that she had thought that. Together, the three of them might have been able to wrap the White Hand in the cord of its unmaking, but the space had been so small . . . they would all have had to be in reach of it. It would have touched them all.

They would not have left her. Not unless they had no hope for her. In taking the hand of White Hand, she had closed their hope — and opened a door, so that they could run.

And they did run. Kestrel. Orca. One of them had dragged the other, shouting, screaming her name — which? Otter could not remember. One seemed as unlikely as the other. Kestrel would not have run. Orca would not have screamed.

She had saved them.

She was turning white. She was very cold.

But it did not hurt. She had expected it to hurt. She'd seen Cricket collapse into the corn hills as if ripped open. She'd seen Fawn die unable even to scream. But it hadn't hurt. It was just — nothing. It was like breathing in nothing instead of air. Like getting nothing instead of love. That wasn't pain. Not exactly.

Fawn — she hadn't been touched by the dead, she'd been caught in a ward. But that was the same, thought Otter. The White Hands, the cords. Two strings in one knot. The same.

And it didn't hurt. Not exactly.

She sat so still that a pair of ravens wandered over to discuss her. She thought they were slip, that she would die like Cricket. But she didn't move.

After a while, one of the ravens hopped up onto her lap and tilted its dark head sideways. Its bright eye met her eye.

It made a disgruntled *caw*, then lifted on heavy wings. The other paused, followed.

The night went on.

"Otter?" It was dawn; pink and gold light flooded over her. "Otter? Can you hear me?" The voice that came to her was ragged and rich, like a pocket-shell rubbed so long that a hole had formed in it.

"*Tveh*," said the voice. "Stand up, can you?" Hands lifted her. Standing, her feet were so numb that it was as if she floated away from the world.

"Are you hurt? Otter?" The boy was holding her up. She did not know his voice. She did not even know the word he spoke: *Otter*. What she knew was the smell. The salt smell that clung to his gear. The oil he rubbed into his boots that was scented with unfamiliar herbs. The thong that held the beads and shells around his neck was made of something fragrant, something buffalo-calf brown, a cord of —

"What is this?" she asked. She reached for the cord.

She saw his throat tense: the muscles bunching, the chin tilting up as he reared away from her.

Then he schooled himself still. His chin stayed lifted. His neck was tight. She could see the life in it, the pulse. The cord lay over that soft pulse, quivering. She reached. Her hands were still brown on their backs, but her palms were dead white. The throat beneath the cord was trembling and still, allowing the touch.

The cord. It was made of something coarse — long strands of something, spun into cordage and then plaited: five strands. Intricately plaited. She knew cords and this was no cord she knew. This was a place far away.

She pushed her thumb against the pulsing skin where the cord twitched. It was alive: It pulsed, it struggled. She pushed harder. The boy that wore the cord held his ground, but his breath came raggedly. "Otter . . ." he said, pleading.

That word again: Otter. She reached after the meaning of it, and as she reached, some power moved in her, and the knot of the cord slipped loose. The necklace came away in her hand, and red beads and silver shells fell into stones at her feet. She held up the thong, empty now, moving slightly in her hand, as if it wished to unplait itself. "What is this made of?" she said again.

"Cedar," said the boy. "Cedar bark. A kind of tree."

The world is larger . . . A voice in her head. A voice that did not belong to something hopeless, something lost.

The world is larger. He comes from the West. There are no White Hands there. The world is larger than we knew, and an end to this is possible.

She took the thong, one end in each hand, and leaned close so that she could give it back, knotting it at the nape of the boy's neck. His hair was short as an animal's. Her arms were around him now. He was shaking. The arms he closed around her were shaking.

"Orca," she said, smelling him, remembering him. "Orca. Help me. Please."

He pulled a little distance from her, and touched her face.

"We do help you. Look —" He pointed across the water, which was shining like a sheet of mica in the early light. "Kestrel makes a fire."

Otter looked at the bright water. She could not cross it. It was . . . not repellant, merely impossible, as if she'd been asked to walk on the sky. She had a Hand inside her now. She was trapped on this island, as she had been for so long, years beyond moon-count, beyond almost the count of the stars.

Her voice did not know how to say it. "I can't —" She gestured at the water, helplessly. At the water, at the whole world. There was a White Hand growing inside her. She would not be able to stay in this shining world.

Orca did not seem to understand that. He answered her very simply, as if it were the smallest thing: "I will help you."

"No one can help me."

"I can," he insisted. "I am an ocean child. I can take a kayak across a riptide. Once I caught a young seal with my bare hands — still I have the scar from its mother! Come: I will take you to your friend."

Orca took her across the water.

Otter had had no idea what it meant to be an ocean child, but apparently it meant this — that Orca could swim on his back while holding her close to his body, one arm wrapped around her.

In the water, her body felt both limp and stiff. She half-floated, as a corpse would. She did not struggle. Water sloshed and slopped into her ears, around her face. She could feel Orca's breathing, his body moving under hers. That stirred something in her — something deep and hungry. The Hand inside her wanted something from that moving body: wanted touch, wanted blood-pulse, wanted skin and name. She herself wanted . . . something. She opened her mouth and water went into it. Still she did not struggle.

Orca pulled her out of the lake and set her on her feet. For a moment she stood dripping, feeling nothing. Then she started to cough. Water went flying from her mouth, she doubled up. Orca caught her, held her while she coughed out the water. And when she was finished coughing, he scooped her up as a mother might a child, and carried her toward the camp.

It was warded, just barely warded. A single binder's cord ran between sticks that were thrust roughly into the moss. Orca simply stepped over it. Otter felt it, though: a jerk like the jerk that ends a dream about falling. Beyond the ward, Orca stopped and set Otter down.

Kestrel stood there. The fire behind her was almost a bonfire: It leapt up and gave her wings of flame. Her face was full as a full moon, glowing in the dawn light, her eyes bright with tears. There was the barest hesitation — fear — and then Kestrel reached out and touched Otter's face, tracing the white handprints that crept fingers-first into her hair. Otter shivered under the soft tracing, and then felt Kestrel fit fingers around one ear. "Otter," she whispered.

A human touch, a strong one. Kestrel's touch. Otter leaned.

"Oh, Otter," Kestrel said. "What must we do?"

They sat Otter on a boulder beside the fire, and she let them do it. The stone under her was cold. The fire in her face was scorching. The sun was up now, but the light was still soft, and the great bowl of the caldera was full of shadows. Otter's shadow jittered around her in the leaping light. It was as if her shadow were a second skin, mostly numb but catching here and there on a sharp stone, with a little prickle of awareness that was like pain. It was as if her whole body had fallen asleep: Her skin felt larger than it should have, and farther away.

She understood, though it was hard to understand, that the fire was a defense: a light against the ones who feared light, the ones whose skins were shadows. It was not the usual ranger kind of defense; nothing quiet and competent here. It was fear, pure fear. Kestrel's fingers were tight around her staff. Orca stood with his drum in both hands.

And Otter sat. She wanted to put her face into her hands and weep. But her hands were white and not quite her own. She did not want them to touch her eyes.

She was dying. Worse than dying. The Hand would eat her from the inside out. It would take her mind and self. It would make her into a horror. It was better, it would be better, to die on the end of a knife than to face what was waiting for her.

"We do not need to do it today," said Kestrel, watching her.

Otter felt her eyes fill with tears. She had three times three days.

"Not today," said Kestrel, crouching in front of her. She made as if to take Otter's hand, but hesitated over the fish-white palms. She lifted one finger instead, and brushed the beads of tears from Otter's eyelashes. She whispered again: "We won't do it today."

Watching them, Orca's eyes crinkled in puzzlement. "Do what?"

Kill me, Otter thought — even tried to say. But she was so frightened that her throat felt stiff and narrow as a bone flute. Air whistled when she breathed and words would not come out.

"How can you not know?" Kestrel twisted around to look at him, her voice tilting from puzzlement to anger. "You must know."

"Uneh," said Orca sharply. "Yes: I am lying to entertain you." He shook his head, spraying the last drops of water from his loose hair. "Do you not see — this wrongness, this White Hand — it is new to me. These handprints on your friend's face — I do not know them. What I know is that I owe you and Otter my life. So: Tell me what we must do."

Otter was looking mostly at Kestrel, who was still kneeling in front of her. But she spoke to Orca, or to the air, her words heavy. "I am touched by a White Hand," she said. "You will have to kill me."

While I am willing, said her mother's voice in her memory, said some ghost inside her. *Promise me it will be you.*

Kestrel stiffened at the words. "I . . ." she whispered. Otter could feel the knots of her friend's body tightening and pulling. The body was knots — Willow had said that.

The body was all knots. "My hunting — training —" Kestrel made an aborted gesture at Otter's throat, her face green and sick. "I can do it quickly."

Orca said something short and sharp that Otter could not understand.

"What?" said Kestrel.

"I said *no*." Orca grabbed Kestrel's shoulder and wrenched her up and around. "Mother Cedar, no! How can you think it!"

Kestrel spun in his grip, digging her thumb into his elbow and striking with her other arm at the nape of his neck. Orca stumbled, dropping his drum — one hand flew up to the place Kestrel had hit him. The other arm was wrenched out behind him by Kestrel's hold on his elbow. She let him go and he fell onto the moss. "Don't touch me," she said, cold.

Orca lay sprawled for three heartbeats. Otter could see the bunched muscles across his shoulders. She watched as — slowly, deliberately — he let the tension go. He rolled over and sat up. "That I haven't fought you, Kestrel, doesn't mean that I can't. Lift your hand against Otter and you will learn exactly what I can do."

Otter heard the rhythm behind his voice, felt the power she knew he could call on. Inside her, the White Hand stirred and tightened, listening too.

Orca stood up, and snapped both wrists in the air as if shaking off water. *The body is knots*, thought Otter. He was still trying to loosen his. Trying to put off his anger. She could almost see it fly from his fingertips. The leather of his leggings was wet and clung to the long muscles in his legs.

His loose, long shirt was almost black in its wetness: the black of dried blood. The bottom hem was fringed with tiny shells.

From nowhere she remembered the night Tamarack had died, how she'd leaned with Cricket into the flank of an earthlodge, the summer cheatgrass prickling her back. She had pressed into his warm body and wished they were younger. She did not wish for that now. Not to be younger. But she felt the same twist of wish and fear. She was not sure what it meant. It was not exactly hunger.

Changing — she was changing. She had nine days.

Kestrel had picked up her staff; she stood silently. Orca pulled his coat from where it was folded on a nearby stone. He made as if to flip it on — then changed his mind and draped it around Otter. She was wet; the air was cold. She should have been cold. She wrapped her arms around herself, rubbing the silky stuff of the strange pelts between her fingers, trying to feel cold so that she could get warm.

Orca sank down in front of her, balancing on the balls of his feet. She saw his eyes flicker, looking at the white handprints that marked her. The prints flared cold under his gaze: the opposite of a blush. She thought he would touch them, but he spoke instead, almost a whisper. "*Cu xashi*, Otter," he said. "Thank you for my life." Feather soft, he put a finger on her lips.

Chapter Twenty-Four

NOT YET

It took them most of the day to walk along the eastern shore of the lake, halfway around the island that had once been Eyrie.

Otter could only go slowly. She felt light as if her feet had been cut off. She felt heavy, as if her shadow were a weight. It fell in front of her and she watched it darken the bright-green moss. It had a human shape. It had hands. Sometimes it seemed to take a grip on a stone and jerk itself forward. Otter stumbled after it.

Orca had his drum out. Kestrel lifted her staff in both hands.

But nothing came at them in that sunny, safe place, the safest place in the world. The sun swung up from the rim of the caldera, and then back down toward the western ridge, and then they came to the holdfast. And Otter thought: *Here is the place where I am going to die.*

Evening came. In the holdfast, Otter sat by the fire and watched the stars come out beyond the birch poles. One by one. Three times three days. Nine days.

Or, eight days now. One was gone.

Then, suddenly, something touched her face. She jerked around. It was Orca. He was so close she could feel his breath, but he did not pull away. One finger swept up her cheekbone, then traced the white blotches at the corners of her eyes — the places where the Hand had touched her. The skin of the blotch was cold. The skin that bordered it shivered and blushed. Orca pushed softly with the pads of his fingers and said: "Does it hurt?"

She leaned back, out of his reach — his touch made her feel strange, as if something were twisting inside her. "No," she said. "It is numb. No."

"Numb . . ." The firelight made his tattoos swirl: For a moment he looked utterly alien. Then he gave her a little slip of a smile. "I took a sting, coming across the dry hills — a spiny-haired spider, do you have them here?"

Otter shook her head.

"It hurt like a spear going through me. And then it was numb."

Otter did not know what to say. The fire crackled. Kestrel was tending the stewpot, and the holdfast smelled of leftover goose melting into wild carrot — a rich, yellowy smell. At last Otter offered: "I have never seen a spiny-haired spider."

"Otter," he said, choking on it — and then, unexpectedly, he laughed, faint as starlight. "I cannot kill you," he said. "No more than water can run uphill. We must find another way."

"There isn't another way." Otter was trying to be brave, to look this in the eye. She didn't dare look in any other direction.

He took hold of both her hands — her white hands. "We must try."

"What do you know of this?" said Kestrel. Otter heard her stirring stick clunk against the clay pot, hard. "You know nothing."

"This is your shoreline, not mine." Orca let go of Otter and extended his forearms toward Kestrel, palms up. The gesture was foreign, but it seemed to read: *I am unarmed.* "You know its currents and its tides. I respect this. But — surely — to kill a friend: This is wrong on all the beaches. This would be wrong in the open desert."

"You know nothing, storyteller." Kestrel spat out the title. "Otter's mother died of this. Willow. The greatest binder of the age. She was touched by a White Hand. She *died*."

Orca looked to Otter. "Is this true?"

"You don't need to make her speak it," said Kestrel. "I say it and that will be enough for you."

And Otter whispered: "It's true."

Orca was silent a moment, his head tucked. Then he said: "Did she die, or did you kill her?"

Otter stood up. The movement felt sudden, sharp — as if she were a spider leg unfolding. As if her shadow could shift and harden like the edge of an axe. The White Hand: She was turning into a White — Otter bolted for the open night.

Outside, she took a dozen stumbling steps toward the lake edge. It was better outside. She had not known it, but now that she was released, she could feel how much the knots of the holdfast had been pressing around her. Turning on her. As if she were already one of the dead.

She bent forward with her hands on her knees, breathing hard. Warmth stirred around her: the breath of the lake. She looked up at the dark bulk of Mad Spider's island. The sliced moon setting behind it.

She did not turn until she heard footsteps behind her. *Kestrel*, she thought. But when she turned, it was Orca.

He stood silent for a while, then offered: "Kestrel said if you were crying she would murder me. I thought: best to go check."

She could only see him as a shape against the darkness. He must not have been able to see her expression either, because he came forward. In one step, she could see his face. In the next, his thumbs brushed her cheeks. "You are," he said. "That's a pity, because I —" But whatever joke he'd been about to make he dashed aside, with a sudden snap of his other wrist. "*Cu mullen*, Otter. I'm sorry. *Cu mullen*. Don't cry."

"I killed her," said Otter. "We killed her. Oh, Orca — I don't want to die."

There was a drumbeat of silence, and then Orca said: "Then don't."

"I can't — you don't —" She drew deep for air. "Are there no horrors where you are from?"

He turned away. She could see the line of his nose and lips against the starlight.

"Horrors enough," he said.

She waited, but he said nothing more.

The restless lake murmured and shushed. At last, Orca

held out a hand to her: "Come and have stew, before Kestrel hunts me down."

So she put her hand in his. It was bigger than hers, bony, warm. They went in and had stew. Otter lay down and drifted above the surface of sleep, listening to Kestrel murmur to Orca about how they had murdered Willow. She lay very still, as if lying in snow, which was said to be a gentle death. Eight days.

Seven days.

The madness rose in Otter like a bog welling into a footprint. Anger: Willow had been angry. Silence: Willow had been silent. Otter understood that now. It was like having water in the ears: There was thickness and pressure between her and the world.

In that thickness, Orca asked question after question. What had happened to Willow? How? When? In what order? Had they ever seen another of the touched? What had they tried? He asked and asked until Otter wanted to smash his head with a rock. "Stop," she begged him. "Please, please stop."

And he would stop and play his drum softly, or do some useful thing — hauling in driftwood for the fire, catching fish — but soon enough he would start again.

When night came, Otter could not sleep. She could feel the prints the Hand had left in embracing her, the prints hidden on her back. They were numb, but they were like lying on stones. She tossed on her bed of ferns until Kestrel came and sat beside her, holding her hand. In the dimness, the ranger looked weary as a wounded deer. She was holding still. She was watching the wolves come.

Kestrel sat and Otter clung to her. But it was not enough.

"Orca," Otter whispered. The name was strange. It wanted to break into its two sounds, drop free from meaning like beads from a string. She put her hand to her throat as if to catch them, and felt the word move there again. "Orca," she said to the boy whose silence she'd begged for. "Orca, tell me a story." And Orca did, a lullaby of a story, with a murmuring drum. But it did not catch her attention; it did not comfort her. The White Hand inside her had heard it before.

She reached sideways and wrapped her hand around one of the birch poles. One by one, in the darkness, the yarns there unwove themselves and came to wrap around her hand.

/\/\/\/\/\

Six days. Otter woke late and the holdfast was empty as a cup of bones.

Of course there was foraging to do: Even the dying must eat. They must be foraging, her friends — for a moment she could not remember their names. She was losing herself.

From somewhere nearby came a *tick* and *tap*, like a bird breaking a snail against a stone. But louder, sharper. She got up and followed the sound toward the lake. The ground had a give as if half-thawed. The speedwell was blooming, blue as if scraps of the woven sky had fallen. Otter walked and felt so strange that she could have been upside down. Walking in the broken sky.

Kestrel was sitting on stone. Her coat was off in the fine morning. Her back was to Otter, bent, moving. She was making a knife.

She had a chunk of obsidian already shaped into a blade like a willow leaf, and she was knapping it sharper. A round stone in one hand. A bit of leather across her knee to work against. She struck the stone. Shook the new fragments off the leather. They fell, and jingled as they fell, like black teeth.

Kestrel was no flint worker, but the black glass of obsidian was easy to work. The knife on Kestrel's knee was sharp already. So sharp that it would be fragile. The kind of blade that could be used only once.

Sharp. Once.

And Otter knew exactly what the knife was for. She could feel it against her throat already.

The delicate rasp and tap of the strike-stone against the blade. The jerk of Kestrel's shoulders.

The body is knots. Otter had power over knots. She could undo them all at a touch, as Willow had undone the ward — as Willow had undone Thistle's hand. Otter could unmake Kestrel with one touch.

She took one step. Her hand out.

Kestrel turned around.

She looked at Otter. Her eyes darted to the blade. Then she looked back into Otter's face. Her eyes were strong and clear, behind their sudden tears.

"Thank you," said Otter. The knife. It was practical. It was kind. It was Kestrel. "I need it to be you," she whispered.

"Not yet," said Kestrel.

Six days.

The whiteness spread across the back of Otter's hands, pushed up her arms in roots and streaks of infection. It opened up her back. It bled out from her temples. One of her eyes turned blue.

Five days.

Orca and Kestrel fought until Otter wondered if Kestrel might test her new knife against that foreign skin. Orca did not understand the White Hands; he did not understand that Otter needed — *wanted*, she told herself, *wanted* — to die. That it would be better if she died.

But Orca did not think so. He questioned and argued until his voice became like a rope around Otter's neck.

"But it is not a monster, or not merely," he insisted, as they built up the fire against the chill evening. "On the island, the White Hand listened to stories. And it spoke to you, Otter: You said."

There was a long pause. Otter was watching Kestrel's face: She was struggling to accept this impossible news. At last she asked: "What did it say?"

Otter tried to find an answer, but before she could, the word whistled out of her as if she were hollow. "Binder," she said. "Daughter. Binder." The voice had not been hers. It was a moan and a hiss. It was a cold draft under a door curtain.

Both Orca and Kestrel looked at her, their eyes wide.

Orca murmured something in his own language, then said: "Is that a curse? Binder?"

"No," said Kestrel. "It is — it is what we call the women of power, the women who tie the knots."

Orca mimed holding up a cradle-star. "This?"

"That, but more than that."

"The bones in the string," said Orca. "On the island. That?"

The image flashed before Otter like something lit by lightning: the ancient ward fragment, thick with shadows. A human skull with a binder's cord moving, impossibly, through its eyes. *Is it still standing?* Willow had once asked, and Cricket had said she was right to ask.

"It's called a ward," said Kestrel. "It's meant to keep out the dead, not trap the living. But — yes, that."

"And?" said Orca. There was a deep crease between his eyes: puzzlement, concentration. Perhaps disgust.

"We bind the dead," said Otter — and again the voice moved out of her, coiling and knotting, tightening and chilling.

Orca looked at her carefully. "What does that mean?"

"We bind the dead," said Kestrel. "We — when we die, our bodies are tied to a scaffold. Up in a tree."

She looked at Otter as she said it. Between them pulsed the memory: Cricket. *Don't bind me.*

"Merely the body?" said Orca.

And the White Hand inside Otter answered: "More."

"Otter," said Kestrel. Otter felt a touch at her elbow, distant — and then one on her hand. Kestrel's hand wrapped around her dead white one. "Otter. Come back." Fingers squeezed hers. Living heat burned against her cold palm. "Not yet, Otter," said Kestrel. "Come back."

"Perhaps you should let it speak." Orca had his drum out. It sat silently in his lap, but it drew Otter's eye as if he were holding the moon. "Perhaps we need to know."

"Not yet. I won't let her be a Hand. Not yet."

"More," said Otter again. She closed her eyes, but behind them was only pulse: red cords pulsing. Her mother's wrist, her dead hand moving. Was this madness? Was this hand — this Hand — the thing that would claw out of her? She could feel it moving inside her, moving in the pit of her body. "Mad Spider bound her mother too tightly," she said. "There is something wrong with the knots."

And Cricket said — No, it was Orca, he was Orca. He said: "Tell me the story."

Behind Otter's eyes the red pulsed. She could see finger-nails. The swelling of death around the nail beds. Her mother's wrist bloating around the cords. She opened her eyes, but the red pulse was still there. Knotting around the faces of her friends.

And all at once, something came rising in her with a rush of horror. "Don't bind me," she said. "After you kill me, Kestrel, don't bind me. I've been trapped. It's terrible. The cords." The cord growing through the sockets of the skull. She could feel it moving inside the softness of her eyes.

Kestrel's fingers twitched around hers. "That's what Cricket said," she whispered.

There was a pause as long as a moonrise. And then Orca said: "Who is Cricket?"

Kestrel rounded on him, her arm thrusting out to strike — the heel of the hand, against the throat, against the nose — but this time Orca moved to meet her. He swept his arm in half a circle, catching Kestrel's wrist with the strongest part of his forearm, knocking her blow aside. *"I said, who is Cricket?"*

Kestrel had pulled back, cradling her wrist with her other hand. "And I said, say his name and I'll break you."

"Yes," said Orca. "I remember. On the island. I stood for three days. I was exhausted and nearly helpless, and you said you would break my leg and leave me to the monsters. Now things are different. We are in safety and your friend is in need. And so I ask: Who is Cricket?"

"Storyteller," said Otter, trying to fight free of the red knots in her mind and keep her friends from hurting each other. "A . . ." she had no words for what Cricket had been.

"But who, to you?" pressed Orca.

Anger was coming up in Kestrel, like sap rising in the spring. It was oozing out of her as sap oozed out of a tree: through the wounds. She stood up, still holding her wrist, and said nothing. Thick, vital nothing.

Orca tilted his chin up and studied her face. Then he made his *I-have-no-knife* gesture again, holding his arms out toward her, palms up. "You think I would not understand. But I have also lost . . ." He swallowed, and finished: "People."

"Should we trade our dead, then?" snapped Kestrel. "Like dried meat?"

"No," said Orca.

"Then I will go get the axe stone," said Kestrel. "You pick a leg for me to break."

"We are caught in a story," said Orca, "and the story may save us. I need to know it, and so you need to tell it. For Otter's sake, trust a storyteller and begin it here: Who is Cricket?"

For a moment there was only silence: starlight and wind.

"*Okishae*," said Kestrel. "My *okishae*."

Orca, for once, was utterly wrong-footed. "I don't know —"

"As an eagle loves another eagle," said Kestrel. "As a wolf loves a wolf."

Orca made the palms-up gesture again. "As a hand," he said, bringing his left hand on top of his right. "To another hand." He wove his fingers together. "Separate, but —"

"Coupled," said Kestrel. Anger was melting away from her like spring ice. "Coupled, always."

Orca lowered his hands into his lap. There was another moon-long pause. "He is dead, then?"

"Yes," said Kestrel. Anger had changed her as a storm changes the sky. She looked washed clean, emptied. She turned toward the open night. "He is dead."

"Don't —" Otter stood up and caught Kestrel's arm as she slipped toward the doorway. Holding on to Kestrel made the red knots loosen, made language come back into her ears. She knew it was only for a moment, but still, when she spoke her voice was entirely her own. "Don't go — it's dark."

"The moon's coming up," said Kestrel. She put her hand over Otter's hand. "Let me go, Otter. I won't walk into the lake."

"Not after, either — after you've killed me, you won't . . ." Otter did not want Orca to hear — but the holdfast was so small.

"With stones in my pockets — no, I won't," said Kestrel. That she had thought about the methods of drowning herself enough to deny the thought was an uneasy thing. Otter gripped her arm tightly. "Cricket would murder me," said Kestrel. "He'd hate anyone who harmed me. I will do nothing that would earn such hate."

Otter caught her other arm, and they leaned their heads together, mingling breath. "I love you," said Otter. "I know it is nothing."

Kestrel touched her face. "It's not." She pulled back, reached for her staff. "Tell Orca I know it's not his fault."

Orca could, of course, hear for himself. But Otter said: "I will."

And Kestrel went out.

Otter watched her out of sight: the dark figure disappearing into the darkness. The world turning silver under the rising moon. It was a while before she sat down again, across the fire from the storyteller who was not Cricket.

"What is the word?" said Orca. "Kestrel's eagle-hearted word?"

"*Okishae*," said Otter.

"*Mullen*. I am sorry that I did not know it."

"It's a rare word," said Otter.

And Orca, looking into the fire, answered: "It's a rare thing." He looked at her then, and his strangely angled, strangely sad face softened into a beautiful smile. No one had ever smiled at her quite like that, though what the difference was in his smile, she could not name. "Cedar knows: It is more than I deserve."

He dropped his gaze.

Five days.

Chapter Twenty-Five

SKINS

The fifth day after she was touched by the White Hand, Otter hurt someone for the first time.

That morning was the first morning when spring seemed something more than a fragile visitor. The sun was warm as a blessing, and high clouds blew fast across the blue sky. They walked along the lakeshore, looking for more of the deeply stupid geese that had fed Kestrel and Otter when they first tumbled, stunned by grief, into the deceptive safety of the caldera. The geese had grown more wily as they considered matings and nestings, and so the trio walked some way.

As the sun came high, Orca shrugged off his coat.

Otter stopped in her tracks.

His shirt — his shirt was woven.

The people of Westmost wore leathers and skins. What yarns they had, they hoarded. There was enough yarn, just barely, to make the bracelets everyone wore, to knot the rangers' staffs and spears and arrows. No one would dream of using yarn to make cloth. Kestrel and Otter had never seen anything that was woven.

"What is that?" said Kestrel, touching the cloth gingerly. They had seen his shirt once before, but it had been in darkness. They had noticed only its dried-blood color, and its little hem of shells.

Without the coat Orca looked younger, well-muscled and long-limbed. "Cedar," he said, and his hand went to his throat, where once he had worn a string of beads. He let it fall. "Cedar bark, again. My people say the cedar is our mother, and she is kind."

". . . Kind?" Otter was caught in fascinated horror, like a rabbit before a snake. "How is it kind, to wear a skin of knots . . . ?" Her voice came hollow and whistling, and she reached her white hand for him.

Orca stepped backward — putting one boot into the lake. He stopped.

Otter drifted to him. "Why are you not strangling?" She touched his shirt, above his heart. The cloth was both rough and soft. Under her fingers the yarns of it stirred. And deeper than that . . .

Orca stifled a gasp. He did not step back again, but he was shaking.

"Otter," said Kestrel. "Otter!"

Otter blinked.

"Let him go," said Kestrel. "You're hurting him."

Otter let go.

Orca staggered backward, splashing into the lake. There was a hole like a scorch in his shirt. Under it was a blossoming bruise: the rootlings and branch tips of blood vessels had come untangled under his skin. Otter's fingerprints were there: bloody blisters.

"Come out of the water," said Kestrel mildly.

Orca didn't look at Otter. He came out of the water and jerked his coat on.

Otter spread her hands against her face and pressed her fingertips hard against her cheekbones. "I'm — I'm —" She curled her nails into her skin, trying to feel something. Sharpness. Something —

Orca darted forward, catching her wrists. "Don't!" He pulled her hands away from her face.

She looked at him.

"You're bleeding," he said softly.

She could feel hot blood trickling from the moons her nails had dug. It was running down her face. It was good to feel something.

Kestrel wiped the blood away.

Something. Anything.

/\/\/\/\/\

Orca was silent after that, silent even through the splash and comedy of catching a goose. They built a fire outside the holdfast — a big one — and dug a roasting pit. Orca hauled driftwood and was still silent, though he hauled so hard and so carelessly that his hands were bruised and cut.

They sat on stones by the fire, Kestrel plucking feathers, with her staff leaning ready against one knee, and her new knife nowhere in sight.

Orca sat thinking. And Otter sat looking at her shadow. It seemed thick to her, in the bright light, thick and slimy, like wet-rot leather.

Orca's voice came to her as she looked, and it too seemed thickened, changed. "What's going to happen to Otter?" the storyteller asked. "More, like that moment by the lake edge?"

Otter could not even lift her head to answer.

"More," said Kestrel. "Worse."

Otter looked up. Orca was staring at her. He had slipped his fingers into the hole she'd unknotted in his shirt. She looked back down.

"Maybe there is a tale to make of it," said Kestrel. "But the stone truth is: more, and worse."

Otter's heart twisted and clenched. "Not yet," she said — and it sounded like begging.

Kestrel was silent for a beat too long.

"Not quite," she said.

Otter shivered and her shadow seemed to bubble like porridge.

"What does it look like?" said Orca. Otter couldn't bear to look at him. "How — how will we know?"

Again, a silence. So long that Otter's shadow moved of its own power, as if the sun had shifted. She lifted a hand and the shadow lifted its hand.

"I will tell you when —" began Kestrel.

And Otter said: "It looks like this."

She folded downward and picked her shadow up off the ground.

Otter put her hands into the shadow hands. Into the moss, it should have been — but the moss rose and met her. Fingers wrapped her fingers. She looked. Her white hands were holding darkness. A darkness too thick to see through. It looked sticky, clotted. But it felt — warm. She knew it. It was soft, but with hard places, like the calluses a binder's hands got from long winters braiding the rawhide. Palms fitted in her palms. Long fingers folded around the back of her hands; thumbs stroked the curls of her fingers. Large hands holding her small hands. Her mother's hands.

"Otter." Kestrel's whisper was horrified.

Otter looked up. The hands she was holding were human. The face she was facing was not. It was made of holes.

Her shadow stood in the air as if it were a swarm of insects. It had a mouth and eyes and ears and they were all just holes.

Otter stood up slowly, face-to-face with the thing she was becoming.

Kestrel was standing too, the dead goose at her feet, her staff in her hands. She moved slowly, like a stalking cougar, and slid the staff into the shadow's back.

Otter felt it. It slid through her spine and through her heart, and she jerked back screaming. The shadow thing jerked with her, slapped against her like a wet coat, went into her like . . . like . . . Otter went down, the world whirling and darkening. *Not yet, not yet, not yet,* she cried inside herself. *Come back. Please not yet.*

And then she did come back. She was on her hands and knees in the moss. Black and gray feathers were blowing around her. The ground was damp. Kestrel's fallen staff was under her hand and all its knots were writhing and popping open.

"*Tveh,*" said Orca. His voice was almost in her ear. A string of words bounced off her, and none of them made sense: They hit her like hail. She felt his hands on her shoulders.

"Don't touch me," she warned, even as Orca jerked back as if burned. Otter sat up. "Don't touch me. I can't —" The bracelets on her wrists were twisting, moving on their own. They wanted to tighten against the thing inside her. The seam of her shirt was opening, stitch by stitch. That could be Orca's skin, opening. Orca's blood and muscle and nerve coming untangled under her fingers. "Don't touch me," she whispered.

Orca took a step backward.

Kestrel stood watching, her face green, the black knife in her hand. "Now?" she said. She was not shaking.

It was sunny, bright. A beautiful day.

And Otter, kneeling in the moss, knew she had to say *yes*. Had to say *now*. Her throat knotted. She swallowed. She said —

"— No," said Orca. "By the Stone. If I had wanted to be a killer, I would have killed my *father*. I have come too far and I have left too much and I will not see the story end this way."

"Oh," said Otter: a word as hollow as a skull. She rose like smoke and twisted around. "A story."

Whatever Orca saw in her face stunned him. His eyes went round. His face went blank as the drum face.

The White Hand spoke through Otter's mouth, then a voice like a wind over a smokehole. "I thought you were emptied, storyteller. Tell me that story."

Orca looked wildly at Kestrel, who said: "Ch'hhh. Tell it."

He paused one more moment, his fingers fumbling at his drum bag as if they were very cold. Otter drifted toward him, and he raised his drum up like a shield — and spoke.

/\/\/\/\

Orca, son of Three Oars, who spun his stories at the edge of the world.

It was cruel to wrench this story from him. But Otter, empty and wearing a shadow that was not hers, was past all cruelty. The drum played its too-fast heartbeat, and Orca's voice flowed and caught.

Orca, son of Three Oars. A village by the edge of the Great Sea, whose walls were made of shells chosen for their shining — for the dead were shy of shining — whose walls were made of shells, and of stories. Any child in that place could tell a small tale that would make the dead stop and listen. A little riddle that might catch those lost hearts in puzzlement. Who knew why it worked? It worked. Orca had often wondered, and sometimes asked, but never been answered.

"I thought it was only the White Hands that listened," said Kestrel.

"You thought there was only one magic in the world," said Orca. "You thought nothing came from beyond the mountains. From the Great Sea. The world is bigger than you knew."

Far away, on the true edge of the great world. By the bounty of the Great Sea. Under the cedar trees. A prosperous place. The oilfish running at the end of winter. The salmon, when they ran, thick enough to walk on. Seal meat; hunters in kayaks; the restless, dangerous peace of the sea. And the little dead, always the dead. Called the jellyfish kind, because they were nothing more than dark made substance, as jellyfish were a kind of congealing of the water. And because they stung — a burn of the nerves, a permanent numbness. The little dead that were everywhere and always, because the world is not perfect.

The storyteller kept them back, whispering his stories to the shells, so that they sounded not with the ocean but with drum echoes and whispering stories. Within the shining wall of stories and along the crash of the sea, Orca had been almost unafraid.

Almost.

Orca here struck the drum's center, and it rang out with all its voices. His hands faltered, and resumed. A triple beat. Otter's bracelets were spread across her white fingers — blue on the white, like the sky streaking through clouds. She cast the cradle-star, the tree, the scaffold. The sky.

"But there was another thing, not a White Hand, but a different horror. Horror enough," said Orca, and laughed a little, low and bitter.

A madness that came out of the forest, that made men eat other men. Even their friends. Even their children. A mad hunger that made them grow taller, leaner. *Nalisque*, they were called. The bottomless. They were holes into which you could pour the sea.

Rarely, yet too often, the *nalisque* came. Rarely — and yet too often — one of those that traded the fish oil overland would come back across the wall wild-eyed and drum-skinned, tall and hungry. The storytellers wrapped them with stories and weighed them with stones and helped them walk into the sea. Learning, little Orca had done that. At his father's side.

Learning the stories of before the world was made; the stories of after. All the stories: thousands. The bone needles dipped in black ashes: the tattoo, the pain. Taking a name. Making a drum. Dancing on the stones by the edge of the sea.

Orca's left hand added a brush and tap to the triple beat, and suddenly the drum was playing the sea. *Slip* and *hish* and *crash*. Stones rolling. Breakers.

A two-man kayak. Orca and Three Oars, who was his father. They had gone to gather listening shells from one of the unhumaned islands. And something came from the red shadows of the cedars, out onto the beach, something very tall, thin as lightning. Something past listening. Even to Three Oars, greatest teller of the age.

Three Oars, my — Three Oars, his father.

They fought it and they lived. But his father was torn across one ear. Bitten. Bleeding. All the way Orca rowed them home while his father slumped, bleeding. Salt into salt.

He unfolded from the kayak taller.

And soon enough he was hungry.

Otter, leaning her whole heart into the story, made the casts again and again. The tree, the scaffold. There was something wrong with them. There was a horror in the knots: Mad Spider bound her mother too tightly.

Orca, son of Three Oars, too young, but the teller of stories. The weights he'd been meant to tie around his father's ankles. The story he'd tried to tell, about the man who became a whale and went deep.

But I —

But he couldn't.

I couldn't. I had to, and I couldn't, and I ran.

"*Any* story. Any story can have more than one ending." Orca's voice was passionate, low and rough. His hands trembled on his drum, making the heartbeat rhythm flutter. "And I don't know how my father's ended. If he walked into the sea or into the forest. If something taller and hollowed walked back. There was a horror tale that followed me. I heard it on the trade trails, before I left my country behind. But I don't *know*."

He lifted his eyes.

Sitting there, listening: something that was both a binder and a thing to be bound. White hands wrapped in blue thread. The body seemed human but the face — slashed and shadowed by Otter's hanging hair — did not bear looking at. The silence of the thing was a hole into which the drumbeat was pouring like the sea.

"That is my last story," Orca said to that silence. "I do not know how it ends. But it is all I can tell you." He struck the drum, center, edge, center, edge. Slower. Softer. Center. Edge. His voice, when it came, could hardly be heard. "I don't want to die. Not like this."

Center.

Silence.

The White Hand that was Otter stood up. She felt herself do it, felt herself unfold, felt her too-soft body stiffen like an insect after molting.

"Please," whispered Orca. "Please come back, Otter. I don't want to die. Please come back." But he did not step away from her. And he did not strike the drum.

"Otter," said Kestrel sharply, "what is in your hands?"

Otter looked down. Around her birch-bark fingers the blue yarn made a familiar pattern. The tree, the scaffold. The sky . . .

As if from far above, she watched as the pattern moved backward. The sky, the scaffold, the tree, the cradle — and forward again. The white, alien fingers worked restlessly, like a child with a question, like a wolf with a skull. Mad Spider bound the dead too tightly.

What if they could be unbound?

Otter blinked. Looked up. Her face grew softer. Became human again.

What if the dead could be unbound?

Orca was still standing there, only a step away. He was trembling with fear as if with fever. His chin was tilted up as it had been when she'd broken the beads from his throat. But as he had not then, he did not now back away.

Brave, she thought. *He is brave.*

"It was not wrong," she heard herself say. It was a soft voice, a human voice. "To let your father go. It was not wrong."

She stepped close to him.

"I'm afraid to touch you," Orca whispered. He knuckled tears off his cheekbones, leaving a smear of damp that made the black tattoos shine. "Do we really have to kill you?"

"Yes," she said.

And then, a small hope broke her heart. *Any story can have more than one ending.* Any story, and she was caught in a story. Her voice came out like a small child's: ". . . Any story . . . ?"

"Any story," said Orca. He lifted his shaking hand and drew a blessing circle in the air between them. And then he leaned forward and kissed her.

It was Otter's first kiss, and Orca was no craftsman. There were things they didn't know, such as what to do with noses. And yet they kissed each other, both of them frightened and broken — but their brokenness seemed to fit together to make a whole. Their noses found their tilts. The soft brush of lips just missing lips became something dead center, something sure and hungry. Otter felt it rise up from the deep places of her body, like the binding power finding the perfect balance in a knot. Orca made a grief noise in his throat and knotted his fingers in her hair. His thumb went under her cheekbone, pressing as hard as if he were sculpting her. She felt her tears pool against his thumb joint. She was crying. They were both crying.

The binder's yarns tangled and snared her wrists and hands.

Chapter Twenty-Six

THE EMPTY NOOSE

When Orca and Otter pulled apart, they were both wide-eyed and gasping for breath — and both entirely human.

"Well," said Kestrel. There was a nudge of Cricket's laughter in her serious voice. "Well. It seems a shame to kill you now."

"What?" gasped Orca. "I —" Beneath his tattoos, his swirling strangeness, he suddenly seemed about twelve years old. His voice squeaked. "What?"

Kestrel laughed at him, though not unkindly. "What do you think, Otter? Would he be any good at hoop-and-lance?"

"Oh . . ." Otter felt a ridiculous smile split her face. A blush began at her heart and moved both down and up. "He might be."

"Well," said Kestrel again, and Otter was startled to see tears welling and dripping in the corners of her eyes. She was not sobbing, though: Her face was aglow. "I suppose there is a night — maybe night and a day — I suppose you could find out."

"What?" squeaked Orca again. But Otter understood.

Kestrel had held Cricket as he died. She had kissed him hard. If Otter had only a day or two left, then Kestrel would wish it to be spent in kisses.

Otter looked down again, at her entangled hands. There was a binder's knot tied around one wrist. It was, she saw, sorrow's knot: The noose that bound the dead.

Looking at that noose, she said: "No."

"Why not?" said Kestrel softly. She could hardly be heard over the *snap* and *chat* of the big fire. "There's little enough I can give you, Otter — a little time, that's all I can give you. Why not?"

"Because I need to hear a story," said Otter. "Tell me 'Mad Spider Bound Her Mother,' Kestrel. Tell it quickly. Tell it now."

Kestrel's smile swallowed itself. The secret story. The story for which Cricket had died.

"But . . ." said Orca. He tugged at the hem of his shirt, smoothed back his rumpled hair. "But, on the island. The White Hand . . ."

Yes. On the island, Otter had started to tell the story and the Hand had tightened; had reared and struck. Even now she could feel the thing she was becoming coil itself up like a rattlesnake. Mad Spider. . . .

She jerked on one end of the knot and the noose bit into her wrist, bringing her back into herself with a bite of pain. "Tell it now."

And Kestrel did.

Orca stood very still, listening. A line formed between his eyebrows, and grew deeper. Otter pulled and pulled on that string, using the pain of it to keep herself listening. Keep herself human.

Give herself hope.

∧∨∧∨∧

Kestrel told Mad Spider's story as goose feathers eddied around them and the roasting fire chuckled and snapped. A dark story on a beautiful day.

Mad Spider was afraid, and she did not want to let her mother go. She bound her too tightly. She left her up a tree in the moonlight. She left her in the living world.

When the story was finished, it was still a beautiful day. The three of them stood in silence and the caldera held them like a cupped hand.

It was Orca — at last, and of course — who spoke: "Then it is the tying of the dead that makes these things. Mad Spider bound too tightly. Her dead became things that could not leave the living world." It took a stranger to see it. A traveler, in a land to which no travelers came. A storyteller, in a land where stories could be deadly secrets. "Why do you bind the dead at all?"

"Since before the moons were named," said Kestrel, "always and always, we've done this."

Otter pulled on the cord that caught her wrist. The white skin was bulging around it now. Her fingers throbbed with each heartbeat, a frostbite pain. *My heartbeat,* she thought. *Human. Living. Mine. Stay here.*

But the heartbeat was slow. Loud as a drum. Pounding against the knots. Too strong, the knots. And quite suddenly,

came the voice: *Since I was a child, they have been too strong.*
Willow had said it: *There is something wrong with the knots.*

"Just a drying line," Otter said. "Just something from which to hang our coats."

Otter did not know who she was, and so it felt like a memory. Not something she had heard. Someone she had been. Her brothers waking up covered in dust and sneezing. . . .

Orca and Kestrel both stared at her. Orca in pure bafflement. But the lights of thought were moving in Kestrel's eyes.

Otter's heart — her heart was slowing. Its four-fold knot drawing tighter and tighter. Too tight to pulse.

Too strong. There was something wrong.

"Too strong," said Otter, and her tongue moved thickly, like the tongue of the dead.

"Too strong," repeated Orca, bewildered. But Kestrel — very slowly, Kestrel nodded.

"The binders," she said. "With Mad Spider, since Mad Spider, they became too powerful. They made our scaffolds into snares."

"We bind the dead too tightly," said Otter. Her white hand twitched. Her voice seemed to come from the hollows of her bones. "We need to let them go."

It took a binder to see it, a binder who traveled like a ranger, a binder who knew a storyteller's secrets. Moons of moons it had been, years of years, since such a woman had walked in the world. "We need to let them go," Otter said again.

And her heart stopped.

Kestrel said: "How?"

And from beyond death, Otter answered: "This."

She pulled the cord around her wrist.

The noose closed onto her skin.

And then it closed through her skin.

And then the knot — as nooses do, when closed on nothing — pulled through itself, undid itself. And was gone.

Otter dropped the unknotted cord and folded inward, clutching her hand to her chest. It had been so numb, as if it were made of twigs and fingernails, and now it blazed as if on fire. She could not even feel the other hand against it — only pure instinct made her push it, protect it, hide it. Her shoulders were pulling in, her knees were buckling —

Kestrel and Orca dove to catch her.

Otter breathed heavily through her nose. She shook. It was sickening, impossible — the cord had gone right through her skin.

Kestrel stuck a hand under Otter's armpit and took a firm hold. Otter leaned, and felt safe leaning: Kestrel could hold up a tree.

Seeing Otter steadied, Orca crouched down to examine the squiggle of yarn that lay in the goose feathers and the moss. It looked as if it had lain there, dropped like a snakeskin, for a moon-count of years. The blue dye had faded. The strands had frayed.

The storyteller looked up at Otter, his head tilted, his eyes dark. Then he touched the yarn with one finger. It did not grab at him. The fibers were loosening, as if no drop spindle had ever whirled them. Orca poked the yarn and it fell apart — smaller than speedwell blossoms, tufts of faint blue among the black flight feathers and the drifting down.

Orca looked up. "What does this mean?"

Kestrel, meanwhile, had caught hold of Otter's forearm, just above her blazing hand. She coaxed it away from Otter's body. "Look."

Otter's hand was brown.

Human.

Young.

The binder's calluses that she herself had earned. Her own constellations of freckles and scars.

It hurt — Otter finally recognized the feeling — it hurt as if she'd slept with it pinned, with not enough blood in it. It hurt worse than that, hurt as if no blood had been in it for days. She shook it. Made a fist and then flared the fingers open. The roar of the nerves began to fade.

"Look." Kestrel stepped away but kept her grip on the transformed wrist. She raised Otter's newly human hand and lowered her own face into it. Otter felt her tears. "Oh," said Kestrel, her eyes closed. "Look."

But Otter stretched out her other hand. It was still made of twigs and fingernails; it was still white as teeth. And it was holding, by the hand, another hand — a hand made of shadow. The White Hand was beside Otter, a shadow standing free in the air. *Sisters*, Otter thought. For a moment, they stood hand in hand, like sisters.

Orca looked up at the shadow. His eyes went round, his body tight. The White Hand, the monster that had already almost killed him. It had him — it had all of them — in easy reach. "It —" he stuttered.

"Cricket was right," said Kestrel, exultant, eyes closed, heedless of the danger. "Cricket was right."

"Otter . . ." whispered Orca, his face rigid with fear.

Otter shuddered — and then breathed in, letting the shadow thing, the White Hand, move back into her body. Suddenly her heart was pounding, beating in her ears, louder than a funeral drum. Dead — she'd been dead.

"I tied my mother in a tree," she said, the Hand inside her said. "She tightened like drying leather. She rotted like a rope. We must go and save her."

Willow, mother of Otter.

Hare, mother of Mad Spider.

Fawn, no one's mother.

All the bound-up dead.

Kestrel opened her eyes and said: "Yes. We must go."

/\/\/\/\

Before they went, of course, they cooked the goose.

Even those caught in stories need to eat, and roasted meat can be carried better than raw. Kestrel sat with her staff on her knees, redoing the knots. Otter watched her, trying to remember a time when she herself had made those knots — when holding a ranger's staff had seemed like a terrible risk. When a cord keeping its secrets had seemed like something right, something sacred.

She'd been wrong. All her life. About everything. Wrong.

It was a very big thing. She sat with it awhile. Her hands on her knees were quiet: one white, one brown.

With a thumb and two fingers, Orca was tapping something high and sweet as a lark's song on the edge of the drum. Otter listened to the notes looping themselves higher and higher, like the geese lifting from the lake at dawn, that seemed to pull up the sun.

It was music to dream to.

Otter spun her bracelets around her dead wrist with her living hand.

"Why do you not pull it through?" said Kestrel.

Otter held out her hands and said: "Try." She flipped off the bracelets and tied sorrow's knot in one of them. She slipped her white hand into the noose. "Try."

Kestrel pulled her eyebrows together. She set aside her staff and came over. Took hold of the tail of yarn. Pulled softly.

"Try," said Otter, again.

Kestrel pulled harder. Harder still.

The noose bit into the white wrist. Into skin that did not dimple and fold, but crinkled and split.

"Try," whispered Otter.

Something came out of those splits that was not blood.

"I —" said Kestrel.

And the yarn tail snapped.

Otter lifted her alien hand. Worked her living fingers into the broken noose, loosening it. The not-blood stained her, stuck to her like pine resin.

She remembered Cricket's and Kestrel's hands glued together with sap. *Look, this is where light comes from.*

"You knew that would not work." Orca had set aside his drum.

"Look at me," said Otter. She lifted her head. As if she stood outside herself, she knew what they saw. The white that washed across her face like funeral paint. Her bleached eyes. She stood and turned around, pulling off her shirt. "Look at me."

The White Hand had held her in its arms. It had put handprints on her back. They had spread their ache and roots, they had become —

"You have wings," said Orca. His voice was awed and close. All at once his fingers brushed her bare shoulder — her body shivered — she should not be bare —

And then Orca's coat enfolded her. He wrapped it around her, covering her, warming her, softly. He turned her around. "They look like wings."

Kestrel looked at her, her face pale. "I thought you were saved."

"Where would you tie the noose, Kestrel? What would you pull it through?" *My head and my heart*, she did not say. *My body itself.* "The White Hand is still inside me. The body is knots. It is caught in those knots. And they — there is only one moment at which such knots come undone."

"Death," said Orca. A word like a fist against the heart of a drum.

They stood there for a moment, the three of them, with the good goose smell all around them and the feathers at their feet.

Otter looked down at her single living hand. Without the brownness of her eyes, the light seemed dazzling, full of lances.

"I was dead," she said. "For one moment. I was myself and not myself. I was inside out and the light went through me. The knots went through me."

"I thought you were saved," said Kestrel again — and went down. Her knees went out from under her, and she sat hard in the moss, feathers puffing up around her like milkweed seeds.

Otter stared, then knelt to her. Put hands — one human, one not — one on each of her shoulders. They stayed there a moment. Orca was silent.

"We need to save them, Kestrel," whispered Otter. "The bound-up dead. We need to set them free."

Another silence. Finally, Kestrel closed her eyes, crossed her arms, and put her hands on Otter's hands, and nodded.

Only then did Orca speak. And he asked: "How?"

How? Otter swallowed the word. It felt like swallowing an acorn with the cap still on. It stuck and scratched and made her shudder. "We must go to the scaffolds," she said. And stopped.

The furrow between Orca's eyes — it was quirked to one side, Otter noticed suddenly, and suddenly, absurdly, she loved that. The furrow between Orca's eyes deepened. But he spoke very gently, like fingers barely brushing a drum. "How?"

He was coaxing her. *We must go to the scaffolds . . .*

Orca the storyteller, who knew the next words were *and then.*

Otter could smell the goose, feel the heat of the roast pit come up through the earth like the potter's fires.

"It was a potter who made the earth, and a weaver who made the sky," she told him.

Orca nodded. "By the Cedar and the Stone, we say. By the Cedar and the Stone and the Great Sea."

All the kind and dangerous things of the world.

"And then," said Otter, because that was how the story went. "And then we must — When we come to the scaffolds, we must —" She swallowed again, hurt again, shook. But she said it: "You must tie me to a burial tree."

It was as if she had thrust a spear into her friends.

Kestrel leapt to her feet, snatching Otter's arms, dragging her up too. "No," said Kestrel, "no," even as Orca spoke over her, the word in his language — did it mean "yes" or "no"? Kestrel seized both of Otter's hands. The yarn on Otter's white wrist spun of its own accord, as if it would tangle the two girls together.

"Otter," said Kestrel. "If you — if we cannot free you — if you need to die —"

"I need to die," said Otter.

"There is . . ." stuttered the ranger. "I made a knife. There is a knife. But not — not like that."

"Please," said Otter. The scaffolds. It was something she'd seen in the translucent moment when the cord had passed through her like every light in the world. It was something she knew in her hands and her bones. But she did not have the courage to say it aloud. Not twice. "Please," she said again. She broke free from Kestrel and pulled Orca's coat tight around her.

"In my country," said Orca slowly, "we say those who take death by the hand gain power in the dancing."

"We're not in your country!" Kestrel snapped.

"But she took death by the hand!" he flared back. Then he shook himself, like a wolf shaking off water, and his voice went back to calm. "Only: Think on it. The White Hands are caught, tied between death and life. What release is there for them, but to finish that journey?"

"You're the one who said not to kill her." Kestrel made no attempt to shake herself calm. "And now —" she sputtered. "Alive! Up a tree!"

"I saw a cord go through her hand. I think we need . . ." Orca swallowed. "I think we need more of those cords. I think we need to tie her . . . everywhere."

"You're a coward," snarled Kestrel. A wild stab to a soft place. "You're a runaway. You're a fool."

Orca rocked back. "Yes." He dipped his head. "And yes. And yes."

Kestrel suddenly dropped her hands to her sides and took three steps backward. "Oh, Otter," she whispered, "are you sure?"

Otter tried to say yes, and failed. She took the three steps forward, to mingle breath with her friend.

"Otter . . ." Kestrel whispered. She reached up and touched Otter's white temples. "Are you sure?"

Otter put her hands over Kestrel's hands. Pressed her forehead to Kestrel's forehead. Rested there. "I am sure."

"You loved a storyteller, *okishae*, Kestrel," said Orca. "Has this not the sound of a story?"

Otter turned to him. He stood face-to-face with her for a long moment, with the fire glowing through his hair. She thought he might kiss her, but he did not. "And look at her," he said — to Kestrel, but his voice was soft, and his eyes were on Otter's eyes. "Has she not the look of hope?"

Chapter Twenty-Seven

TOWARD HOME

Together, Otter and Kestrel and Orca left the holdfast and the lakeshore, and the island that had once been Eyrie, and climbed up to the rim of the caldera. The valley of the River Spearfish lay spread at their feet: black pine, thrusts of gray rock. The river itself was a dip and a thinning in the pines, a stitching of brilliant aspens, just budding out, and here and there a glimpse of water glittering like beads.

Far away, and yet surprisingly close, was the smudge of smoke that was Westmost. They were on the edge of the world. And yet they were nearly in sight of home.

They picked their way down the path of the waterfall. Otter had to lean on Orca and Kestrel. She was cold, dizzy, clumsy with fear.

Deciding to die is one thing. Walking to your death with your eyes open is another.

It was three days back to Westmost, two to the scaffolds. The first night, under the huge willow tree at the foot of the waterfall, Kestrel cast a small ward. It pushed at Otter; it clawed at her. She lost language; she could say nothing. She kept opening and closing her human hand.

Kestrel cooked, Orca fidgeted. And Otter tried to breathe.

She gulped air in and hiccupped it out. She held her breath until the world went dim. The new willow wands were a violent green. They hung like the cords of a ward, all around her. They seemed to stir inward. She thought she would die, right there.

And then Orca started to play his drum.

He had it braced against a boulder. One hand held the edge, the fingers keeping high loops of edge voices soaring. The other hand added a center voice. It was loud, louder than the waterfall, and strange, and very beautiful. Otter's life had been full of music — bone flutes and turtle-shell tambourines, deer-hoof rattles sewn to dancing shirts. But no one had ever played a drum like this: like a dozen heart-beats, like a hundred footfalls, like breath and life itself; a moon balanced on the round back of a stone.

"Otter," said Orca. "Stay with us. Otter. One more day."

She stayed.

Dawn. They hurried down the river.

They passed a place where the raspberry canes were torn out of the ground. It would be nothing to notice. They noticed it.

Inside Otter, the White Hand opened like a hide in a dye pot. It had almost all of her. And yet, from some huge distance, she could still feel the skin of her human hand. The

White Hand stirred into it. From within, it seemed, it took her hand and held tight.

They found the little creek and the path of bare stones. They went up toward the scaffolds.

No one played the burial drum. No one played the bone flutes. No one came with them. The waning curl of the Sap-Running Moon was drifting pale in the pale sky, like the dead, out of place in the world.

In the scaffolding grounds, Otter came back to herself. It was the knots that did it, the inward push of the red ward that was strung around the place. It pushed her into herself, pushed the spreading darkness back into her lungs, until she choked on it and came back gasping.

Otter blinked and shivered, looked around. Clear light. The trees black around her. Below, the black eye of the high lake. One dark eagle turning in the sky above. Cold. It had been earliest spring in the caldera, where the heat came up through the earth. But it was still winter here; the last turn of winter. There were scales of snow in the pine needles, icy rings around the drifted bones.

Kestrel had already lowered a burial frame. Otter stared at it.

"Can you hear me?" It was Orca's voice. She realized that he had said it over and over, through half the day. She turned from the terrible square of the frame and looked at him. Faint as a blush, he smiled. "There you are."

"Otter." Kestrel, at her other hand. "I — Are you sure?"

"It's . . . It's . . ." The curdled darkness had filled her lungs. It was hard to speak.

But she was sure. She was a binder born. She knew knots. The way to undo a noose was not to unwind it. It was to empty it. And pull it shut.

She held up her two hands, one of them human, and one of them white. She unlooped her bracelets and showed Kestrel the cast: the cradle, the tree. The scaffold. The fingers of the white hand were longer, thinner, than her human fingers: She fumbled. She cast the sky.

She moved her two hands apart —

And the pattern exploded, all its crosses coming undone in an instant, until all that was left was the yarn, looped from hand to hand, hanging harmless and slack.

Kestrel stared.

"Sorrow's knot," said Otter. The voice made a hollow of all her bones. "Like this." She made a small noose with the yarn. She showed it to Kestrel one, two, three times. "This. Tie it like this."

And Kestrel — weeping and practical — Kestrel did.

Being lashed to the scaffold was every horror she'd ever known. Every knot. It was the thing in the corn that had struck Cricket and then crawled up into the yarns of her hands. It was the tangle of power that had killed Fawn. The White Hand on the island, hissing and striking. The dream of the cords growing into her mother's wrist.

That dream.

Her wrists tied.

Her ankles.

Every bump against the frame made her shudder, but she couldn't move. Her breath was gristly with fear. *May the wind take me . . .* The words shuddered up into her mind, but she couldn't find breath to say them.

She closed her eyes, opened them. Orca.

His face was tipped and his hair fell into it, but in her eyes he shone like a raven. "Listen," he whispered. His fingers were on his drum. She could see them move, but the sound they lifted was so soft it hardly reached her. He spoke with equal softness.

Once on a riptide
I was swept out to sea
Once with no oar
I was swept out far
The fog came
And the dark came
And the fear came
Thickly

All night I breathed it
And I was so afraid
Water smacked all around me
And the waves seemed to seek me

I thought it was sharks
But it was the oar of my father
I thought it was seal
But it was the boat of my mother

I thought I was lost
But there was love all around me

First the lamps of my people
Then the great light of day

They were private words, a seashell to hold to her ear. Orca swallowed. "An old song . . ." He shuddered. Softly kissed her. Said: "Forgive us."

And then they hauled her up.

Chapter Twenty-Eight

COLD AND EMPTY, THE SKY

Cold and empty, the sky.

Otter lay on her back and looked at it. The White Hand was with her, but it seemed to simply lie over her, heavy as a buffalo skin, heavy and still. Mad Spider, her mother, mother of them all. Her mother, keeping her warm. Her mind was clear and cold and empty.

High in the tree, the burial frame swayed. She could feel the knots at her wrists and ankles, and beyond them, bare to the cold, her hands and feet pulsed slowly — pain, numb; pain, numb. They were swollen already. Swelling up toward death. She could feel the rough pole against her spine, pressing like a dulled knife. She could feel the cross braces under her shoulders and hips and knees.

The tree swayed.

Pain, numb; pain, numb. It was worse; it would get worse.

The other scaffolds. Willow was tied there. Otter could see the hand, just the hand, in the red wrappings. The skin coming off like a glove. Did it move? Did it twitch?

Did I do this to you, Mother? she asked silently. *Were you awake for it? Are you awake? How long did it take? How long did it take you to become a White Hand? How long will it take me to die?*

Sudden as falling into freezing water, she was afraid. She was afraid it would take a long time.

She pulled at the knots. Pulled hard. Hurt herself. In the caldera, the cord had come through her hand. It had freed her, given her back to herself.

The ropes cut into her skin.

If only they would go through her.

But they did not. And they did not give way.

There was something bound inside her. The body is knots. The self is knots. They had to be undone, so that she could set the bound thing free.

Otter's hands spasmed. It was as if they were being crushed with axe stones. Crush, numb; crush, numb — the slow drum of her heart. Ravens were gathering above her.

Mother, she thought.

Fists and fists of sky.

A bad moment: the tree shifting and shaking, the pole sawing at her spine, the axe stones hitting her. Noises. The ravens lifted and whirled.

And Orca's face came into view, his body: the woven shirt, the bruise of his heart, the drum at his hip.

"What . . . ?" She couldn't speak to him.

"Kestrel. She cannot climb: her wrist. But she — neither of us — would see you up here alone." He tried to come closer to her, onto the platform, but it wobbled and swayed under his weight. She moaned thickly. He froze, drawing back. Even if she had not been tied, he would have been too far away to touch.

She heard his breath shudder. Her vision swam with red and darkness. She could not see his face.

Crush, pain. Crush, pain.

"Storytellers —" he said. "In my country, storytellers — one of our powers is to ease death. To drum down the heart. Do you —" his voice caught. "Do you want me . . . ?" He reached for her. The branch lurched.

Hold still, she begged him, unable to speak. *Hold still, hold still, stay with me, hold still.*

He held still. He stayed.

Shivering ran over her body, clawing at her. Muscles spasmed. Her breath grew shallow.

There was drumming.

Sorrow's knot.

A noose that has nothing inside it will knot itself away.

The pain floating above her, lying on top of her like a heavy hide.

Mother.

"Tell me something," she said. "Tell me something wonderful."

The heartbeat of the drum. Distant as the sea.

". . . And the fog came up," said Orca's voice, "and we lost sight of the land."

She had not heard this story; the Hand that she half was had not heard this story. It was not even a story, just a voice, a memory, a boy from the sea clinging now to a treetop, far beyond the edge of his world.

The sea made its waves of shuddering in her body.

". . . And they came up like sea swells," he said. "Like the islands when the world was being made, they rose on every side. They were gray whales, among the little fishes. Singing. And I no longer cared that I was going to die."

The whales blew their spray over her; the taste of tears. Otter took air.

And went under.

/\/\/\/\\

In the stories they told later, they said the Unbinder, the girl who remade the world, took a deep breath, and pulled her wrists away from the burial frame.

The cords went right through them.

The knots pulled themselves closed, closed on nothing, and so — opened.

And all around the scaffolding ground, the cords gave way.

Skulls fell from the trees with a patter like a drum. Finger bones fell like rain.

But from the newest scaffold, from Willow's scaffold, something rose.

That was the story. What the storyteller said was a bit different.

Orca saw Otter shudder and then shiver and then still. He recognized the moment — he had drummed more than one death — and his fingers struck a loud last drumbeat, slid across the drumhead, and then . . .

And then, something black and sludgy came out of her. It lay over her like a blanket, for just a moment. For just a moment, it had hands that held her hands. And then it rose. Like a curl of smoke. Like a whirl of raven feathers.

Orca looked at Otter's white — no longer white — hand. It twitched. Her fingers unfurled.

Orca forgot his fear, forgot how Otter's pain had kept him from touching her platform. He dropped his drum — it went tumbling down through the branches like the moon falling — and swung out onto the frame beside her.

The platform swayed like a whale-bumped boat. He clung to it, shouting: "Kestrel! Kestrel! Get us down!"

The ravens that had been gathering croaked and complained. Wings flapped heavily.

Otter raised her swollen hand. The fingers — they were almost the color of blueberries, a blue with blood in it — twitched. Orca heard something falling around them. It wasn't until much later that he knew it was bones. The cedar weavings of his shirt stirred, moving over his skin. The point of numbness on his ankle, where once he'd been bitten by a spiny-haired spider, flared into painful life.

"Otter," he said, touching her face. "Otter. Don't die. Please don't die." The frame shook and creaked under them. Otter moaned.

He was from a people who knew cold, Orca. He had grown up on mist-shrouded, storm-wracked islands that rose humpbacked from the cold sea. He knew, therefore, how to save her. He inched his body over until it lay against hers on the wild, swinging scaffold. He took her in his arms. And he kissed her.

/\/\/\/\

To Otter, it was another kind of drum.

The warmth went into her. The cold went out. The breath came into her like warmth, like tears and milk, like love itself. And the cold went out.

"Otter. Otter."

The warmth went in. The cold went out.

Her hands. Her feet. Pulse, numb. Pulse, numb.

Orca's kiss. The warmth going in. His tears, the taste of the sea. Pulse, numb. Pulse, numb. The warmth went into her, and the cold went out.

The lamps of my people. The great light of day.

The light and the lamps — the light and the lamps . . .

And finally, Otter, wanting to see them, opened her eyes.

/\/\/\/\

All around her, the world rocked. She was lost, like a kayak in the fog; things rose around her like the world being made new. It was nearing sunset. There were shouts and voices — later she learned it was the rangers. Kestrel, half expecting the freed dead to come climbing facefirst down the trees like bats, had lit a smudge fire, and rangers had come. The women were casting lines up to Otter's scaffold, working to get what should have been her dead body lowered to the ground.

But Otter did not understand this. The first thing she saw that she understood was Orca, who had one arm wrapped tight around her. The other hand was clinging grimly to the point where once her wrist had been knotted.

"Otter!" he gasped, seeing her open eyes. "Hang on. Hang on. We'll be down in a moment." His body was hot against hers, and hers was awake and shivering. "Otter," he said. "Otter, I have you. Stay."

The platform lurched and dropped an arrow's length. Orca's hand dug into her back.

"It is beyond foolish," he said, breathless, "after all this. But — I am afraid of heights." The platform lurched again. Orca pressed Otter's body closer to his.

"By the Cedar," he said. "And the Stone. And the Great Sea."

Chapter Twenty-Nine

A MUSIC LIKE DRUMS

Rescued from her scaffold, Otter lay pinned under her body's cold and pain.

Orca and Kestrel took turns holding her head, holding her hand. And the rangers warmed her. They built a fire right there in the scaffolding grounds. They warmed stones in it, then wrapped them in hides, tucking them against her.

All that night the company sat with her, murmuring and awake, with the firelight leaping over the new-fallen bones. There was something new in the scaffolding grounds: a deep, still peace.

/\\/\\/\\/\

Thistle, captain of the rangers, was not a woman of great imagination. But she had seen the skulls fall, and she had seen something rise, something more than ravens, something both darker and more shining.

She sat and listened. The rangers had questions and Orca had stories. Kestrel kept silent. Finally, at dawn — out of the pale, clear sky at dawn — a snow began to fall, small flakes wandering down, like a condensation of brightness.

Thistle stood up and — with her one good hand — gestured like a queen. "We must take her back to Westmost."

So the rangers took the burial frame and piled it high with pine boughs, and laid a deer hide over that. And they carried Otter back.

/\/\/\/\/\

They went to Thistle's lodge, of course. Where else was there to go? In the slow, smoky days that followed, Otter wondered if the old lodge had ever held a jumbled, busy life, and if Thistle had ever wished for one. There had once been years, many years, when Thistle hardly came to Westmost, but haunted the forest, making her way in rangers' holdfasts and Water Walkers' islands. In the forest, she trained her rangers and kept down the dead and became almost a figure of legend, shut outside the ward she had not wanted her daughter to cast. She'd become so strange and so estranged that as a child Otter had glimpsed her only rarely, as if she were some rare kind of bird.

Now Otter wondered if small Willow had grown up inside these walls, in the days before the smoke turned the wattle black. The many years of blessing knots scattered around them — had any been tied by her mother?

But whether or not the lodge had ever seen a jumble, a family, it held one now. Thistle — fierce, hawk-wild Thistle — turned out to snore. She could also cook. From somewhere she begged a larger cookpot, and made for them stews of corn and dried squash and berries. She roasted walnuts and grouse. She fed Otter herself, in the early days before Otter's hands could grip a gourd spoon.

"A privilege," she said gravely. Her second hand — freed now of its splints and swelling, withered away to bones and skin — rested limply on the blanket beside Otter. "I missed your babyhood, granddaughter. You must let me catch up."

Otter was too proud to admit she liked it. But Orca smiled.

Kestrel said nothing at all. Because Kestrel had seen — as Otter had not — the moment Thistle had met Orca. She'd seen Thistle take him in, piece by piece: His tattoos that exaggerated the strange planes of his face. His child-short hair. His coat of long-traveling. His voice whose shape suggested another language.

"Who are you?" Thistle had asked, tipping her staff at Orca as if it were a spear.

"Don't touch him!" snarled Kestrel, swinging up her own staff, smashing Thistle's out of line. As Thistle squinted at her, puzzled, Kestrel whispered: "Don't touch him."

Because Thistle had already killed one storyteller.

Cricket. Otter had not forgotten. But she didn't feel the weight of it as Kestrel did — Kestrel, tying her knots around her staff, eating from the same stewpot as the woman who had killed her *okishae*.

As Otter came back to herself, the meaning of Kestrel's tight silence was easy enough to unravel. With Thistle as captain of the rangers, how could Kestrel be a ranger again? But if she was not a ranger, what was she? What would she do?

Kestrel, not a ranger. And Otter, not a binder. What would they do?

∧∨∧∨∧

Otter grew stronger slowly.

The Moon of Blossoms came, and winter broke like a fever. Suddenly the world was young and green and tender. Then the Water Walkers came with the spring trade, and turned the careful pinch into feast and festival.

Otter limped out to the fires, some nights, to hear new stories, to breathe the green air. Kestrel sat beside her, behind her, giving her an arm to lean on, giving the others short answers when Otter grew tired enough to tremble.

Everyone had questions.

Otter tried to explain, but it was too big to say. Who could accept it — that since the time of Mad Spider, the binders had used their powers backward? That in knotting out the dead they had in truth tied them to the living world? It was too big to say, though Otter tried to say it. She was not eloquent.

This time, it was Orca who had fallen silent.

It was, of all people, Newt the bonesetter who slowly turned the pinch around.

She came often, plying Otter with teas of blue flag and partridge berry, liniments of prairie-smoke root, bitter chews of black-birch gum. Otter liked having less pain. But no matter what else had happened, she would never like Newt.

Still, Newt had power that was sister to a binder's power, a power over knots. And she had sat by many a deathbed. She understood how the living held the dying, sometimes, too tightly. Had seen how the dying needed to be let go. She had secrets in her cord: She knew that a bonesetter's knots could be used wrongly, could trap a dying woman on the bitter edge of death.

Newt understood. And it was she who named Otter the Unbinder.

The girl who had risen alive among the dead, and died there. And come back.

Orca, through all the coming and going, through the feast of storytelling and fires, through all the times when he could have been a hero, sat quietly on the sleeping platform opposite. He was rebuilding his drum, which had been slashed in its fall from the burial trees. He had traded some of the beads from his coat hem to one of the Water Walkers for an elk skin. For most of a moon he sat cross-legged and speechless, working first to cure and stretch the hide, and then to stretch it over the frame.

Otter was baffled, hurt. Orca had saved her with the warmth of his own breath. He had not touched her since.

Finally his drum was finished. Smoke-cured, the drumhead was mottled gray. It had a different tone than his old drum: more somber, its center voice braver, but with an undertone of trembling — a drum that could weep. He sounded it softly with his fingertips, and the sound rose to the round roof like a deep breath.

He played it a little, experimenting: a rain-on-the-corn patter from the rim, the heartbeat of the edge and center, the rising triples that made Otter think of her strange dream: whales rising.

He played the whales. And, then, suddenly, he was in tears.

Kestrel stared. It was Otter who stood, who went to him. Who helped him to his feet, the drum like a shield between them. She had to nudge it aside to hold him. His body trembled like a tree.

"I let you die," he whispered to her. "I — tied you." He swallowed, his tattoos showing the twitch of the muscles in his jaws. "As I could not tie my father."

He was weeping now, openly, the whales on his cheekbones rising.

"And then what happened . . . to him? To my people?" He bent his head and buried his face in her hair. "Otter, I have been such a coward."

She wrapped a hand around the back of his neck — the vulnerable hollow place there, the feather sleekness of his hair.

"I will make a story of you," he promised, a fierce whisper. "It will go over this country like a tidal wave. The girl who remade the world."

"Oh, wait a bit," she said, in Cricket's voice. "You have not yet seen the ending."

That night, Otter took out her red shirt — the one that had been her mother's, the one with an embroidery of bones, the one binders wore for funerals — and waited.

It was not every binder who had the strength to tie the dead to the living world, Otter explained. Most did not. But among the free women of the forest, once or twice in every moon-count of years, there would be one who did.

Those strong binders made White Hands. Mad Spider had been the first with such strength. She had made a White Hand out of her mother, Hare, and more out of the other dead among her people, and finally had become a Hand herself, touched at last by the things she made. Willow had made a White Hand of Tamarack. Otter herself had made one of Willow, and another of Fawn, though those ropes had not been left long enough to rot.

Mad Spider, who had been wrong, but who had been powerful and clever and brave, had freed the Hands of her time. Other binders had made and freed other Hands. Otter had freed Mad Spider. In her death on the scaffold, she had freed the Hand that was caught inside herself, freed Willow, freed Fawn, freed all of Westmost's restless, twitching dead.

There was one left. Solitary as a daytime moon.

Trapped as Otter had been, on the scaffold, with her hands pulsing.

Otter knew she would be coming.

And she came.

In the dark pause between the Moon of Blossoms and the Moon of New Grass, as the spring fires burned their highest and the Water Walkers rolled their tents to travel and told their last tales, the White Hand came.

The pinch came running for Otter, of course. She might have strange ideas, she might be at the center of a strange story, she might be young, she might even be mad — but she was the binder of Westmost.

So Otter put on her funeral red and walked out into the evening. She went to the water gate, the gap in the ward where her mother had stood on the day the river had frozen. Here, Willow had slipped. Here, Willow had fallen into the hands of a White Hand. *This* White Hand.

"Don't go," she called to the women who were running, to the rangers who were herding the children of Westmost to the binder's lodge, where they could — if they had to — make a desperate stand. "Stay," said Otter. "This needs witnessing."

Some of them went anyway. But most stayed, rangers holding their staffs, Water Walkers with wide eyes, the ordinary women of Westmost waiting in the safety of the running water. It was nearly full night: The sky beyond the birches of the ward was like water saturated with blue dye, dark but full of shining. The ward itself was just a shiver in the twilight.

Outside the ward was something darker than the darkness, hanging at the edge of the black pines. They could see its hands.

Otter took off her spring slippers, eased into the water, and walked out toward it. At the forest edge she climbed onto the bank. She stood in a patch of marsh marigold, bright and soft under her feet. She held out her hands toward the White Hand — a foreign gesture, but one that read *I am unarmed* — and let her voice ring.

"Welcome home, Tamarack. Binder of Westmost."

Otter stepped closer to the Hand in the darkness. It drifted toward her out of the pine shadows, into the scrub meadow. Almost to the ward. She could barely see it: only the hands. The hunch of what might be shoulders, carrying something heavy. "I am sorry," she said. Her hands were still out. "I am sorry that we kept you here. I am sorry that we bound you up. To all of your kind. My kind is sorry."

She stepped forward one more time. The yellow flowers cast petals at her feet, like a dapple of moonlight, though there was no moon. The ward was at her elbow. The gathered rangers behind the strings. The women of Westmost. The silent men of the Sunlit Places.

Otter slipped off her bracelets. She cast nothing. She looked at the cord for a moment. The White Hand seemed to look too. Then Otter made a single slip knot, with a loop no bigger than might hold a cradleboard. "Tamarack?" she said. And held it out.

The pale hands stirred in the darkness like moths. Fluttered, fumbled. Plucked.

The loop lifted from Otter's fingers. She felt the air stir as the white hands moved next to hers, but not so much as a moth's feeler touched her. And then the loop was around one white wrist. Around both.

Otter stepped closer still and took the free end of the cord. "I loved you in life," she said. "I let you go."

She pulled the loop closed.

There was just one moment where the noose bit in, held. Then it went through the shadow stuff of the White Hand as it had once gone through Otter's own wrist. There was a fluttering, an urgent movement, like quail flushed from the grass.

And then nothing. The blue yarn fell into the flowers.

Otter lifted her chin and let her voice rise, ring out over the silent pinch. "We will never bind the dead again," she said.

And then she picked up her slippers and walked back to her lodge.

"It is a good story," said Orca, leaning on the flank of Thistle's lodge, watching the chaos near the ward — rangers, dyers, Walkers, children — a fuss of voices and torches such as serious, stable Westmost rarely knew. "A good ending."

Too much time walking with death had robbed Otter of her quick tongue. On the other hand, she'd become better at listening. She turned to Orca. "But . . . ?"

"I —" He ducked his head aside. "I must go, Otter. I must go back."

"To your people."

"To my father. To find out what happened. To put right what I can."

The great fire of the spring festival was burning in the palm: It made Orca's tattoos leap and change, though he was holding very still. Otter said nothing. To go back — it would be a terribly hard thing. But she had little standing to argue against doing terribly hard things.

"I will make the story first," he promised. "Your story. When I am done, those who hear it — those who hear it will weep. They will never tie a binder's knot again."

Otter thought about this, silently.

Orca had pulled a bit of bindweed. The flower was closed against the night, a curl of softness against one of his fingernails. He looked down, then up. His eyes were dark and serious. "It will break me, Otter. It will tear me like the drumskin, to leave you."

For a moment, she felt her own heart tear. Then she blurted: "But I'm coming with you."

His face fell open. It was a perfect mirror of Cricket's look of foolish surprise, and behind her, Otter heard Kestrel laugh.

"Of course she is, storyteller," she said, coming over. "Did you not see that coming? Otter and I are going west. We have been for some time."

"Otter *and* you?" Orca tried to gulp down his gape, which made him look even more foolish.

"I have left enough of myself here," said Otter.

"If she goes without me, she will probably be eaten by a bear," said Kestrel. "She has no woodcraft. And she's stupid with love."

Orca tucked his chin, blushing. "Is she?"

"I don't know yet," said Otter.

"Hmmm." Kestrel pointed across the gardens to where Newt the bonesetter was trying to keep back a small pack of women who looked likely to storm over to the unbinder and demand answers. "I'd best help take care of that."

She left, and Otter found herself alone, watching Orca spin the bindweed in his fingers as if he were making a rope. He was blushing deeply, and the waves on his jaw quivered as he tried not to let himself smile. "You don't know . . . ?" he murmured, his head bent as if speaking to the sealed flower.

"I just came back to life, Orca," she said. "You must give me some time to find out." She stepped in front of him, trapping him against the earth wall. He glanced up at her, shivering as if with fear.

"Take time now," he said, his voice rough. He put one hand on the flare of her hip.

She slipped a hand behind the back of his neck. She felt him tense, and then — as she kissed the point on his jaw where the waves turned to whirlpools — she felt the fear knots in him releasing.

Something rose in her, certain and sure, as she sought out his mouth. She slid her hand around him until her fingers curled over his collarbone. She pulled herself up on tiptoe, and pressed the other hand over his heart. His heartbeat matched hers.

Their hearts, together, made a music like drums.

ACKNOWLEDGMENTS

A few years ago, my then-five-year-old daughter asked: "What's taking you so long with your book, Mommy? Is it all the words?"

There's a lot of words in my life, and I want first to thank my husband, James Bow, who has loved me through more than a million of them. Thanks also to my early readers Rebecca, Seánan, and Susan, who walked me through chapter by chapter, step by step. Seánan in particular was there for long Internet chats, usually in the middle of the night her time, in which she helped me feel my way to the story in a dozen lost-in-darkness places. Thanks and love to my in-person writers' group, the Hopeful Writers — Kristen, Nan, Pamela, Susan again, and our much-missed late friend Esther — who read bits and held hands. My online friends at Wri, too many to name, listened to me whinge about stuckedness. Thank you all.

Now, research. As my last book was set in a fantastical world that was recognizably Eastern European, this one is set in a fantastical world that's recognizably North American. (It's worth noting, though, that the Shadowed People are not meant to represent any particular indigenous culture.) It takes a lot of research to build a rounded world. My characters and I would like to thank the folks at the ethnobotany project at the University of Minnesota, for tending to our aches and pains; wild food and foraging experts Mike and Christine, for keeping Kestrel and Otter from starving; ancient technology expert Ashti, for tending to the fires; and sacred drummer Nicholas, for helping Orca find his beat. The late Buffalo Bird Woman's ethnographic testimony gave Westmost its lodges and gardens. There were more folks lending a hand along the way, setting dyes, knapping flint, ruining cities, and more. A thousand thanks to all of them.

This book took some time to find its shape. Thanks to my agent, Emily, who believed in it when it was shapeless. And thanks to Arthur, the other Emily, and the rest of the folks at Arthur A. Levine Books and Scholastic for their keen editorial eyes. I hope that Otter's book is sharp, strong, and sweet — but if it is, it's because Arthur and Emily helped me see.

Finally, this book in which so much family stuff goes wrong would not be possible without a life in which family stuff goes right. Thank you to my parents, who thought they were raising a scientist but embraced the writer without hesitating, and only occasionally express their worry that I will end up under a bridge. And thanks to my own two lovely little girls. Vivian, Nora: You are the music of my heart.

This book was edited by Arthur Levine and Emily Clement. It was designed by Jeannine Riske. The text was set in Berling, designed by Karl-Erik Forsberg for the Berling Foundry in 1951. The display type was set in Augustea Open, designed by Aldo Novarese and Alessandro Butti for the Italian Nebiolo Type Foundry in 1951. The book was printed and bound at R. R. Donnelley in Crawfordsville, Indiana. Production was supervised by Starr Baer, and manufacturing was supervised by Angelique Browne.